THE C♠RDTURNER

ALSO BY Louis Sachar

Holes
Small Steps
Stanley Yelnats' Survival Guide to Camp Green Lake
Dogs Don't Tell Jokes
The Boy Who Lost His Face
There's a Boy in the Girls' Bathroom

THE C♠RDTURNER

LOUIS SACHAR

A Novel About
a King, a Queen,
and
a Joker

Delacorte Press

All rights reserved. Published in the United States by Delacorte Press, an imprint of Random House Children's Books, a division of Random House, Inc., New York.

Delacorte Press is a registered trademark and the colophon is a trademark of Random House, Inc.

Visit us on the Web! www.randomhouse.com/teens

Educators and librarians, for a variety of teaching tools, visit us at www.randomhouse.com/teachers

Library of Congress Cataloging-in-Publication Data is available upon request.

ISBN 978-0-385-73662-6 (hc)—ISBN 978-0-385-90619-7 (lib. bdg.)
ISBN 970-0-375-89647-7 (e-book)

The text of this book is set in 11-point Sabon.
Book design by Trish Parcell Watts

Printed in the United States of America
10 9 8 7 6 5 4 3 2 1
First Edition

To Nancy Joe, Nancy Jo Gordy, Marilou Powell, Paul and Beth Tobias,
Jerry Bigler, Claudette Hartman, Alex Kolesnik, and Ruth Sachar.
It's been a joy sitting across the table from you

(even if a bit trying at times),

and to all my friends at the Austin Bridge Center,
opponents and partners alike,

and to anyone, anywhere, who is struggling to figure out
whether a bid of four clubs is Gerber or natural . . .

A Note from the Author

Imagine you were abducted by aliens and taken away to their home planet. After living there awhile, you learn to speak their language, and then actually become a pretty well-known author. You were a huge baseball fan back on Earth, so you decide to write a book about baseball. You know that none of your alien readers have ever heard of baseball, but you think it will make a great story, and besides, you really love the game. . . .

As you attempt to write it, you quickly find yourself entangled in words with multiple meanings, like *ball* and *run*. When you try to describe a triple play, you get so bogged down explaining the rules about force-outs that the excitement of the play itself is lost.

That was the predicament I put myself into when I wrote *The Cardturner*. It's not about baseball but about bridge, a card game that was once extremely popular but that, unfortunately, not too many people play anymore, especially not young people. In fact, the people who do play bridge seem to live in their own alien world.

My publisher, my editor, my wife, and my agent all said I was crazy. "No one's going to want to read a book about bridge!" they told me on more than one occasion.

Still, I really love the game. . . .

THE C♠RDTURNER

1

My Favorite Uncle

Ever since I was a little kid, I've had it drilled into me that my uncle Lester was my favorite uncle. My mother would thrust the phone at me and say, "Uncle Lester wants to talk to you," her voice infused with the same forced enthusiasm she used to describe the deliciousness of canned peas. "Tell him you love him."

"I love you, Uncle Lester," I'd say.

"Tell him he's your favorite uncle."

"You're my favorite uncle."

It got worse as I got older. I never knew what to say to him, and he never seemed all that interested in talking to me. When I became a teenager I felt silly telling him he was my favorite uncle, although my mother still urged me to do so. I'd say things like "Hey, how's it goin'?" and he'd grunt some response. He might ask me a question about school. I imagine it was a great relief to both of us when my mother took back the phone. Our brief conversations always left me feeling embarrassed, and just a little bit creepy.

He was actually my great-uncle, having been my mother's favorite uncle long before he was mine.

I didn't know how much money he had, but he was rich enough that he never had to be nice to anyone. Our favorite uncle never visited us, and I think my mother initiated all the phone conversations with him. Later, after he got really sick, he wouldn't even talk to her. My mother would call almost daily, but she could never get past his housekeeper.

I had only met Uncle Lester face to face one time, at his sixty-fifth birthday party. I was six years old, and to me, his house seemed like a castle on a mountaintop. I said the obligatory "Happy birthday" and "I love you" and "You're my favorite uncle" and then steered clear of him.

"His heart is as cold as a brick," my father said on the drive home.

That phrase has stuck with me, I think, because my father used the word *cold* instead of *hard*.

My elementary school was a brick building. Every day on the way home, I would drag my fingers over the hard, and yes, cold surface.

I'm in high school now, but still whenever I walk by a brick building, I feel compelled to touch it. Even now, as I write this, I can almost feel the hard coolness, the sharp edges, and the roughness of the cement between the bricks.

2

A Turn for the Worse

Uncle Lester has taken "a turn for the worse." That's a phrase I heard a lot around the first of this year. Another phrase that came up a lot was "complications resulting from diabetes."

I wish I could report that these words brought great concern and sadness to our household. True, when my mother spoke of our favorite uncle's unfortunate turn, her voice had a somber tone, and sometimes she would place a hand on her heart, but I would say the overall mood was one of anxious anticipation. Once, I actually saw my father rub his hands together when he mentioned that Uncle Lester was not long for this world. December 25 might have come and gone, but there was a sense that Christmas was still just around the corner.

To be fair, I should mention that my father worked for a company that manufactured and installed insulation material. He often complained how the synthetic fibers made his hands itch, and that could have been the reason he was rubbing his hands together.

Nevertheless, the only person who seemed genuinely worried about our favorite uncle was my sister, Leslie. She was also the only one of us who had never met him, unless you count his sixty-fifth birthday party. She was about four months old when we went to his dark castle on the mountain. My mother put extra emphasis on the first syllable of my sister's name when she introduced Uncle *Les*ter to his new grandniece, *Les*lie.

Leslie was eleven when Uncle Lester took his turn for the worse.

"What's diabetes?" she asked me.

"It's kind of a disease," I answered. "It has something to do with your body not being able to turn sugar into insulin."

"Why do you need insulin?"

I didn't know.

"Is Uncle Lester in pain?"

Complications-resulting-from-diabetes was just a string of words to me, and I never gave much thought to their meaning. Unlike me, Leslie could feel the suffering behind the words.

A week later I found out just how complicated his condition was. My uncle Lester had become blind.

"I guess he won't be playing cards anymore," my father said, rather callously, I thought.

It was the first time I'd ever heard anything about my uncle and cards.

According to my mother, we were Uncle Lester's closest living relatives. By this, I think she meant we lived the closest, which I doubted had any legal significance, but she seemed to think this was important if, God forbid, any-thing should happen to him.

He had no children of his own. He had one brother and two sisters, and they all had children (including my mother), and their children had children (including Leslie and me).

That was a lot of people with whom to split any inheritance, but my mother seemed especially concerned about Mrs. Mahoney, Uncle Lester's longtime housekeeper. "I think there's more going on there than just housekeeping, if you know what I mean," she said one evening during dinner.

She was speaking somewhat cryptically because of Leslie. I knew what she meant, of course, and I'm pretty sure Leslie did too, but I really didn't want to think about my old uncle and his aging housekeeper while I was eating.

There was somebody else who was even more worrisome to my mother than Mrs. Mahoney. That person was Sophie Castaneda.

I'd heard about the Castaneda family all my life, "the crazy Castanedas," but I never quite got my uncle's relationship to them. It was complicated, to say the least.

From what I understood, Sophie Castaneda was the daughter of Uncle Lester's ex-wife's crazy sister.

When Uncle Lester was in his twenties, he had been married for less than a year. His wife had a sister who went insane. The sister had a daughter named Sophie King, who later changed her name to Sophie Finnick, and then became Sophie Castaneda when she got married.

See what I mean?

According to my mother, all the Castanedas were bonkers. I met Toni Castaneda, Sophie's daughter, at my uncle's sixty-fifth birthday. Toni was about six years old, and I remember I was glad to find someone my own age to play with. Toni ran up to me. She covered her ears with her hands, her elbows sticking out, and shouted, "Shut up! Leave me alone!" and then she ran away.

She didn't do that just to me. I watched her tell other people to shut up and leave her alone too. I thought she was funny, but when I tried playing that game, I got in trouble for saying shut up.

3

By the Way

This is very embarrassing.

Have you ever been in a situation where you've been with someone for a while and you don't know that person's name? It's too late to ask, but you know the longer you go without asking, the more awkward it will become. So even though you feel really stupid, you finally just have to bite the bullet and say, "By the way, what's your name?"

That's how I'm feeling right now, only in reverse.

By the way, my name is Alton Richards.

A talented author would have skillfully slipped that in earlier, probably on the very first page. "Alton, come tell your favorite uncle how much you love him." Something like that.

Part of my difficulty, you have to admit, is my name. If I tried to slip *Alton* into the conversation, you might not have recognized it as a name. You might have wondered, "What does that word mean?"

And if I tried to slip in my last name, chances are you

would have thought my name was Richard Alton. A number of teachers have called me that.

I'm seventeen years old. I am five feet, ten and a half inches tall, and I weigh 150 pounds. My hair is brown, and more fluffy than curly. I have dark, "intuitive" eyes and a "warm" smile.

My ex-girlfriend, Katie, is the one who described my eyes as intuitive and said my smile was warm. That was before she dumped me. Afterward she probably would have said I had a pathetic stare and a goofy smile, but since I'm the one writing this, we'll stick with intuitive and warm.

I asked Katie what she meant by "intuitive eyes." She said I could see right through all her phoniness and I always knew exactly what was in her heart.

The truth is, I never had a clue.

Maybe that's why I fell in love with her. People are attracted to mystery. No doubt I once seemed mysterious too, but by the time we broke up, I was to her, just as I am to you, an open book.

4

And, And, And . . .

By mid-March Uncle Lester's health had taken another turn, whether for the better or worse depends on your point of view. Sophie Castaneda had installed some kind of New Age nurse in my uncle's household. This nurse, Teodora, put him on a vegetarian diet and had him doing yoga and meditation.

"She's just prolonging his suffering," my mother said, and maybe she really believed that.

Mrs. Mahoney didn't like the new nurse either, and complained to my mother that Teodora paraded around the house half naked.

"Which half?" I asked.

My mother ignored my question. "When Mrs. Mahoney suggested to her that she might want to dress more appropriately, do you know what Teodora said? 'What does it matter? He can't see me.'"

"What does it matter?" asked Leslie.

"It's disgusting, that's what" was our mother's reply.

I mentioned earlier that my mother didn't trust Mrs.

Mahoney, but you wouldn't know that from listening to her end of one of their daily telephone conversations. She'd chat and laugh and say things like "Isn't that just like a man?"

Mrs. Mahoney was her only source of information. It wasn't until after my mother hung up that the smile would leave her face. Then she'd wonder out loud if Mrs. Mahoney told Uncle Lester how many times she had called, or if Mrs. Mahoney had relayed even one of her dinner invitations.

My father was wrong when he said that Uncle Lester would never play cards again.

"He's been playing cards four days a week with Toni Castaneda," my mother informed us one evening, her voice stewed in bitterness.

I didn't see how that was possible.

"What can they play?" Leslie asked me later in my room. "Go Fish? 'Do you have any sevens?' Then what? Toni looks at his cards to see if he has any sevens. She could cheat like so easily!"

"Why would she cheat an old blind man who's about to die?" I asked. "It's probably just the opposite. He asks her if she has any sevens, and she says, 'Darn it, you got me again,' and hands him a six and a king."

"And then he changes his will and leaves her all his money," said Leslie.

Leslie had come into my room for the computer, but I was still using it. I had priority, not just because I was older and the computer was in my room, but because I usually waited until the last minute to do my homework, and so I had a greater urgency. Leslie did her homework the day it was assigned, and therefore could wait.

I know it's not fair. I'd get rewarded for my laziness, and she'd get punished for her diligence, but that's how it was.

"Well, I guess we'll soon be able to afford a second computer," I said.

"I guess so," Leslie agreed.

Neither of us wanted to sound overly excited about the prospect.

"And we'll probably be able to download all the music or movies we want," Leslie added.

"Probably," I agreed.

"How much money do you think Uncle Lester has?" she asked me.

"I have no idea."

"More than a million?"

"Definitely."

"More than fifty million?"

I shrugged. "It's not like we need a lot," I said. "Still, it would be good to get the pool finished."

Leslie agreed with that.

We currently had a big hole in our backyard, with some warning barriers around it. Our parents were involved in some kind of lawsuit with the pool company, although it had never been quite clear to me who was suing whom.

"And I can get my own phone," said Leslie, "with unlimited text messaging!"

"And I can get my car fixed," I said. "Or maybe even a new car."

"Or a new house that already has a swimming pool," said Leslie.

"And a hot tub," I said.

"And a game room, and a pool table," said Leslie.

"And a giant TV with surround sound, and every kind of video game."

And, and, and . . . That's the trouble with money.

5

Cliff

Whatever Teodora was doing for my uncle must have been working, because by the end of the school year, our hole in the ground was no closer to becoming a pool. My best friend, Cliff, landed a job as a lifeguard at the country club, so I figured I could probably sneak in there if I wanted to go swimming.

The reason I haven't mentioned Cliff before now is because even though he and I had been best friends since the third grade, we had stopped spending too much time together. He had a new girlfriend.

Her name was Katie.

If that name sounds familiar to you, yes, it's the same Katie who told me I had intuitive eyes.

I don't know why it hurt more to think about Katie with Cliff than Katie with somebody else, but to put it lightly, it tore at my insides.

That was my problem, I realized, not Cliff's. It wasn't his fault she broke up with me.

Cliff had asked my permission the first time he went over to her house. "You don't care if I go to Katie's to study for the French test, do you?"

What was I supposed to say—"No, you can't study with her, even if it means failing the final exam"?

I said some pretty terrible things to Katie when she dumped me. I called her awful names. Then I begged her to take me back. Then I called her more bad names. And then I begged some more.

It wasn't my finest hour.

I often wondered if Katie had told Cliff any of that. Did she tell him I cried?

If she did, Cliff never mentioned it to me. He was too good a friend.

I've gotten way off track here. When I started this chapter I was simply trying to relate my state of mind at the end of my junior year, and then I somehow got started on Katie again.

I guess she'll always be a part of my state of mind.

It was the second-to-last day of school. I didn't have any summer plans, just a vague notion about getting a job. I had just driven Leslie to her friend Marissa's house, and when I got home I heard my mother say, "Alton would love to spend time with his favorite uncle!"

I froze.

"Yes, he's an excellent driver," said my mother.

I should point out that whenever my mother rides with

me, she grips the armrest while slamming her foot on an imaginary brake.

"I think I just heard him come in. Alton, is that you?"

She walked into the kitchen where I was standing. Her eyes were filled with delight. She placed her hand over the phone and whispered, "It's Mrs. Mahoney. She wants you to play cards with Uncle Lester on Saturday. He and Toni Castaneda got into a big fight!"

I brought the phone to my ear. "Hello?"

"Do you know the difference between a king and a jack?" asked a gruff voice that did not belong to Mrs. Mahoney.

"Uh, yes, sir," I said.

My mother's eyes widened when she realized to whom I was talking. "Tell him he's your favorite uncle," she urged.

"Do you know how to play bridge?" asked my uncle.

I didn't, but thought that maybe I could fake it.

"Tell him you love him," said my mother.

"No," I said to my uncle (and to my mother).

"Good!" barked my uncle. "It's better that way!"

"I could probably pick it up by Satur—" I started to say, but Mrs. Mahoney was back on the line.

"Hello, Alton?" She told me that Mr. Trapp needed to be at his club by one o'clock, and that I should pick him up no later than twelve-fifteen. I would be his cardturner, which meant, as far as I could tell, that he would tell me what card to play and I would play it. It didn't make a lot of sense, but I was having trouble concentrating on everything Mrs. Mahoney said, because my mother, think-ing that I was still talking to Uncle Lester, kept telling me what to say.

"Well?" my mother asked once I hung up.

"I'm supposed to take him to his club on Saturday and play bridge with him."

My mother put her hands on my shoulders, looked me straight in the eye, and gave me her best motherly advice.

"Don't screw it up, Alton."

6

Are You Sure?

I knew that bridge was a card game, but that was about it. It seemed dull and old-fashioned. Maybe, at one time, bridge might have been some people's idea of fun, but that was before computers and video games.

I called Cliff, and hoped Katie wasn't with him. I'm always amazed by the stuff he knows. If anybody could teach me how to play bridge by Saturday, it would be him.

He was no help. According to Cliff, bridge was a card game little old ladies played while eating chocolate-covered raisins.

"Anyway, your uncle's blind," Cliff pointed out. "So he won't be able to tell whether you know how to play or not."

I wasn't quite sure about that. I went online and found a Web site that sold bridge books. There were hundreds of books on bridge, possibly a thousand. There were books for beginners, and for advanced and expert players. Just your basic how-to-play-bridge book was over two hundred pages, but even if I wanted to read it, I wouldn't get it in time for Saturday.

Mostly, the whole thing struck me as very odd. Why would there be so many books about one game?

I found another site that had the rules of bridge. I learned that bridge was a game played by four people. All the cards were dealt, so each person got thirteen cards. You were partners with the person who sat across from you.

I was lost after that. There were two parts to a bridge hand, *the bidding* and *the play,* but I couldn't tell you what you were supposed to do in either part. There were also things called a *contract,* and *trump,* and a *dummy,* and the directions north, south, east, and west seemed to have something to do with it.

"Didn't Uncle Lester say it was good you don't know how to play?" Leslie asked me, looking over my shoulder.

"I guess," I muttered, but that didn't make a whole lot of sense either. "How are we supposed to be partners?" I complained. "He can't see the cards, and I don't know the rules!"

"Don't yell at *me,*" said Leslie.

Saturday, my mother made me wear a jacket and tie. This despite the fact that it was over eighty degrees outside, and also despite the fact that *"He can't see what I'm wearing!"*

"You're taking him to his *club,*" replied my mother.

She let me take her car, thankfully, since mine wasn't all that reliable, but first I had to wash it. That made even less sense to me than wearing a jacket and tie. What, would all the other people at the club be looking out the window to make sure he arrived in a clean car?

My Internet directions said it would take forty-three minutes to get to his house, but it took me over an hour. Once I left Cross Canyon Boulevard, I had to follow a labyrinth of winding roads up a hill, and most of the street signs were hidden behind trees and flowering shrubs. I followed this simple rule: when in doubt, go up. My uncle's house was at the very top of the hill.

The house wasn't the castle I remembered from when I was six, but I could see why it had made that impression on me, all stone and wrought iron with giant beams of wood. Nor was the hill a mountain, although there were great sweeping views in all directions.

Not that the views were much good to him now, I thought somewhat morbidly.

An iron knocker in the shape of a goat's head, horns included, was attached to the massive front door. I was tempted, but used the doorbell instead. A dog barked inside.

Mrs. Mahoney opened the door. "Well, aren't you a handsome young man," she said, no doubt referring to my jacket and tie. "Hush, Captain!" she said to the dog, who did not hush.

"You'll have to excuse Captain. He's gotten a lot more protective since Mr. Trapp lost his eyesight."

Mrs. Mahoney was dressed in a peach-colored pantsuit and wore a jade necklace. At first glance she seemed very refined and genteel, but the way she grabbed Captain by his collar revealed a woman with muscular arms and a strong grip.

She invited me inside.

Captain was a mixed-breed, with just enough Doberman pinscher to make me wary about entering. However, my hope of seeing the half-naked Teodora was greater than my fear of my uncle's dog.

"He knows I've never played bridge, right?" I asked.

"Don't worry about that," Mrs. Mahoney assured me. "He will tell you which card to play."

"And you will play that card!" declared my uncle, coming through an archway. "You will not hesitate. You will not ask, '*Are you sure?*'"

For someone who was supposedly on the brink of death, his voice was loud and strong. He was a large man, both in height and weight. His hair was cut short, but there was still some black mixed with the gray. The only clue that there might be something wrong with him was his dark sunglasses.

"But you are to wait until I tell you what card to play, before you play it," he continued. "Even if you are certain what that card will be. Even if a diamond is led, and the ten of diamonds is the only diamond in your hand, you will wait until I say 'Ten of diamonds' before you place it on the table. Because if you play that card before I call for it, then everyone will know it's a singleton, won't they?"

I shrugged, which, I realized, was as meaningless to him as his words were to me.

"Mr. Trapp takes his bridge very seriously," said Mrs. Mahoney.

Captain continued to stare threateningly at me as my uncle rubbed him behind his ears. "What's your name?"

"Alton. Alton Richards."

"Your niece's son," said Mrs. Mahoney.

"Does he know Toni?" asked my uncle.

"Ask him yourself."

He didn't ask. Instead, he launched into a tirade of bridge gibberish.

"Dummy's got king, queen, ten of spades, and I'm sitting behind it with ace, four, doubleton. Declarer leads the deuce, partner plays the seven, and declarer calls for the king from dummy. 'Four of spades,' I say, without the slightest pause for thought. And what does Toni do? Does she play the four? No. She *hesitates*. She asks, '*Are you sure?*' A few lessons and she thinks she knows more than I do!"

"Toni doesn't think that," said Mrs. Mahoney.

"Well, she just told the whole table where the ace was, didn't she?"

I hoped that question wasn't directed at me, because I had no idea what he was talking about.

"What's your name?" he asked me again.

"Alton Richards," I said.

"*Are you sure?*"

I wasn't sure what to say.

"Dumb question, ain't it? Hah!"

7

Teodora

Teodora came drifting through the same archway as had my uncle, although he hadn't exactly *drifted*. The only half of her that was naked was below the knees and above the neck. She wore five ankle bracelets, all on the same ankle.

I should mention that my interest in Teodora, and what she was or wasn't wearing, wasn't due entirely to my total lack of maturity. I was required to report back to my mother on whether or not she was "alluring."

Teodora reminded my uncle to breathe, and to focus on the Here and Now.

She was about half my uncle's age, about twice mine. I wouldn't call her alluring in the normal sense, not that it was a word I would ever use. She was plump, and had a pockmarked face, yet when I shook her cool hand, I found myself looking into her dark and—there's no other word for it—*alluring* eyes.

I found her voice alluring too, which probably mattered a whole lot more to my uncle than her complexion. When she introduced herself to me she said her name was "Day-o-daughter," with the *gh* in *daughter* not quite silent. She called Captain El Capitan.

She confused her singulars and plurals too. As my uncle and I were about to leave, she put her hand on my arm and told me not to let him eat any "cakes or cookie." "And no *café*!"

I led him to the car, his left hand holding my right elbow. I was unsure whether I should open the front or back door for him. Was I his chauffeur, or were we family? It seems silly now, but as we moved closer to the car I really agonized over it.

Finally I just asked. "So, do you want the front or the back?"

"Shotgun," he said, "so I can watch the road."

I guessed that was a joke. I smiled politely, which, I realized once again, meant the same to him as if I had stuck out my tongue.

Mrs. Mahoney had given me directions to the club, but unfortunately they began by telling me to head back down the hill the way I had come. Even on normal, right-angle roads, I get confused when I try to follow directions in reverse. It was nearly impossible to try to figure out my way through the tangle of streets.

My uncle must have realized I was having problems. He suddenly asked, "What street are you on now?"

I edged past a shrub so I could read the street sign. "Skyflower," I said.

"You're not too far off. Turn right, then make another right on Ridgecrest."

I did as I was told.

"It's easy to get lost up here," he said. "I moved here for the view. Hah! Doesn't do me much good now, does it?"

That was exactly what I had been thinking earlier, but it didn't seem right to agree with him. "Well, you can still kind of feel it, can't you?"

"What does a view feel like?" he asked.

I felt foolish, but I pressed on. "An aura," I tried. "Can't you still kind of sense, in some way, that you're on top of the world?"

"I could be living across the street from a junkyard," he said matter-of-factly, without a trace of bitterness.

8

The Club

If you were expecting a fancy club, with plush carpeting, leather chairs, wood paneling, and people sipping brandy and smoking cigars as they discuss the stock market, then you've come to the wrong place.

Maybe I should have realized that earlier, when I saw that my uncle was not dressed up like me, but I think I chalked that up to his blindness. I guess I thought that blind people could get away with wearing anything. Other people would just assume they made a mistake getting dressed, and would be too polite to comment.

My second clue was the club's location. Mrs. Mahoney's directions took me through the parking lot of a carpet warehouse, and then into a complex of industrial offices. I parked in front of building number two, then led my uncle up some concrete steps to the second door on the right, where the words BRIDGE STUDIO were stenciled on the glass.

Three rows of square tables. Eight tables per row. Four chairs at each table. Computer printouts posted on the walls. And all around me, people were speaking bridge gibberish.

"I'm the only one to bid the grand, which would be cold if spades weren't five-one."

"Unless you can count thirteen tricks, don't bid a grand."

"I had thirteen tricks! Hell, I had fifteen tricks, as long as spades broke decently."

I asked my uncle where we were supposed to go, and he told me he always sat at table three, South.

In the center of each table was a laminated placard that indicated the table number and the directions: North, South, East, and West. Each direction corresponded to one of the four sides of the table.

As I negotiated our way to table three, a woman wearing a big hat approached my uncle. "Trapp!" she demanded. "One banana, pass, pass, two no-trump. Is that unusual?"

It sounded unusual to me.

"That's not how I play it," said my uncle.

A moment later a man in shorts and a torn T-shirt came up to him.

"Trapp, can I ask you something?"

"Go ahead."

"Do you remember that hand from last Monday, when you were in four hearts, and dummy had six clubs to the king?"

"King, nine, eight, six, four, three," said my uncle. "Your partner led the five, clearly a singleton."

"Could I have set you?"

"You needed to cash the king and ace of spades before giving your partner his club ruff."

"I didn't have the king."

"Your partner did."

"How was I to know that?"

My uncle gave a half-smile as he raised his left shoulder about an inch, then lowered it.

Even though I didn't understand what they were talking about, I think that was my first inkling that bridge wasn't just a simple game, and that there maybe was something extraordinary about my uncle.

When we reached table three, there were two chairs in the South position. My uncle told me to take the one closer to the table, and then he sat in the chair to my left and a little behind me.

"Well, I see you have a new cardturner," said the woman sitting across from me in the North seat. "Do you think maybe you can keep this one?"

"He's perfect," my uncle said. "He knows nothing about bridge, and even better, he knows he knows nothing."

I wasn't sure whether I was being complimented or insulted.

"Well, aren't you going to introduce us?" asked the woman.

My uncle didn't say anything.

"You don't know his name, do you?" accused the woman.

He remained quiet.

She reached her hand across the table. "I'm Gloria."

"Alton," I said, shaking her hand.

"Don't feel bad, Alton. I've been Trapp's partner for eighteen years, and he only just learned my name last Wednesday."

"Hah!" laughed my uncle.

9

Shuffle and Play

Gloria was an elderly woman with blond hair. She wore lots of jewelry, including earrings that looked like cards, the queen of hearts and the queen of clubs. She was nicely dressed, as were most of the women in the room. It was mostly the men who were slobs.

You know what? I'm not going to describe anybody else as *elderly*. Let's just say that if you take my age and double it, I would still have been the youngest person in the room, *by a lot*.

A man came around and placed two metal trays on each table. The room, which had been abuzz with bridge gibberish, began to quiet down.

"There are fourteen tables," the man announced. "We will play thirteen rounds, two boards a round, with a skip after round seven. Shuffle and play."

I didn't know he was called the *director*, or that the metal card-holding trays were called *boards*. This isn't easy. I'm trying to relate my overwhelming sense of

28

confusion and at the same time let you know what was going on—even though I didn't.

A board is a small rectangular tray, with four slots for the cards. The slots are labeled *North, South, East,* and *West.* Each board is numbered. Our boards were numbered five and six.

One thing did become clear to me. Gloria was my uncle's partner. I was to be his assistant, his cardturner. Before each hand, I was to take him aside and tell him what cards he held, and then he would tell me which card to play.

That made more sense.

Sort of.

The cards were shuffled and dealt; then each hand was placed back into the slots on the board. I learned later that this would be the only time all day that the cards would be shuffled. The same hands would be played over and over again at different tables.

We began with board number five. Everyone removed their cards from their corresponding slots. Since my uncle and I were in the South position, I removed the cards from the South slot. The bridge studio was now as quiet as a library.

It may seem silly, but I suddenly felt very nervous.

I stood up and led my uncle to the coffee alcove. I think that was why he always sat at table three. It was the one closest to the alcove.

No, I didn't let him have any *"café."* Even if my family did hope to inherit his fortune, I wasn't about to do anything to speed up the process. The coffee alcove was just a place where I could tell him his hand without other people overhearing.

I spoke quietly, slightly above a whisper. "Nine of spades, king of hearts, three of clubs, jack of spades, ten of di—"

"Stop!" he suddenly shouted, covering his ears. "What do you think you're doing?"

"Just telling you—"

"Are you a moron?" he asked. "Or are you just trying to drive me insane?"

I didn't know what I'd done wrong. Everyone in the room had stopped what they were doing to look at us.

The director hurried over and asked if there was a problem.

"Yes, there's a problem," said my uncle. "My new card-turner is an imbecile!"

"Keep it up, Trapp," the director warned, "and I'm going to penalize you half a board."

"Yes, penalize him," said Gloria, entering the alcove. "Maybe he'll learn some manners." She said this even though penalizing my uncle would also have meant penalizing her.

My uncle threw up his hands. "He just starts rattling off cards!"

"Well, did you explain how you wanted it done?" asked Gloria.

He sputtered a moment, then admitted he had not.

"Then I suggest you do," said Gloria. "But first you owe him an apology."

She gave me a sympathetic smile, then returned to the table.

He didn't apologize, but he did explain how I was supposed to tell him his cards. I had to sort them into suits first, and then tell him his spades, highest to lowest, then his hearts, then diamonds, then clubs. Always that order.

"You got that?" he asked.

"Spades, hearts, diamonds, clubs," I repeated, trying to sound bored and uninterested, as if I found the whole thing beneath me. I was angry that he'd called me a moron and an imbecile in front of everyone.

I gave him his hand as directed. "Spades: ace, jack, nine, three, two. Hearts: king, nine. Diamonds: ten, six, four. Clubs: ace, queen, three."

"Is that better?" I asked, filling my voice with contempt, both for him and for his stupid game.

He didn't seem to notice my tone, or care about what I thought. His mind was focused on those thirteen cards.

We sat back down. On each corner of the table there was something called a bidding box.

Gloria reached into her bidding box, took out a green pass card, and placed it on the table. "Pass," she said aloud. At every other table, the bidding was done in silence.

The man next to her, in the East seat, also passed.

"One spade," said my uncle.

I reached into my bidding box, removed the 1♠ card, and set it on the table. "One spade," I repeated.

I should mention that nobody bothered to explain bidding boxes to me. I figured out what I was supposed to do all by myself, but do you think my uncle gave me any credit for that?

No.

Over the next two and a half hours we played twenty-six hands of bridge. "Nine of hearts," my uncle would say, and I'd set the ♡9 on the table. "Queen of clubs," and I'd lay down the ♣Q. He never once forgot what cards he held. His voice remained flat, so I had no clue how well he was doing, but after a while I got the impression that my uncle and Gloria were doing very, very well.

Each time, one of the hands became the dummy. That hand was placed faceup on the table for everyone to see. The dummy's cards were said aloud for my uncle's benefit, once and only once, always in the same order: spades, hearts, diamonds, then clubs. So not only did he have to memorize every card in his own hand, he had to memorize all of the dummy's cards too. That's twenty-six cards, half the deck.

Every North-South pair was a team, and every East-West pair was a team. When we finished a hand, everyone would place their cards back in their original slots on the board. We played two boards each round; then the East-West pair would leave and a new team would sit down against us. We would pass the boards we had played to table two and get new boards from table four.

It was like some sort of odd dance, with the people moving in one direction and the boards moving in the other. After the seventh round, every East-West pair skipped a table to avoid playing boards they had already played.

At least three women commented on Trapp's "handsome" new cardturner. Gloria always had to introduce me since my uncle still didn't know my name.

It might not have been just the jacket and tie. Women over a certain age tend to think I'm handsome. Girls under twelve too. According to Leslie, all her friends think I'm hot. Whenever her friends are over, I can hear them giggle when I walk past. The first few times it happened, I checked to make sure my fly was zipped.

When it was all over, Trapp and Gloria had played against every East-West pair except for the team that had skipped them. (I'll call him Trapp, since that's what everyone else called him.) They'd played twenty-six of the twenty-eight boards. The director gathered all the score sheets and entered the results into the computer.

"Did you win?" I asked.

"We'll have to wait and see," said Gloria.

It was odd that after playing for almost three hours, we had to wait for the computer to tell us who won.

"Thank God for computers," said Gloria. "In the old days, we had to wait around for almost an hour while the director tallied the scores by hand. Sometimes we didn't find out until the next day."

Gloria explained that the final score depended on how she and Trapp did on each board, compared with every other North-South pair. So even if they only took two tricks on board nineteen, they would still get a high score on that board if most other North-South pairs only took one trick.

I liked that. I was unlucky when it came to cards. Cliff always beat me at poker. He must have won close to a hundred dollars off me, and we only played for quarters.

I guess that was the one good thing about him being with Katie. We hadn't played any poker for a while.

But in this game, luck wasn't a factor. It didn't matter if Trapp was dealt bad cards. It was just how well he played those bad cards, compared to every other person sitting in the South position, who had to play the same bad cards.

A woman came up to my uncle and asked his result on

33

board fourteen, a hand we probably played an hour and a half ago.

My uncle thought for no more than seven seconds. "We set three no-trump two tricks."

"You set it? They made an overtrick against us!"

"You have to knock out dummy's king of spades," said Trapp, "and then hold up twice on your diamond ace."

But he still couldn't remember my name.

The printer spat out the results, and the director posted them on the wall. The scores were given in terms of percentages. Trapp and Gloria won with a 65 percent game. That might not sound like much, but second place was only 56 percent.

I take back what I said about luck. The East-West pair who skipped table three was very lucky.

10

An Apology of a Sort

We drove back in silence, which was just fine with me. I was having a difficult enough time trying to follow the directions from his house to his club, in reverse.

"I'm going to give you thirteen letters," he suddenly said. "I want you to repeat them back to me."

Before I could even say *"What?"* he began rattling off random letters. *"G-b-c-d-i-o-a-o-r-y-t-g-l."*

I gave it my best shot—"Um, *g, b, c* . . ."—but then stopped. "Look, I get it," I said. "Your memory is better than mine."

"It's not memory. It's context. I'm going to give you the same thirteen letters, but in a different order. Concentrate really hard now."

I sighed.

"G-i-r-l, b-o-y, c-a-t, d-o-g."

I didn't bother saying them back to him.

"Hah!" he laughed, then said, "They're the same letters. I just sorted them into suits for you."

Half an hour later we were parked in his driveway and I escorted him to the front door.

"How much did Mrs. Mahoney tell you?" he asked.

About what? I thought, then noticed him fumbling with his wallet. "She didn't say," I said. "Just whatever you paid Toni is fine."

"This has nothing to do with Toni. We have a different arrangement. How about seventy-five?"

"Sure."

He handed me his wallet. I removed three twenties, a ten, and five ones, then gave it back to him.

Teodora opened the front door. "Thank you so much, Alton," she said as she shook my hand, using both of hers. "This means so much to him."

"It's just a card game," groused my uncle.

She led him inside, and I returned to the car.

Okay, I admit it. When he handed me his wallet, the thought did occur to me that I could take any amount of money I wanted and he wouldn't know the difference. Not that I would steal from a blind person. Not that I would steal from anybody, even if he was so rich he'd never notice, and even if he did call me an imbecile and a moron in front of a roomful of people.

Besides, I was no longer angry at him, and it wasn't just because he paid me. I think the girl-boy-cat-dog thing was his way of apologizing.

"You will return that money!" my mother said the second I stepped into the house.

She had obviously chatted with her dear friend Mrs. Mahoney.

"Get back in that car, drive straight to his house, and tell him you have no interest in taking any money from him. You're doing it for the joy of spending time with your favorite uncle."

"He'll think I'm crazy!" I protested.

"No, he'll respect you for your integrity."

"I'm not being unintegritary," I replied. (Don't bother looking up that word.) "I've been gone for almost six hours. Seventy-five dollars is barely minimum wage. And then there's the price of gas."

I thought "the price of gas" would be my trump card. I couldn't remember a single day when my parents didn't complain about gas prices—not that it stopped my father from buying an SUV.

"You think you're doing this for a measly seventy-five bucks?" asked my mother. "Seventy-five dollars is squat! In a few months Uncle Lester will be . . ." She didn't finish her sentence. For a brief instant I thought I saw a flash of sadness on my mother's face, as if the words she was about to say suddenly meant something to her. But that was only for an instant. "All right, you can return it to him on Monday."

"What's Monday?" I asked.

"He goes to his club every Monday, Wednesday, Thursday, and Saturday."

So this wasn't a onetime thing.

"What about my job?" I asked.

"What job?" she scoffed.

37

"I was going to get a job this summer."

She stared at me, hands on her hips.

I turned and skulked into my room.

Okay, I was too lazy to get a job, and my mother knew it, but I wasn't as lazy as she thought I was. I was fairly certain that I could have packed groceries or hauled boxes from one end of a warehouse to the other with as much vim and gusto as anyone. My problem was I couldn't get motivated to actually get into my car and drive to every supermarket, restaurant, movie theater, and appliance store just to ask to fill out a job application. Especially since I was pretty sure they'd throw my application in the trash the second I walked out the door.

I phoned Cliff and told him about the bridge club. "It's crazy," I said. "These people are like from a different planet. Planet Bridge. They even speak their own language."

"They're just a bunch of old people," said Cliff. "It's either bridge or bingo."

For some reason I felt offended by that remark. Bingo was just a game of luck. Bridge seemed more like a sport, a mental sport, like chess, only with a partner. And my uncle was a superstar of the sport.

"My uncle is amazing," I told Cliff. "Everybody's always coming up to him and asking 'How should I have played this hand?' or 'How would you bid this hand?' And he can't even see the cards."

Cliff wasn't impressed. "You told him what cards he had, right?"

"Right, then he told me which card to play."

"Well, what's so amazing about that?" Cliff asked. "Now, if he could somehow know his cards without you telling him, that would be amazing."

I tried again, but he showed little interest. In fact, he didn't seem all that interested in talking to me, quickly dismissing whatever I said.

Then it hit me: Katie was over there.

I can be such an idiot! I told him I had to go, and hung up.

11

Tiger Woods's Caddy

I didn't have to return the seventy-five dollars after all, thanks to Leslie. She pointed out to our mother that if I returned Uncle Lester's money, he might think we were so rich we didn't need it. Then he wouldn't leave us anything in his will.

I drove Trapp to his bridge club Monday, Wednesday, Thursday, and Saturday, and continued to get paid seventy-five dollars each time. Maybe I should have given Leslie a cut.

I no longer wore a jacket and tie, but my mother worked during the week, so I had to drive my car. One time it lurched a bit, and almost died, but I doubted Trapp noticed. We were driving back to his house after the Wednesday game, so his mind was on some bridge hand.

Every bridge hand is a unique puzzle. If Trapp failed to solve the puzzle at the table, he would figure it out on the way home. He would think not only about what he should have done differently, but also about what the opponents should have done, and what he would have done if they had done that. I could have driven into a ditch and he wouldn't have noticed.

Gloria was Trapp's partner on Monday, Thursday, and Saturday, but on Wednesday he played with Wallace, a tall black man who taught physics at the university. Wallace and Trapp argued with each other after every single hand, saying things like "I asked for a club switch! If I wanted a spade returned I would have led a low one," and "How could you bid three spades? Didn't you hear my double?"

Listening to them, you would have thought they were in last place, but they ended up with a 72 percent game, which was huge. Apparently it was very rare to break seventy percent.

I learned what I was supposed to do if Trapp was dealt a hand with no cards in one suit. I'd say the word *void*. So when telling him his hand, I'd say something like "Spades: ten, nine, eight, seven, six. Hearts: king, queen, jack. Diamonds: *void*. Clubs: ace, nine, six, three, two."

I also began to understand how the game was played. I learned what *trump* meant. I wouldn't admit it to my uncle, but the game began to intrigue me. I would sometimes try to guess what card he'd play before he told me to play it, but don't worry, I never asked, "Are you sure?"

Toni Castaneda must have been out of her mind.

In all, we came in first three times and finished third once. I say "we" because I began to think of myself as part of the team. I imagined I was like Tiger Woods's caddy. I had once heard Tiger Woods on TV saying how important his caddy was to him, how he wouldn't have won some golf tournament without him.

Trapp never actually said anything like that about me, but he wasn't big on compliments. One time I heard him say "Nicely played" to an opponent. That was it.

12

The Basics

Do you see that picture of a whale? It's going to be our secret code. (Okay, maybe it's not so secret.)

This past year I had to read *Moby-Dick* in my Language Arts / English class. It seemed like a pretty good adventure story about a monster killer whale, but just when I started to get into it, the author, Herman Melville, stopped the story and went on page after page describing every tiny detail of a whaling ship. I zoned out. I never finished the book and had to bluff my way through the test.

The reason I'm telling you this is because I'm about to attempt to explain the basics of bridge. My guess is that there's going to have to be more bridge in this book as well.

I'm not going to try to teach you how to play bridge. There's no way I could do that. I'll just try to explain enough of the basics that if you want, you might be able to understand some of the bridge stuff that happens.

I realize that reading about a bridge game isn't exactly thrilling. No one's going to make a movie out of it. Bridge is like chess. A great chess player moves his pawn up one square, and for the .0001 percent of the population who understand what just happened, it was the football equivalent of intercepting a pass and running it back for a touchdown. But for the rest of us, it was still just a pawn going from a black square to a white one. Or, getting back to bridge, it was Trapp playing the six of diamonds instead of the two of clubs.

Well, there's nothing I can do about that. I'm sorry my seventy-six-year-old blind, diabetic uncle didn't play linebacker for the Chicago Bears.

So here's the deal. Whenever you see the picture of the whale, it means I'm about to go into some detail about bridge. If that makes you zone out, then just skip ahead to the summary box and I'll give you the short version.

There are two parts to a bridge hand, the *bidding* and the *play*. For now, I'm just going to explain how the play works.

It's all about taking tricks. Somebody sets a card on the table. Then, going clockwise around the table, the next three people all must play a card of that same suit, in turn. After all four people have played, the person who played the highest card wins the trick.

That person is then *on-lead* for the next trick. That means he or she chooses any card to play, and once again everyone else has to *follow suit*.

As I mentioned earlier, one of the four players is the dummy. The dummy hand is set out on the table for everyone to see. When it's the dummy's turn to play, the dummy's partner tells the dummy which card to play. So when Trapp's hand is *dummy*, Gloria tells me which card to play.

Everyone begins with thirteen cards, which means there are a total of thirteen tricks for each bridge hand. Since Trapp and Gloria are partners, it doesn't matter whether Trapp wins a trick or Gloria wins it. It counts the same.

"What happens if you can't follow suit?" Leslie asked me when I explained this to her.

You have two choices. You can *discard*, which means you just choose some card in your hand that's no good anyway and basically just throw it away. Or you can win the trick by playing a *trump* card. Trump cards are like wild cards in poker.

Let's say diamonds are trump. Somebody leads a club, but Trapp doesn't have any clubs left in his hand.

He can win the trick by playing a diamond. Any diamond will do. The ◊6 will beat the ♣K. That's called *trumping* or *ruffing*. Everyone else still has to play a club if they have one.

"Why are diamonds trump?" Leslie asked me.

I just used that as an example. A different suit is trump for each hand. It had to do with the bidding, which I still didn't quite understand.

A person plays a card and the next three people all have to play a card of that same suit. The person who plays the highest card wins the trick. If you can't *follow suit*, you can either *discard* or *play* a *trump*. There are a total of thirteen tricks in each hand of bridge.

13

In the Garbage

I got to thinking. Toni Castaneda had been Trapp's card-turner before me, before she asked, "Are you sure?" But how could she have taken him to the bridge studio during the week? School had only just ended.

"She's homeschooled," my mother explained. "Uncle Lester taught her bridge as one of her courses. They wouldn't let a girl like her into a real school. She'd freak out!"

"Why? What's wrong with her?"

"She's nuts. The whole family is nuts. Her mother, her grandmother. Did you know they could be extremely wealthy, but Sophie threw their money in the garbage? And I don't just mean a few million dollars. I'm talking real money."

I always thought a few million dollars was real money. "What do you mean she threw it in the garbage?" I asked.

"Just what I said," said my mother. "In the garbage!"

She then explained that Sophie Castaneda's father had been Henry King, one of the wealthiest men in America.

"Sophie didn't appreciate her parents and all they did for her. She ran away from home when she was fifteen, and when she turned eighteen she legally divorced them."

"You can do that?" I asked.

"Don't be smart," said my mother.

Sophie eventually married Martin Castaneda, and they had a daughter, Toni. Sophie had refused to let her father ever see his granddaughter, or even talk to her on the telephone.

Sophie's father's lawyers sent her a letter, trying to arrange a meeting between grandfather and granddaughter. They offered Sophie five hundred thousand dollars for a onetime visit, and one million dollars per year after that for regular monthly visits. In addition, her dad promised to include both daughter and granddaughter in his will.

It was the letter that Sophie had thrown in the garbage. She sent a short note back to the lawyers. *My daughter is not for sale.* When Henry King died, years later, he didn't leave them a penny.

14

National Championship

Cliff wanted to know how much money Trapp got for winning.

Nothing. He earned masterpoints.

Gloria explained it to me after the game on Saturday while Trapp was in the men's room.

She said there are bridge clubs in almost every city in the United States, and that they're all part of the American Contract Bridge League (ACBL). The results of each and every game are sent to the ACBL. That organization keeps track of who won, and awards masterpoints.

That first day I was his cardturner, when Gloria and Trapp won, there had been fourteen tables, so they won 1.4 masterpoints. Notice the decimal point. That's one and four-tenths. You need five hundred masterpoints to become a Life Master.

"Is Trapp a Life Master?" I asked.

"Oh, yes," she said.

"Are you?"

She said she was. I asked her how many masterpoints she had.

"A little over five thousand."

"Wow!"

"There are higher rankings than Life Master. At one thousand points you become a Silver Life Master. At 2,500 you're a Gold Life Master, and you need 5,000 to be a Diamond Life Master."

"So you're a Diamond Life Master," I said.

She shrugged as if it were no big deal, but I could tell by her smile that she was proud of her accomplishment.

"How many masterpoints does Trapp have?"

"Eleven thousand."

I wasn't surprised.

"How about Wallace?" I asked. I wondered if there was some sort of competition between Gloria and Wallace.

"I don't know," she said. "I think about eighteen hundred. He's a very strong player. Much better than I am. He just doesn't play as often."

"What's the highest rank you can get?" I asked.

"Grand Life Master," said Gloria. "You need ten thousand masterpoints for that."

"So Trapp's a Grand Life Master."

She shook her head. "No. To be a Grand Life Master, you also need to win a national championship."

So far, I had just taken Trapp to club games. It turns out there are also bridge tournaments, where you can earn a greater number of masterpoints if you win, but the competition is much tougher.

There are three types of tournaments: sectionals, regionals, and nationals. In order for Trapp to win a national championship, he would have to win a major event at a national tournament.

"Has he ever played in a national?" I asked.

"Only one time, but listen to me, Alton," she said, suddenly sounding very serious. "You must never ask your uncle about that."

"Why, what happened?"

She stared at me a moment, then just shook her head. "That was over forty years ago," she said. "It's best to let sleeping dogs lie."

"Well, do you think he'll ever try again?" I asked.

"I think that's the reason he's started playing again, despite his illness, or maybe *because* of his illness. He wants to give it one last shot." She looked me straight in the eye and said, "That's why you're here."

In the back of my mind I heard my mother's sweet and loving voice: *Don't screw it up, Alton.*

15

The Perfect Partner

Trapp came out of the men's room. "How'd we do?" he asked.

"Fifty-nine percent," I said. "Second place."

"I should have switched to the ten of clubs at trick two," he said.

He was speaking to himself. He knew I didn't know what he was talking about. He was still muttering about club switches and heart tricks as I led him out to the car.

Gloria probably shouldn't have told me not to ask him about the last time he played in a national tournament. As I drove him home, it was all I could think about. *What wouldn't Gloria tell me? After all, what's the worst that can happen at a bridge tournament?*

"So, who's your partner going to be for the national tournament?" I asked. "Gloria or Wallace?"

(Gloria didn't say I couldn't ask him about that tournament, just not the one forty years ago.)

"What!" he snapped. "Who said anything about playing in the nationals?"

"Gloria just mentioned—"

"Gloria's a dreamer. How am I supposed to compete against the best players in the world when I can't even see the cards?"

"You see the cards better than anyone," I said.

"Hah!" he scoffed, but I noticed a hint of a smile. "You may find this hard to believe, Alton," he said, "but bridge is tiring. I get worn out after just one session. That probably sounds strange to you. From your point of view, all I do is sit on my keester for three hours."

"No, I know," I said. "It's like I told my friend Cliff. Bridge is more like a sport than a game. A mental sport."

"At tournaments you play two sessions per day," he said. "I don't know if I'm up to it. I don't know if they'll even let me play."

"They have to let you play."

"Tournaments have strict rules," he said. "The club is willing to accommodate me and my cardturner. You may not be allowed to sit with me at a tournament."

"That's not fair," I said.

"There's a sectional tournament in two weeks," Trapp said. "Gloria's checking with the ACBL to see if I'll be allowed to compete."

"So then she'll be your partner?"

"*If* I play."

We drove in silence for a while. He could sue them, I thought, if they wouldn't let him play in the tournament.

"Gloria has more masterpoints than Wallace," I said, "but she says that's because she's played a lot more. She says he's a better player than she is."

"They're both excellent players," he said. "I'm honored to play with them."

"But you're better," I said.

"They can see the cards," he said, as if that made a difference.

"You had a seventy-two percent game with Wallace," I said. "I think he should be your partner for the nationals."

He sighed.

I thought that would be the end of it, but then he said, "Wallace can play the cards better, but Gloria is a better partner."

I didn't understand.

"Like you said, bridge is a sport," he explained. "But it's a *team* sport. You and your partner have to work together. Wallace is like a basketball player who's always shooting the ball. He can make some amazing shots, but he wouldn't have to take those shots if he passed the ball more often."

It was too bad, I thought, that Gloria couldn't play the cards as well as Wallace, or that Wallace couldn't be as good a partner as Gloria.

"I guess it's hard to find the perfect partner," I said.

"Wallace and Gloria are still looking," he replied.

I doubted that.

We drove in silence for a while, but then he said, "It's easier to find a wife."

I turned off Ridgecrest onto Skyline, then made my way up the tangled web of streets toward his house.

I thought our conversation had come to an end, but he surprised me. "I used to have the perfect partner," he said. "Used to have a wife, too."

53

"Were they the same person?" I asked.

"No, sisters."

I waited for more, but there was no further explanation. I glanced over. His jaw was set tight and it seemed as though his face had turned to stone.

16

The Milkman and the Senator's Wife

As I drove back to my house, I tried to put the pieces together in my mind. About forty years ago, Trapp had been married. His wife's sister was his "perfect" bridge partner. Then something happened at a bridge tournament. Trapp's partner went insane, he and his wife got divorced, and he never played in a national tournament again.

His wife's crazy sister, his perfect partner, was the mother of Sophie Castaneda, who was the one who threw the letter in the garbage.

Sophie was the mother of Toni, who had yelled "Shut up! Leave me alone!" at me when we were six, and who had also made the terrible mistake of asking Trapp, "Are you sure?"

I don't know if that makes any sense to you, but it didn't to me.

When I got home I asked my mother how long she had known Sophie Castaneda.

She flinched at the name. "I've known *of* her for a very long time. I've only met her a few times."

"Did you ever meet Sophie's mother?"

"No."

"Then why do you think she was insane?"

"I don't just *think* she was insane," said my mother. "She was sent to an asylum."

"Is that why Sophie divorced her mother?"

"Sophie didn't divorce her real mother," my mother corrected me. "Senator King remarried after Sophie's mother was put in the insane asylum."

"Sophie's father was a senator?" This was news to me.

"He would have made a damn good president, too," my mother added.

"So what kind of crazy things did Sophie's mother do?"

"Everything. The way she lived was crazy! She was the reason Henry King never became president. Mind you, I was just a little girl at the time, but I heard stories. One time, she gave the milkman a thousand dollars for his clothes."

I had never heard of a milkman. I supposed it was like being a mailman, only with milk instead of mail.

"He was still wearing them at the time," my mother continued. "She paid him to take off his clothes and give them to her. And then she made him wear her dress and all her underneath things."

"And he wore them?"

"For a thousand dollars, he did. That was a lot of money in those days."

I thought it was a lot of money in these days. I walked down the hall into my room and tried to make sense of what my mother had told me. I wondered if she had her story straight.

I hate to say this about my own mother, but she doesn't always know what she's talking about.

I picked up a deck of cards and practiced shuffling. Gloria had taught me how to shuffle cards so that they'd flutter perfectly together.

If it was something my mother had heard when she was just a little girl, then who knows who told it to her, or how much of it she understood? It seemed to me that maybe the senator's wife had been doing something else with the milkman, and the senator came home unexpectedly, and they both just grabbed whatever clothes were the closest. That made a little more sense, but either way, my uncle's "perfect partner" sounded a bit weird, to say the least.

17

Finesse

Besides trying to find out what happened forty years ago, I was also trying to figure out bridge. I never admitted it to my uncle, but I paid attention to every card he played and listened closely to all the bridge gibberish, trying to make some sense out of it.

I learned what it meant to *finesse*.

Suppose Gloria is dummy, and has both the ace and queen of spades. (We won't worry about her other cards.)

Dummy (Gloria)
♠ AQ

West   East

Trapp (South)
♠ 42

Trapp would like to win two spade tricks. The ace will win one, of course, but he also would like to win a trick with the queen. But how can he do that? One of the defenders still has the king of spades.

The answer lies in a play known as a *finesse*. It will only work if the West hand is the one with the king.

Dummy (Gloria)
♠ AQ

West
♠ K5

East

Trapp (South)
♠ 42

Trapp will lead the ♠2. Let's say West plays the ♠5. Then Trapp will tell dummy to play the ♠Q, which will win the trick. If instead West plays the ♠K, Trapp will play the ♠A from dummy, and then win the next trick with the ♠Q. No matter which card West plays, he's screwed.

"That's so cool!" Leslie said when I showed this to her. I thought it was cool too.

It only worked because West had the ♠K. If East had the king, then she'd be able to win a trick with it. A finesse gives you a 50 percent chance.

Once I understood it, I noticed finesses popping up a lot.

Dummy (Gloria)
♡ 98

West   East

Trapp (South)
♡ AQ

This time Trapp hopes that East has the ♡K. If so, he
can finesse it by leading the eight from dummy. If East
plays the king, Trapp plays the ace. If East doesn't play
the king, Trapp plays the queen.

You can also finesse queens.

Gloria (North)
♣ 654

West   East

Dummy (me)
♣ AKJ

Gloria leads the ♣4, and hopes that East has the ♣Q. If
East plays a small club, Gloria can win the trick with
dummy's jack.

By the way, when I showed this to Leslie, I used real
cards, not a bridge diagram. If you find it difficult to follow the diagrams, try using a real deck. For the first hand,
you can also try dealing East the king of spades instead of
West, and you will see why the finesse won't work.

A *finesse* is a cool play that allows you to win two tricks with the ace and queen of a suit, even though one of your opponents holds the king. It has a 50 percent chance of success, depending on which one of your opponents holds that king.

18

The Housing Crisis

Nights were the hardest for me. I usually didn't think too much about Katie, or Cliff and Katie, during the day, and even if I did, I was strong enough to handle it. I was weaker at night and sometimes came close to calling her even though I knew I'd regret it.

I had to force myself to think about something else. Sometimes I would deal out bridge hands. I'd play all four hands, pretending I didn't know which cards were in each hand. Leslie would sometimes join me, but on this night, I was alone.

It was Wednesday. Trapp had played with Wallace earlier in the day, and they had won with a 61 percent game. They had argued after every hand, but not as much as they had when they'd had their 72 percent game.

There was a knock on my door. A moment later my parents entered, Leslie in tow. Her eyes were red, and my parents wore very somber expressions.

My first thought was that Uncle Lester had died.

"What's wrong?"

My father got right to the point. "My company is having to cut back," he said. "I was fired."

"You weren't fired," said my mother. "You were laid off."

I'd heard vaguely about something called "the housing crisis," but it didn't mean much to me until that moment.

What happened was this. A lot of banks made bad loans. People couldn't pay them back, and many people lost their homes. The banks lost a lot of money and stopped making new loans, which meant people stopped buying houses, which meant builders stopped building houses, which meant nobody needed insulation material. Which meant my father was out of a job.

"Are we going to have to move?" Leslie asked.

"We'll be fine," my mother assured her, or maybe it was herself she was assuring. Then, turning to my father, she said, "You hated that job anyway, always itching all the time."

"So, how are things going between you and Uncle Lester?" my father asked me. "Are you two bonding?"

"I guess."

"Has he mentioned his will?" asked my mother.

"No."

"Do you know if he even has a will?" asked my father.

"No, Dad, strange as it may seem, Trapp and I haven't talked about his will."

"Well, you need to find out if he has one," said my mother.

"And when it was last updated," said my father.

"A lot of people don't like to think about death," my mother said.

Yes, I was one of them.

"And so they don't make the necessary preparations," she continued. "You may have to remind him to make sure he completes all the paperwork."

"What, if he doesn't fill out all the forms, they won't let him die?" I asked.

They ignored my sarcasm.

"You can be very clever when you're not being stupid," said my mother, her version of a compliment. "I'm sure you can figure out some way to bring the subject up with him. Mrs. Mahoney says he listens to audiobooks. Find out what books he likes. People die in books all the time. Maybe he likes murder mysteries."

"Start with that," said my father, "then guide the conversation around to wills."

I realized my parents were worried because my father had been fired. Hell, I was worried too, but what did they expect me to say to him? "Hey, Trapp, you're going to die soon, which is too bad for you, but my dad lost his job, and we could really use a few bucks, like maybe ten million dollars."

"And quit calling him Trapp," said my mother. "It's disrespectful. He's your *uncle Lester*. You need to remind him that you're family."

Leslie remained in my room after our parents left. We looked at each other, but didn't know what to say. We were both scared.

64

Leslie noticed the cards on the floor. "What's trump?" she asked.

"Hearts."

We played out the hand, without either of us mentioning our father or our worries about our future.

19

Captain and the Radio

I'm ashamed to admit it, but I actually tried to talk to Trapp—excuse me, *Uncle Lester*—about his will. No, I didn't ask him if he liked books that had dead people in them. But as my mother says, I can be pretty clever when I'm not being stupid. I decided I'd get him talking about religion, because if you think about it, most religions are all about death.

"Why don't you play bridge on Sunday?" I began as we drove to the bridge studio.

"Four times a week is about as much as I can take," he said.

It wasn't the answer I had hoped for. "Do you go to church on Sunday?" I asked.

"Hah!"

This was getting me nowhere.

"Do you believe in God?" I asked.

Another "Hah!"

Maybe my idea wasn't so great. I once had a teacher

who told me I'd be twice as smart if I was half as smart as I thought I was. I'm still trying to figure that one out.

"I'm aware there is a greater reality, of which I'm totally unaware," my uncle said, surprising me. "I imagine I'm a lot like Captain and the radio."

He explained that he had been listening to his radio earlier, and that his dog, Captain, had been in the room with him. He said there was a report about Barack Obama, then one about global warming and the melting ice caps in Greenland.

"Let me ask you something," he said. "Which part of the radio broadcast do you think Captain understood?"

I didn't think his dog actually understood any of it, but of course I didn't say that. "Maybe global warming," I tried. "Like the way animals can predict earthquakes."

"Don't be absurd," he scoffed. "Do you really think Captain knew what the newscaster was saying?"

"Well, no," I said, feeling stupid. "But that seemed like too obvious an answer."

"Do you think my dog even knew that the noises coming from the radio were *words,* meant to convey ideas?"

"Not really," I said.

"Captain was oblivious," said Trapp. "Not only did he not understand a word the newscaster said, he did not even know there was anything to *understand.* I've got an atlas in my bookcase. Do you think it might help Captain if I showed him a map of Greenland?"

"No," I said. "I'm aware dogs can't read maps."

"Not only can't they read, they don't even understand the concept of reading. Dogs, like every other animal, have evolved to be able to function in their limited world.

They know what they need to know, and are oblivious to everything else. So what makes you think you and I are any different?"

"I can find Greenland on a map," I said.

"Congratulations, you're smarter than my dog, hah!"

I laughed too.

"Humans have evolved in order to function in our own limited world," he said, "just like every other animal. Yes, we're smarter. We couldn't outrun tigers or outfight bears, so we had to out-think them. But just because some of us are smarter than kangaroos, it doesn't mean we know everything."

I laughed at "some of us."

"Of course, I don't have to worry about tigers or where my next meal is coming from," he said, "so I use my brain and its two hundred and fifty thousand years of evolutionary development to play bridge, but that's beside the point."

"And the point *is*?" I asked.

"Okay, you were probably taught there are five senses," he said. "We see, hear, touch, smell, and taste. But how do we know those are the only five? What are the senses we don't have? What are we failing to perceive?"

It didn't seem right for me to point out that he no longer had all five senses. Or maybe, I considered, it was his loss of sight that made him wonder what else he was missing.

"We may be surrounded by some greater reality, to which we are oblivious. And even if we could somehow perceive it in some entirely new way, it is extremely doubtful we would be able to comprehend what we perceived."

"Like Captain listening to your radio," I said.

20

Toni Castaneda

We entered the bridge studio and made our way through the clutter of people, tables, and bridge gibberish.

"Aces and spaces . . ."

"I had nine points, but it was all quacks. . . ."

"Odd-even discards?"

Talk about being oblivious!

This being Thursday, I had assumed Gloria would be Trapp's partner again, but when we reached table three, someone else was sitting in the North seat, someone a lot younger.

"Hi, partner," she said brightly.

I guessed who she was even though I hadn't seen her for eleven years.

"You think you're ready?" Trapp asked as he settled into his seat.

She took a breath, then blew it out the corner of her mouth. "I hope so."

Did you notice that she didn't acknowledge my presence, even though I was sitting directly across from her?

At least she didn't tell me to shut up and leave her alone, like she had the last time I'd seen her.

She was pretty, with shoulder-length dark hair, pale skin with some freckles across the bridge of her nose, and a shy smile. "I'm really nervous," she said, and then, as if to prove it, she knocked over her bidding box. "Oops!"

"What happened?" my uncle asked.

"Sorry. I just knocked over my bidding box. Sorry."

"That's all right. Alton will clean it up."

I reddened. That wasn't part of my job description. Nonetheless, I got down on my hands and knees and began picking up the various bidding cards scattered across the floor.

"I hope I remember everything," said Toni.

"You won't," said Trapp. "That's how you learn. But after you make the same mistake one, or two, or five times, you'll eventually get it. And then you'll make new mistakes."

I gathered all the bidding cards. There were thirty-five possible bids, plus a number of pass cards, double cards, and redouble cards. They all had to be put back in a certain order, placed in such a way that each bid was visible.

"Thanks," Toni said to me when I put the box back where it belonged. "This is my first time, and I'm really nervous. I'm Toni, by the way."

I told her my name, then had to repeat it. She obviously didn't remember meeting me at Trapp's sixty-fifth birthday party, and I saw no point in mentioning it.

"I used to do what you do," she said. "Whatever you do, don't ever ask, 'Are you sure?'" She smiled.

"Hah!" laughed my uncle. "You don't have to worry about that with Alton. He has no idea what's going on. He thinks we're playing Go Fish!"

The director came around and placed two boards on our table. West shuffled one, and I shuffled and dealt the other, placing the cards in their slots when I was finished.

The director made a few announcements, and then the game started.

"Well, here goes," said Toni, removing her cards from the North slot.

I removed the South cards, then led Trapp to the coffee alcove and told him his hand. His Go Fish remark had stung me. And I was mad that he hadn't bothered to warn me about who his partner would be.

I found myself rooting against them. After a hand is over, bridge players often discuss what they could have—and should have—done differently. It's called the *post-mortem*. I remember the first time I heard such a discussion, I felt like screaming, "Why do you care anymore? The hand's over!"

As I already told you, Trapp and Wallace yelled at each other after every hand. So you would have thought that Trapp would have plenty to say to Toni.

Nope.

It wasn't that he was unaware of her screwups. Even when he was dummy, he asked the other players to please say their cards aloud, so he could follow along.

Yet all he said to Toni were things like "That was a very tough hand. At least you recognized the problem." Then he'd compliment her on what she did right.

The worst thing he said to her was "Make a note of board eleven. We'll talk about that one later."

"Uh-oh, I'm in trouble now," Toni said to me, smiling.

I didn't smile back.

I had been wrong imagining myself like Tiger Woods's caddy. A caddy gives advice. Tiger Woods and his caddy discuss club selection, wind conditions, and overall strategy.

Trapp would never take advice from me, I realized. He had no respect for me.

Toni Castaneda was his protégée. I was his trained monkey.

And I hated her for it.

21

Fixed

A *fix* is when your opponents do something really stupid, like make a ridiculous bid, or choose an inferior line of play, but, lo and behold, it works! Most of the time it would be the wrong bid, or the wrong line of play, but because of some lucky distribution of the cards, it turns out to be right this one time.

"We got fixed on that board," Gloria or Trapp would occasionally say after their opponents had left the table. They would never say it when the opponents were still at the table. That would be rude, since basically they'd be calling their opponents stupid and lucky.

I'm bringing it up now because Toni Castaneda must have fixed the opponents at least half a dozen times. Her luck was unbelievable. She'd make a play that even I knew was wrong, so you can imagine how bad it must have been, and then it would turn out to be right. Or else, the play would so confuse the opponents, they'd make an even worse play.

I wasn't just imagining this. Trapp actually apologized twice to the opponents for fixing them.

With Toni's amazing luck, combined with Trapp's ability, they finished in fifth place with a 52 percent game.

"Congratulations," he said to her. "You just earned your first masterpoint."

She beamed.

It wasn't actually a full masterpoint. For coming in fifth, she had earned .29 masterpoints. That's 29/100 of a point. Yet from the look on her face, you would have thought she'd just become a Life Master.

"Nice game, partner," said Trapp.

"Thank you, partner," said Toni.

I wanted to throw up.

Trapp told me to go fetch boards eleven and twenty-three. He didn't actually say the word *fetch*, but that was how it felt to his trained monkey.

I had to sit around for at least another half an hour while they went over the two boards. "I led the five of hearts and you played the queen."

Toni scrunched up her freckled nose. "I did?"

"Yes. You should have played the jack. It might not have seemed like there was any difference whether you played the jack or queen, but when you played the queen, you were telling me you didn't have the jack. Remember, good defense requires teamwork. Every card you play gives information to your partner."

By the way, even though I had to wait around an extra thirty minutes, I still only got paid seventy-five dollars.

22

The Blind Lady Bowler

I was still in a bad mood when I got home, and I took it out on my mother. "You can forget about Uncle Lester leaving us any money," I said, hitting her where it hurt. "Guess who his bridge partner was today?"

She already knew about it, having talked with Mrs. Mahoney.

"She's his protégée," I said.

"It's part of her homeschooling," said my mother. "That's all. I wouldn't worry too much about it. She'll do something crazy and that will be the end of that."

"She seemed normal enough to me," I said. "A little nervous, maybe. She knocked over her bidding box."

My mother nodded knowingly, then said, "You can bet she was heavily medicated."

"She's really pathetic," I told Cliff. "She pretends to be all interested in bridge—'Gee, you're so smart, Trapp, why didn't I think of that'—when really all she's doing is

75

sucking up to him so he'll leave her a bunch of money in his will."

"I thought that's what you were doing," said Cliff.

We were at the country club pool. Cliff had come down off his lifeguard perch and was sitting on the edge of my lounge chair. I had signed in as Robert Mays, a country club member who, according to Cliff, was vacationing in New Zealand.

I hadn't told Cliff about my father losing his job. For some reason I felt ashamed.

"Check out the diving board," Cliff said.

A girl in a pink bikini stood at the far end of the diving board. She shook her hair back, smiled at us—well, at Cliff—then raised herself up on her toes, took two steps, bounced, and dived into the pool.

"Oh, I forgot to tell you," Cliff said. "You'll like this. There was this blind lady bowler on the news the other day. She'd been in a car accident, but before that she'd always been this great bowler. They showed her bowling. Her husband got her all set up, and then she took three steps and rolled the ball down the alley. At first it looked like the ball was headed straight for the gutter, and I thought, you know, *Well, big deal, what's so great about that?* but then, when it was an inch away from being a gutter ball, it suddenly curved back and hit smack in the center of the pins for a perfect strike."

"Great," I said, without a whole lot of enthusiasm.

"Everyone was all excited," Cliff said, "not only the people on TV, but at my house watching it. Katie had tears in her eyes."

"Katie?" I asked, trying to keep my voice at an even pitch.

"Sorry," he said.

76

"No, it's fine," I said.

"Really, she was just leaving," he said, as if that was supposed to remove the sting. "My dad had the news on, and we stopped to watch."

"It's no big deal," I said. "I'm glad you and Katie are together. Better she's with you than some jerk."

The girl in the pink bikini climbed out of the pool and passed right in front of us, this time not looking at Cliff, content that he was watching her.

"She's like fourteen years old," I pointed out.

He blew his whistle and yelled at some kids to quit running.

"You got to admit," he said, "bowling a perfect strike is more amazing than just memorizing a few cards."

Not that there's a contest to see who the most amazing blind person is, but I don't admit that. A bowler does the same thing every time. The same three steps. The same arm motion. It's muscle memory.

Every bridge hand is different. I looked it up on the Internet. There are 635,013,559,600 possible bridge hands. And those are just the cards one person holds. There are 53,644,737,765,488,792,839,237,440,000 possible deals, each one a unique puzzle.

Trapp had to memorize every card in his hand and in the dummy, while at the same time keeping track of every card the opponents played. Hand after hand after hand.

Don't get me wrong. I was happy for the blind bowler. I watched her bowl her strike on YouTube. She was inspirational.

All I'm saying is, I bet she's better at strikes than spares.

23

Bidding

Leslie asked me to explain bidding to her, and it's about time I explained it to you, too, because on Saturday Gloria told us that Trapp had been cleared to play in the sectional tournament with me as his cardturner.

You probably already noticed there's a whale coming up, so you can skip this part if you want, but I think you should at least give it a try.

You already know about trump. If you can't follow suit, you can play a trump card and win the trick. So it's good to hold a hand with lots of trump cards. If spades were trump, you would want a hand with lots of spades.

That's what the bidding is all about.

Bidding is like an auction. The highest bid decides which suit is trump.

You always add six to whatever you bid. So if you bid one heart, you're saying you can take seven tricks if hearts are trump. If you bid two hearts, you're saying you can take eight tricks.

The highest you can bid is seven. If you do, you're saying you will take all thirteen tricks.

The suits are ranked in the same order I always give them to Trapp. Spades is the highest-ranked suit, then hearts, diamonds, and clubs.

So let's say somebody bids one heart. Maybe the next player has lots of spades in his hand, so he might bid one spade. He only has to bid at the one-level, because spades are ranked higher than hearts. But if instead he had lots of diamonds, he'd have to bid two diamonds, because diamonds are a lower-ranked suit than hearts.

The bidding proceeds clockwise around the table. A typical auction might go like this:

North: One heart. (I have a good hand and at least five hearts.)

East: One spade. (Well, I've got a pretty good hand too, with at least five spades.)

South: Two hearts. (I've got some hearts to go along with my partner's hearts.)

West: Three clubs. (To hell with all of you! I've got a boatload of clubs.)

North: Pass. (Even though I still like hearts, I don't want to bid at the three-level. I'm not sure we can take nine tricks.)

East: Pass.

South: Three hearts. (I'm willing to take a chance.)

West: Pass.

North: Pass.

East: Pass.

The bidding ends when there are three passes in a row.

For simplicity's sake, that auction would be written like this:

North	East	South	West
1♡	1♠	2♡	3♣
Pass	Pass	3♡	Pass
Pass	Pass		

The final *contract* is three hearts. Hearts are trump, and North has to take a total of nine tricks (three plus six). If he succeeds, his side will score some points. That's called *making his contract*. If he fails, the other side will score some points. That's called *setting the contract*.

Since North was the first person to bid hearts, he plays the hand. He is known as the *declarer*. His partner, South, becomes the dummy.

As in other sports, there are an offense and a defense. The defenders in bridge try to prevent the declarer from making his contract, just like a football team tries to prevent the other side from scoring a touchdown.

There is a fifth suit I haven't mentioned: no-trump. No-trump is ranked higher than spades.

So the bidding could go:

North	East	South	West
1♡	1♠	1NT	Pass
Pass	Pass		

No-trump means what it says. If the final contract is one no-trump, then no suit is trump. There are no wild cards.

If you can't follow suit, all you can do is discard.

There are two additional bids I haven't mentioned yet: *double* and *redouble*. In the bidding box, the double card is red, with a large white X. The redouble card is blue, with *XX*.

If you double, you're saying you think your opponents bid too high. If they make their contract, they'll get double the points, but if you set them, then you'll get double the points.

I hadn't seen anyone use the redouble card yet, but I suppose it increases the number of points at risk. Leslie put it this way: a double card says "No way!" and a redouble card says "Way!"

One last thing about bidding, and this has to do with keeping score. You don't always want to bid as cheaply as possible. You get a big bonus if you bid *game*.

To bid game in hearts or spades, you have to bid at least four, 4♡ or 4♠. They're called the *major suits*. To bid game in diamonds or clubs, you have to bid at the five-level, 5♣ or 5♢. They're called the *minor suits*. You only need to bid 3NT to be *in game* in no-trump. That makes sense, since it is harder to win tricks when there are no wild cards.

You get an even bigger bonus for bidding a *slam*. That means bidding at the six-level, regardless of the suit. You'll have to take twelve tricks to make your slam contract.

A *grand slam* is when you bid seven. You have to take every single trick, but you get a huge bonus for it.

It's not enough just to take every trick. You first have to bid it.

You may wonder how anyone could bid a slam unless they were dealt practically every ace, king, and queen in the deck. But each bid you and your partner make gives you information about your hands. When Trapp and Gloria bid, it's like they're talking in code, describing their hands to each other as they try to figure out what suit should be trump and how high they should bid.

One time, they both bid spades, and then at some point in the auction, Trapp surprised me by bidding five clubs. He only had two clubs in his hand.

I didn't ask, "Are you sure?" I kept my face expressionless as I set the 5♣ bid on the table.

Gloria then bid six spades. Trapp never wanted clubs to be trump. His bid had somehow told her that he held the king of clubs, which was all she needed to hear to bid slam.

She made her contract, and scored 1,430 points for it.

Every other pair who had played the same board also took twelve tricks, but most had only bid four spades, so they only scored 680 points. One pair didn't even bid game. They stopped at two spades, and scored 230 points for taking the same twelve tricks.

The bidding determines which suit will be trump, which player will be the declarer, and which player will be dummy. After the bidding there will be a *final contract*. You always add six to the number bid, so if the final contract is four hearts, it means that the declarer needs to take ten tricks, and hearts are trump. If the final contract is three no-trump, it means the declarer has to take nine tricks, and no suit is trump.

24

My Sick Fantasy

You're probably wondering why I didn't tell my uncle I understood, sort of, how to play bridge. I was getting better at predicting what card he would play. Why not let him know? Why not ask him to teach me the finer points of the game? I could be his protégé too, instead of his trained monkey. What better way to "bond" with him than to show an interest in the game he loved?

You're right. That would have been the normal and sensible thing to do.

But in case you haven't noticed, I have a deranged personality. I don't like people telling me how to do things. It makes me feel stupid. I have this need to figure things out for myself.

Ask my mother, she'll tell you. "You can't tell Alton anything!"

Besides, after my uncle's Go Fish remark to Toni, I wanted to prove to him just how wrong he was.

I had this fantasy. He's playing in a real important game, maybe for the national championship, when suddenly

Gloria gets sick. Nothing serious, mind you, but she has to leave the table.

"Well, that's it," he says. "We'll have to forfeit."

Then I say, "I suppose I can fill in."

"You? Hah! We're not playing Go Fish!"

"I've been watching you play," I say. "It doesn't look too hard. Besides, what have you got to lose? It's better than forfeiting."

So he reluctantly agrees. Leslie takes my place as his cardturner, and I take Gloria's seat. I then astound him with my brilliant play, and of course, we win, thanks to me. I know, it's sick.

25

Lab Rats Pushing Buttons

Trapp wasn't perfect. He didn't always win. The following Wednesday he played with Wallace again, and this time they had a 48 percent game. More than half the field did better than them. Everything that could go wrong did go wrong. The funny thing was that he and Wallace hardly argued at all.

While I was driving Trapp back to his house, I felt the gas pedal start to vibrate, which was always the first sign of trouble. I increased my pressure on the pedal, but helplessly watched the speedometer go from sixty, to fifty-five, to fifty. . . .

Cars were speeding past me on both sides. The guy behind me was right on my tail. I swerved into the right lane, nearly getting us killed.

"If I returned a club, he could have discarded his losing spade," my uncle muttered.

My foot was pressed to the floor and the speedometer was down to thirty, but I had to be careful. This had happened before. At any moment something would catch and I'd be going ninety.

Suddenly the engine roared, the car lurched, and just as suddenly it died. I managed to coast to a stop on the side of the highway.

"Am I home already?" asked Trapp.

"Not quite," I said, then explained the situation. "Don't worry," I assured him. "It happens all the time. We just have to wait about twenty minutes while it fixes itself."

"It fixes itself. That's quite a car."

"That's what happened the last time," I said. "I don't know," I admitted. "I guess I know as much about cars as Captain knows about global warming."

He laughed a double "Hah! Hah!" then asked me if I had one of those new cell phones thingamajig.

He had me call a tow truck. He was going to have the car taken to a certain dealership he knew on Jackson Street.

I tried to tell him that car dealerships overcharge for repairs, and that I knew a good mechanic who was cheap.

"If he's so good, then why does this happen 'all the time'?"

"Good point," I said.

He told me not to worry; the owner of the dealership was a bridge player. I took that to mean she'd give me a good deal on the repairs.

While we waited, he asked me what I thought of "this game of bridge."

I wasn't sure how much I wanted to tell him.

"You don't have to answer," he said. "I'm sure it seems boring to you. No flashing lights."

"No, it seems very challenging," I said.

"So, what do you like to do?" he asked. "Do you play any games?"

Once again, I considered telling him that I'd been dealing out bridge hands, but instead I mentioned playing video games with my friend Cliff. That was a huge mistake.

He didn't think too highly of video games. "You don't play the game," he said. "The game plays you."

I tried to explain that some video games take a lot of thought and skill, but he said it was "like lab rats pushing buttons. A light flashes, and the rat presses his nose against a button, causing a nugget of food to drop out of a chute."

The tow truck arrived and took us to the car dealership. When we pulled into the lot, the owner came out to greet us. She was a red-haired woman wearing boots and a cowboy hat.

She gave Trapp a hug when he stepped out of the tow truck, then immediately launched into bridge gibberish. "I pick up ace, queen fourth, king third, void, and six solid clubs, missing the ace. My partner opens one diamond— my void, of course—and I bid . . ."

That was fine by me. I figured the more they talked bridge, the less she would charge to repair my car.

"Do you play bridge?" she suddenly asked me.

"Me?" I asked. Maybe if I told her I was trying to learn, I thought, she'd fix the car for free.

"Alton likes video games," said Trapp.

So I bet you're thinking that my uncle paid for the repairs?

Nope. He bought me a new car.

I was stunned. I must have babbled incoherently for about ten minutes as I thanked him over and over again. I even asked the dreaded question "Are you sure?" at least five times.

It was one of those fuel-efficient hybrids. "If I'm going to have you driving me to bridge tournaments," he said, "just so I can indulge my ego, it seems, at the very least, we should get good gas mileage. No reason to unnecessarily pollute the environment and waste the natural resources of other people who are struggling to lead real lives."

The owner of the dealership told me to bring her the pink slip for my old car at my convenience.

It was embarrassing getting all my junk out of the trunk of my old car and putting it into the new one. Fortunately, Trapp couldn't see my crumpled schoolwork and dirty socks.

"Who's to say what's a real life?" I asked, once we were back on the road.

You would think my parents would have been happy about my getting a new car, what with my father losing his job and all. You would think.

My mother complained that it would raise the cost of our insurance. My father demanded to know how much I got for the trade-in.

I'm not kidding. He was afraid I got ripped off.

My father doesn't trust car salesmen. He also doesn't like lawyers, bankers, plumbers, electricians, politicians, or swimming-pool contractors.

"We still have the pink slip," he said. "That means it is still legally our car."

He wanted us to go to the dealership and take the car back. He was sure we could sell it ourselves for a lot more than the dealer paid for it.

Once again, Leslie came to my rescue. She reminded him that the woman was a friend of Uncle Lester's. If we made her mad, Uncle Lester might cut us out of his will.

I realize it's a cliché for a teenager to be embarrassed by his parents. Cliff often complained about his parents, but I always thought they were pretty cool. Was it possible, I wondered, that there was somebody, somewhere, who thought my parents were cool?

26

Yarborough

Toni Castaneda was once again Trapp's Thursday partner. She was already in the North seat, smiling brightly as we approached.

"Hi, Alton," she greeted me.

I grunted.

I was shuffling the cards when she suddenly asked, "So do you like your new car?"

"How do you know about that?" I asked.

"Trapp had dinner at our house last night. That must have been scary when your car died in the middle of the highway!"

"It was no big deal," I said with a shrug.

Have I told you how many times my mother had tried to invite Uncle Lester to our house for dinner? Mrs. Mahoney always declined on his behalf. Recently she'd been using Teodora's special diet as an excuse, but Trapp had been refusing my mother's dinner invitations long before Teodora started working there.

Not that I blamed him. I wouldn't eat dinner at my house either if I didn't have to. Still, it bothered me that he went to the Castanedas'.

"I thought you were on some special diet," I said to my uncle.

"We're vegetarians," said Toni.

"Sophie's a terrific cook," said Trapp. "She made a lentil and barley soup that was incredible. With just a hint of mint."

The game got under way, and Toni screwed up on the very first hand. Toni passed, East opened "One heart," and Trapp said, "Double."

I set the red card with the big *X* on the table.

I had seen Trapp make that bid before. It didn't mean he expected to beat one heart.

This was his hand:

♠ AQ98
♡ 7
♢ KJ52
♣ AJ92

His bid is called a takeout double. He was telling Toni that he had a good hand, and the three other suits. He didn't know which suit to bid, so he was leaving it up to her.

His bid basically said, "Bid something. Anything! Bid your longest suit!"

But what did Toni do? She passed.

Toni	East	Trapp	West
Pass	1♡	X	Pass
Pass!	Pass		

The final contract was one heart doubled. If this had been the week before, she probably would have lucked out and gotten a top board. But this week her luck had run out. If anything, her mistakes were magnified. The declarer made two overtricks for a score of 560 points.

> Toni screwed up big-time!

"My fault," Trapp said when the hand was over. "I haven't taught you about takeout doubles."

She should have known anyway, I thought. *I did.*

As the game progressed, Toni continued to make mistakes. I almost felt sorry for her as she and Trapp got one bad result after another.

Almost.

They finished with a 41 percent game. Afterward he had me get boards six, ten, and twenty, and went over the hands with her.

"Take a look at your hand on board twenty," he said.

Toni removed her cards from the North slot and spread them on the table. "Yuck!" she said.

There was not a single face card in her hand.

"You had a very rare hand," said Trapp. "It's known

as a Yarborough, a hand with no card higher than a nine."

I looked again at the spread of cards. There wasn't even a ten.

Trapp said that before bridge was invented, there was a game called whist played in England. "They played for money, not masterpoints, and people were always complaining about being dealt lousy cards. If somebody won, well, that was because of his superior skill. If he lost, it was bad luck. Hah!"

Trapp went on to explain that the Earl of Yarborough got so sick and tired of all the griping that he offered a kind of insurance. He gave thousand-to-one odds. A whist player would give the Earl of Yarborough one British pound, and if that player was dealt a hand with no card higher than a nine, the earl would pay him one thousand pounds.

"Did he ever have to pay off?" I asked.

My question startled him. He had been telling all this to Toni and I think he'd forgotten I was even there.

"Not very often," he said. "The Earl of Yarborough made a lot of money."

"Yarborough," said Toni. "That was the name of your company, wasn't it?"

"Yarborough Investment Group," said Trapp. "We were able to find value in things that other people thought were worthless. And that, Toni, is how you should have approached your hand. When you pick up a hand that seems worthless, you should think: *This is a rare hand. A Yarborough! One in a thousand.* You should ask yourself, *Where is the hidden value?* After all, even Alton would be able to win a trick with an ace or a king.

It takes great focus and concentration to win a trick with a six."

He went on to explain how, if she had discarded diamonds and saved her clubs, she could have won the last trick with the six of clubs.

27

A Phone Call

The second I walked in the door, my mother practically shouted in my face. "Toni Castaneda called! She wants you to call her back. I wrote down the number."

"Okay," I said as I walked past her, then started down the hall.

"Wait, where are you going?"

"To take a leak, if you don't mind. It was a long drive home."

"I mind your attitude."

In the bathroom, I splashed my face with cold water and stared at my reflection.

It's never been easy for me to just call up a girl on the phone. I had to psych myself up first.

You would think it would have been easy in this case, since I hated Toni, and since I was just calling her back.

You would think.

My mother was waiting for me as I stepped out of the bathroom, Toni's phone number in her hand. For someone who supposedly hated the Castanedas, she was awfully insistent.

I went to my room and called Toni on my cell.

"Hello?"

"Toni?" I asked.

"No, this is her father. Who's this?"

For the record, although his initial hello might have been slightly high-pitched, Toni's father had a normal masculine voice.

"Alton," I said.

"I didn't get that."

"Alton," I repeated.

I don't think I've ever said my name just one time to anyone.

A short while later Toni came on the line. "Hi, Alton," she said cheerfully.

"My mom said you called," I said cheerlessly.

"Your mom seems really cool," said Toni.

That answered that question. Of course, everyone knew the Castanedas were bonkers.

I stared out my window at the disaster known as our backyard and waited for her to say whatever it was she had called to say.

She got right to it. "Why do you pretend you don't know how to play bridge?" she asked.

"What do you mean?" I asked, neither admitting to nor denying her accusation. I felt like I'd been caught, but I wasn't quite sure what I was being accused of.

"You knew about the takeout double," she said. "I saw it in your eyes. And you're always trying to guess what card he'll play before he plays it."

"I may have picked up a little, watching him play," I said.

"You need to tell him!" she said. "He'd love it if you played bridge. He's always saying how he wishes more young people would take up the game. He's afraid that bridge is like a dying culture. He's worried that in like thirty years, there will be no one left to play it."

"Well, I've never actually played," I said. "And I never can figure out what bid he's going to make."

"Bidding's not that hard, once you learn the basics. Trapp and Gloria use a complicated system and I'm trying to learn it, but you don't have to do all that. You just have to know which bids are *game-forcing,* which ones are *invitational,* and which ones are just *cooperative.*"

The words meant nothing to me. "O-kay," I said hesitantly.

She laughed. "I can teach you," she offered.

I thought it over.

"Okay, sure," I said.

"Maybe we can have a game," she said. "Do you know two other people who might want to play?"

I knew one for sure. Leslie had been dying to play.

"My sister," I said. "She's only eleven, but she's real sharp. And I have a friend who's really good at cards."

"Great," said Toni. "How about tomorrow?"

I told her I'd check with my friend first and call her back.

It's funny how you can go from hating a girl to maybe liking her, maybe liking her a lot, just because she shows a little interest in you. I pictured Toni in my mind. Her shy smile. The freckles across the bridge of her nose. The way she concentrated so intently when she was playing bridge with Trapp.

I was reminded of the girl who had sat next to me in freshman algebra. We didn't have traditional desks. Two students shared a table. I'd watch her out of the corner of my eye as she tried to factor algebraic equations. She was oblivious to the world around her, oblivious that I was sitting next to her, as she chewed on the tip of her eraser. It made my heart ache, she was so beautiful.

That girl had blond hair, and Toni's hair was dark, but they both had that same look of innocent and total concentration.

I called Cliff.

I should tell you that so far, when I've recounted my conversations with Cliff, I've left out certain *descriptive* words. It's not that we're especially vulgar or crude. It's just that those kinds of words seem worse in print than they do when we would just say them in an offhand way. I think I've been able to omit those words and still give you a fairly accurate account of what was said between us.

However, if I were to try to repeat what Cliff said when I asked him if he wanted to play bridge, I'd have to leave out every other word. Let's just say he wasn't overjoyed with the idea.

Still, he was my best friend, and when he realized I was *serious* (adverb deleted), and that it was *important* to me (adverb deleted), he agreed to *play* (adverb deleted).

"But afternoon only," he said. "Katie and I have plans for tomorrow night."

He normally wouldn't have mentioned Katie. He would have said something like "I'm busy tomorrow night." I think he just wanted to twist the knife a bit, since he'd agreed to do me a favor.

As I expected, Leslie was thrilled to finally get to play bridge. She wasn't too thrilled, however, that Cliff would be our fourth.

"He's a big goof-off," she said. "He won't concentrate on the game. He'll just make stupid jokes."

Leslie was a lot like her uncle Lester. She took her bridge very seriously.

"Besides . . . ," Leslie said.

"What?"

She didn't say, but I knew what she was thinking. She blamed Cliff for what had happened between Katie and me.

Like a football coach getting his team ready for the second half, once again I had to pump myself up to call Toni. You would think it would have been easier for me the second time, but you would be wrong.

She answered the phone this time.

"We're on," I said. "You, me, Cliff, and Leslie."

I told her two o'clock, and she said she was looking forward to it.

"So why did you call me?" I asked, regretting the question as soon as it came out of my mouth.

"What do you mean?"

What I meant was this: we hadn't exactly been friendly

at the bridge studio. She mostly ignored me, and my attitude toward her can best be described as surly. But I didn't say that to Toni.

"Never mind," I said. "I mean, I was just . . . surprised you called."

"My grandmother told me to," said Toni.

"Oh. Okay," I said. "Well, see you tomorrow. You'll really like Cliff."

28

Toni's Grandmother
and President Nixon

I had felt so awkward asking Toni that question that I readily accepted the answer she gave, and really didn't think about what she said until after I hung up. Her answer was even stranger than my question.

Everybody has two grandmothers, I realized; in fact, Toni had three, if you count the woman Henry King married later on. I had no reason to assume Toni was talking about Trapp's "perfect partner," his ex-wife's insane sister. I had also assumed that person had died.

If she was still alive, and living with Toni's family, it would explain why Trapp went there for dinner. But why didn't he play bridge with her anymore? Did she even remember how to play, or was her mind too far gone?

But that wasn't what made Toni's answer so strange. Why would Toni's grandmother (whichever one it was) tell her to call me? I had never met any of them, except perhaps at Trapp's birthday party eleven years ago. To use an expression my own grandmother used to say, they didn't know me from Adam.

Besides, since when does a teenage girl call up a boy at the suggestion of her grandmother?

I wandered back out into the kitchen.

"Well?" asked my mother.

"Well, what?"

"*Well, Toni?*"

When I told my mother about our upcoming bridge party, you would have thought from her reaction that she must not have heard me clearly. She must have thought I had said the Queen of England was coming for tea.

She immediately started cleaning everything in sight as she worried about what she would serve.

"Potato chips?" I suggested.

"Don't be ridiculous," she replied, then ordered me to vacuum the living room.

My father came home in a bad mood. He had spent half the day filling out forms at the unemployment office, and hardly said a word during dinner. Not that I'm such a sparkling conversationalist either. Usually the most they can pry out of me are a few "Uh-huhs" and "Pass the applesauce."

"It's bad enough losing a job," he said finally. "Then some condescending government worker treats you like you're some kind of welfare cheat. It's my money!"

"Pass the applesauce," I said.

"I've paid unemployment insurance for seventeen years," my father continued. "All I want is what's rightfully mine. Those government clerks never worked at a real job in their lives."

My father doesn't like government workers any better than he likes car salesmen and pool contractors. He didn't like people on welfare, either.

My mother interrupted his diatribe to tell him that "the Castaneda girl" would be coming to our home the next day.

"We're going to play bridge," Leslie said happily.

My father withdrew back into his silence.

"Is Toni's grandmother still alive?" I asked. "Or did she die in the insane asylum?"

My mother stared at me like I was the one who belonged in an insane asylum. "Now, don't you go asking Toni a lot of stupid questions about her grandmother. Try to act like a normal human being."

"I was just curious what ever happened to her," I persisted.

"She went crazy," said my mother. "They locked her in an asylum."

"I mean after that. Did they ever let her out? Is she still alive?"

"She's dead," my father said flatly. "She died in the asylum. Nixon led the investigation into her death."

I wondered if I had heard him correctly. "Nixon?" I repeated. "President Nixon?" I had learned about Nixon and Watergate in U.S. History.

"It was before he became president," said my father.

"Senator King was a very important man, from a very prominent family," said my mother. "When his wife died at such a young age, you can be sure there was an investigation."

"What did they find out?" asked Leslie.

"About what?" asked my mother.

"How did she die?"

My parents didn't know.

"I think it was ruled a suicide," said my father.

"Those were different times," my mother explained. "Before CNN. People's privacy was respected. It was bad enough for Senator King that he married such a person. The public didn't need to know all the embarrassing details."

Embarrassing? I wondered. His wife kills herself, and he's *embarrassed?*

29

A Silver Ice Bucket

I didn't know we owned a silver ice bucket. Tiny silver tongs, too. They had been placed on a silver tray, along with several bottles of soda. There was also the box of fancy cookies that had been sitting on the top shelf of a cabinet for as long as I could remember. Leslie and I had been forbidden to open it. Until now.

My mother had gone to a store and purchased a "bridge set," which included two decks of cards and a special score pad with the words *We* and *They* printed on it. She also bought a cheese ball.

"You're wearing that?" she asked me.

I didn't reply. I was wearing what I was wearing.

"Can you at least comb your hair?"

The doorbell rang.

"Well, are you just going to stand there, or are you going to answer it?"

I opened the door to see Toni's nervous smile. "Hi," she said quietly.

"Hi," I replied.

My mother told me to quit standing there like a bump on a log. "Invite your guest to come inside."

"Come on in," I said.

"Welcome to our humble home," said my mother.

"Thank you," said Toni.

"And how are your parents?" my mother asked her.

"They're fine, thanks."

"We go way back, you know."

"Yes, they've told me about you," said Toni.

That couldn't be good, I thought.

"Too bad you never got to know your grandparents," said my mother. "I think it's tragic when a family can't get along."

"It was tragic," Toni agreed.

"Are you still seeing the same psychiatrist?" my mother asked. "What's his name?"

"Don't answer that," I said, then told my mother to "quit badgering her."

"I'm not badgering anyone. I'm just making friendly conversation. She's your guest, and you've hardly said a word. Somebody has to pick up the slack."

"It's all right," said Toni. "His name's Dr. Ellsworth."

"Ellsworth's a good man," my mother said, as if she had a clue. "Are you taking medication?"

"Jesus Christ!" I exclaimed. This from a woman who complained about people's privacy not being respected anymore.

"It's no big deal," said Toni. "Yes, Mrs. Richards. I have a prescription to control my schizophrenia."

My mother shot me an I-told-you-so look. Then she

turned back to Toni and told her she had "wonderful poise. Don't you think so, Alton?"

"Yeah, she's got great poise."

Toni smiled.

"It's wonderful that the world of medicine has come so far," my mother said. "Too bad those drugs weren't around for your grandmother."

For the first time I thought I saw a flash of defiance in Toni's eyes. "There was nothing the matter with my grandmother," she said. "She didn't need medication."

"Well, I'm no psychiatrist," my mother admitted.

I managed to lead Toni away from my mother and into the living room. We sat down at the card table across from each other. She began shuffling one of the decks of cards, and I shuffled the other.

"Sorry about my mother," I said.

"It's okay. My parents warned me about her," Toni said, then instantly put her hand over her mouth. "Sorry. I didn't mean anything by that."

"No, I know," I assured her. "If anybody needs a psychiatrist, it's her."

That was the wrong thing to say. "Sorry," I said. "I didn't mean—"

"I like Dr. Ellsworth," said Toni. "But I don't take the meds."

I started to say she seemed perfectly normal to me, but stopped myself in time. I'd already put one foot in my mouth.

I had told Leslie to stay away until Cliff arrived, so

I could have some time alone with Toni, but that wasn't working out exactly as planned. I'm a lot smoother in my daydreams than I am in real life.

"Are you having a pool put in?" Toni asked, looking at the backyard through the sliding glass door.

"No," I said.

We continued to shuffle our cards.

"So, what else do you like to do, besides play bridge?" I asked.

"I don't know, different things," said Toni. "My friend and I are making a quilt."

"A quilt?"

Her face reddened. "You think that's really lame, don't you? *Who is this loser?*"

"No, not at all," I said.

I tried to think of something fascinating to say about quilts, but nothing came to mind.

Leslie stepped into the room. "Sorry," she said. "I guess Cliff's not here yet. Big surprise."

I told her to come join us.

"You sure?" she asked.

"Of course," I said. "Leslie's been bugging me for weeks to play bridge," I told Toni, "and now she's afraid to enter the room."

That was unfair. For one thing, Leslie was never a pest. She shot me an accusatory glance, but then, not wanting to make me look bad in front of Toni, she smiled sweetly.

"It's a great game," said Toni. "You'll love it."

Leslie went to the ice bucket. She picked up a single ice cube using the tiny silver tongs and dropped it into her glass. *Kerplunk!* Then another. *Kerplunk!* Then another. *Kerplunk!*

From the way Toni and I watched her you would have thought she was performing delicate surgery.

Leslie noticed our stares. "You want a soda?" she offered.

"No thanks," said Toni.

"I'm cool," I said, being anything but.

30

The Life of the Party

Cliff was only about ten minutes late, which was about five minutes early for him.

"So?" he asked, when I opened the door.

"What?" I asked.

"You and Toni? So?"

"She's just here to play bridge."

"If you say so, Romeo."

He walked ahead of me into the living room and sat down at the card table across from Toni, in my seat. "I'm Cliff. You must be Toni. I hear you're quite the card shark."

Toni smiled shyly. "Not really," she said quietly.

"That's what she *says*," Cliff said, "but I saw that twinkle in her eye."

Toni's eye might not have been twinkling before, but it was then.

Leslie looked at me, waiting for me to say something. She knew I wanted to be partners with Toni, but it seemed silly for me to make a big deal out of it. Cliff was already sitting down. Besides, I realized, it probably made more sense this way, since if Toni and I were partners, Cliff would be Leslie's partner.

"We'll have to watch out for these two," Cliff said to Toni. "They have that brother-sister telepathy thing going."

Toni gave us a brief lesson on bidding. She said that bidding is a conversation between you and your partner. The only way you can talk to each other is by the bids you make. No other talking is allowed.

"Can you wink?" asked Cliff.

"That would be unauthorized information," said Toni.

He winked at her.

Toni's cheeks turned pink. "After you sort your hand into suits," she continued, "you count your points. An ace is worth four points. A king, three. A queen is worth two, and a jack, one."

"How about a six?" asked Cliff.

"Nothing," said Toni.

"How about two sixes?"

"Still nothing."

"Three sixes and an eight?"

"C'mon, Cliff, you're not *that* stupid!" said Leslie. "I can understand it, and I'm only eleven!"

Cliff laughed.

You also get points for voids, singletons, and doubletons. Toni had made note cards for each of us.

A = 4   Void = 3
K = 3   Singleton = 2
Q = 2   Doubleton = 1
J = 1

She explained that the points were just used as a way to help evaluate how good a hand you have. If you have thirteen points, then you have a good enough hand to open the bidding. With fewer than thirteen points, you should pass.

"Pass," said Cliff.

"It's not your turn," said Toni. "Alton dealt."

The dealer is always the first to bid. At the bridge studio it's indicated on the boards who is the dealer for each hand.

I looked at my cards.

♠ AKQ
♡ 87432
♢ K9
♣ J92

I had fourteen points. The ace, king, and queen of spades were worth a total of nine points. The king of diamonds was worth three, and the jack of clubs was worth one. I also added one point for the doubleton diamond.

Even though my points were in the other suits, I was supposed to bid my longest suit. "One heart," I said.

"Six spades," said Cliff.

Toni pretended to slap him.

"Double!" shouted Leslie.

Toni told Cliff that if he didn't have enough points to open the bidding, he certainly didn't have enough to bid six spades.

"But I have six spades," said Cliff.

"Just bid one spade," said Toni.

"Too late," said Leslie.

Leslie's protests notwithstanding, we let Cliff take back his bid. Cliff bid one spade.

"One no-trump," said Leslie.

Toni passed, I passed, and Cliff passed too.

One no-trump was the final contract. Toni led a spade, and my hand became the dummy.

Leslie was completely on her own. She had to choose which card to play from her hand, and which card to play from dummy. Watching her, you would never have known she had never played before.

Not only did she make her contract, but she made an overtrick to boot.

"Well done," said Toni.

"Hey, whose side are you on?" asked Cliff.

Leslie's grin was a mile wide.

Toni dealt the next hand. She opened "One club," Leslie passed, and it was up to Cliff. He rubbed his chin. "Suppose I had the nine and seven of spades; four hearts, including the king and queen; the ace and two other diamonds; and four little clubs. What would I bid?"

"One heart," said Toni. "Once your partner opens the bidding, you only need six points to *respond*."

"One heart," said Cliff.

"Uh, hello?" said Leslie. "He just told you his entire hand."

"I didn't say that was my hand," said Cliff. "I was simply asking a hypothetical question." He winked at Toni.

"He just winked!" shouted Leslie.

"I really don't remember what he said," Toni assured Leslie.

Cliff sighed. "The *nine* and *seven* of spades, the king and queen of hearts . . ."

Toni and I laughed, but Leslie wasn't amused.

Cliff wasn't as dumb as he pretended. The final contract was two hearts, and he made two overtricks.

He had played the card game hearts, so he knew all about following suit and taking tricks. It wasn't that much of a stretch to learn about trump.

At the bridge studio, it took my uncle and his group about three hours to play twenty-four boards, one right after another. Leslie, Toni, Cliff, and I played from about two-thirty to six o'clock and maybe got through ten hands.

I got to be the declarer twice. The first time I went down in three clubs, and the second time I made a four-spade contract.

Cliff actually seemed to have a good time. I was glad that he and Toni got along, and after a while even Leslie laughed at his jokes.

Once I got over my initial awkwardness, I was able to throw in a few funny and insightful comments. I know they were funny and insightful because Leslie didn't groan and roll her eyes. More importantly, Toni smiled.

Cliff and I make a good team that way. He breaks the ice; then I'm able to keep things flowing.

"You're a natural card player," Toni told Leslie as we all headed to the door.

Leslie beamed.

"What about me?" asked Cliff.

"You're *un*natural," Toni said.

"You want to do this again sometime?" I asked.

"That'd be good," said Toni.

"Or something else," I said.

She smiled at me and said, "That'd be good too."

I glanced at Leslie, who gave me a little nod of approval.

"Gilliam's having a party tomorrow night," said Cliff. "You guys want to come?"

Toni and I looked at each other.

"Okay by me," she said.

It was then that I remembered Trapp's bridge tournament. "I can't," I said. "The sectional."

In fact, now that I thought of it, Cliff had mentioned Gilliam's party to me earlier in the week, and I had told him I couldn't go.

"Oh, I forgot," said Toni. She placed her hand on my arm and said, "That's more important."

"Absolutely," Cliff agreed. "Trapp's tournament means a lot more than some stupid party."

That wasn't what Cliff had said to me when I first told him I couldn't go to Gilliam's party. Then it was "a stupid tournament."

"You know about Trapp?" asked Toni.

"He's an amazing bridge player," Cliff said sincerely. "I just hope he wins."

Toni nodded.

"He will!" said Leslie.

"You can still come to the party if you want," Cliff offered. "If you got nothing better to do."

Toni looked at me to see if I had any objection, but what right did I have to say she couldn't go to Gilliam's party?

"You'll have fun," I said. "Gilliam's a riot. Gilliam's his last name, but that's what everybody calls him, probably even his mother."

Toni laughed. She turned back to Cliff and said, "Okay."

"Cool," said Cliff.

Leslie's eyes filled with anger. She wasn't looking at Cliff or Toni. Her anger was aimed at me.

31

Smoking Ears

I left for Trapp's house at ten the next morning. The tournament wasn't until one-thirty, but I'd have to pick up Gloria, too, and then it would take an hour after that.

I saw no reason to be mad at Cliff. I never told him I liked Toni, just the opposite. Besides, it wasn't like he was making a move on her. Cliff was just being Cliff. And anyway, he already had a girlfriend, and I had no doubt that Katie would be going to Gilliam's party.

Who would have thought I'd ever take comfort in the fact that Cliff was with Katie?

I must not have taken a whole lot of comfort in it, however, because everything I just told you, I told myself over and over again all night long. It played like an endless loop inside my head.

As I drove to my uncle's, I thought back to earlier in the week when Cliff first told me about Gilliam's party. At the time I was glad to have Trapp's bridge tournament as my excuse, since I wasn't exactly thrilled at the prospect of being there with Cliff and Katie.

That was before Toni. Strange, I thought, how everything can change in just two days.

Thinking about Gilliam's party got me started again on my endless loop about Cliff and Toni, Cliff and Katie, me and Toni. I was able to plug my iPod into my new car's sound system. I turned it up loud so I wouldn't have to listen to my own stupid thoughts!

I parked in the driveway, then rapped on the door using the heavy iron goat-head knocker. Mrs. Mahoney answered with a finger at her lips.

A hush seemed to have settled over the place. Even Captain didn't bark. I smelled cinnamon and cloves.

Trapp lay on the floor. Teodora knelt beside him, holding some kind of burning cylinder. Black smoke poured out the top. The bottom of the cylinder was sticking into my uncle's ear. It was as if the cylinder were a giant fuse and my uncle's head were the bomb.

I watched the small ring of flame move closer and closer to his head. Next to Teodora was a ceramic bowl of water, with images of the moon and stars. When the ear candle (as I later learned it was called) burned down to about three inches from his head, she lifted it away and doused it in the water.

"Is that any better?" she asked my uncle.

"Maybe," he said. "Alton, is that you?"

"Yes."

"Say something," he said. "Say a card."

"Um, six of diamonds."

"Clear as a bell," said my uncle.

"If diabetes and blindness aren't bad enough," Trapp said as we drove to pick up Gloria, "now I have too much earwax. Not too much wax, really—too many little hairs growing inside my ear canal. You need earwax. For most people, it just oozes out, imperceptibly. My ear hairs hold on to it like Velcro, which causes it to build up."

"Thanks for sharing," I said.

"Hah!" he laughed.

He asked me if I'd ever done the experiment in school with an egg and a milk bottle.

I didn't know what he was talking about.

"The idea is to somehow get the egg into the milk bottle. The opening in the bottle is too small for the egg to fit through. You sure you never did that?" He seemed surprised.

"Pretty sure," I said.

"I guess it's all about computers now," he said.

"I guess."

"What you do is, you place a burning piece of paper in the empty bottle. Then you put the egg, hard-boiled, without the shell, on top of the bottle, plugging up the opening. The flame will use up all the oxygen inside the bottle, and this creates a vacuum so strong it sucks the egg right through the hole."

I nodded. You would think I would have learned to stop making useless gestures around my uncle.

"Teodora's ear candles work on the same principle," he said. "The flame creates a vacuum that sucks the wax out of my ear."

"Cool," I said.

I never thought I'd use that word in connection with earwax.

"Do you want some advice?" he asked me. "Don't get old."

"Too late," I said. "I already am."

"Hah!"

A thought struck me. "Did you ever work as a milkman?"

"What?" he asked, following it with an emphatic "No!"

Of course, just because he denied it didn't mean he hadn't. Would you admit to having been a milkman if you'd sold your uniform for a thousand dollars to a senator's wife?

Based on all the jewelry Gloria always wore, you might have thought she was really rich, but she lived in a fairly ordinary condominium complex. "Did you ever do that egg and milk bottle experiment when you went to school?" Trapp asked her when she got into the car.

She hadn't heard of it either. He seemed disappointed, almost sad.

We'd been driving awhile when he suddenly said, "Alton, you have a philosophical bent. I have a question for you."

I didn't know if I was bent that way or not, but I suppose I was glad he thought I was.

"Are your fingers alive?"

I wiggled my fingers on the steering wheel. I considered making a joke about them coming alive and attacking me, but that joke would be mostly visual, and not that funny anyway.

I decided to take his question seriously. "I'm alive," I said, "and my fingers are a part of me."

"But what's the part of you that is actually living?" he asked. "Your heart? Is your heart alive?"

"I wouldn't say it's alive," I said. "But I can't live without it."

"Not the same thing, is it?"

"How about the brain?" Gloria asked from the backseat.

"That mass of gray matter," said Trapp. "The brain's just another organ. Like Alton said, you can't live without it, but that doesn't make it a living entity."

"Then what are you suggesting?" asked Gloria.

"Our bodies are not alive," said Trapp. "The only living entities are *ideas*."

"That's the brain," said Gloria.

"No. What if ideas exist outside the brain? Our brains simply perceive them."

There was that word again, *perceive*.

"You smell a flower, or hear a violin, but the flower and the violin aren't inside your brain. Your brain simply registers the smell or the sound. The same can be said about ideas. They are alive, living outside our brains. Our brain simply perceives and registers them. After all, a brain surgeon can't tell you where a certain idea exists inside your brain. She can't tell you what cells make up that particular idea. She might look at an electronic image of your brain, and she can tell you what part of the brain is active when you listen to music, or eat, or play bridge, but that's the perception of the idea, not the idea itself."

"So how does that make them *alive*?" I asked.

"Think about it," he said. "Ideas evolve. They reproduce. That's the very definition of life."

"They *reproduce*?" asked Gloria.

"Through communication," said Trapp. "Are you aware, Alton, that another word for *communication* is *intercourse*?"

Gloria laughed. I think I might have blushed, but fortunately Trapp couldn't see me.

"The urge to communicate is even stronger than the sex drive," Trapp said. "Why do you think people gossip so much? Why can't we keep secrets? Why have we invented the printing press, the telephone, the Internet? It's so ideas can grow and reproduce. Our bodies, our brains, are just machines that ideas use for a while, then toss aside when they wear out."

"Okay," I said, "but here we are, talking about the idea that ideas are alive, right? So who are *we* talking about that idea?"

(Don't worry if my question doesn't make sense to you. It doesn't make sense to me now either, as I write this, although I think I understood it when I asked it.)

"When you think of yourself, Alton, when you think, *Me*, what comes to mind? Do you think about what you look like? Your arms, your legs, your face? Or is the *Me* that's inside you something else?"

I didn't answer. I have a definite sense of who I am, and it has nothing to do with what I look like, but I couldn't put it into words.

"Your body will wear out someday," he said. "It may deteriorate slowly, like mine, or perhaps one day a piano will fall on top of you."

"Hah!" I laughed, sounding surprisingly like him.

"One way or another, the body of Alton Richards will cease to exist," he said. "But the *idea* of Alton Richards will live forever."

I suppose that was somewhat comforting.

"So what happens to ideas that are not communicated?" asked Gloria. "Do they die?"

"What do you mean?" asked Trapp.

"What if Alton thinks of a brand-new idea, but before he can tell anyone, a piano falls on top of him?"

I was beginning to get concerned about falling pianos.

"Or say a songwriter creates a beautiful melody," continued Gloria, "and then dies before he can play it for anyone. Does the melody exist?"

"An idea doesn't die," said Trapp. "It exists somewhere, in its own dimension, waiting to be perceived."

"How? Where?"

"Who knows? Maybe those are the voices that Toni hears."

"Toni?" I asked. The mention of her name instantly triggered all my worries about Cliff and Toni, Cliff and Katie, me and Toni.

"Toni has a psychological abnormality," said Trapp.

"I don't think you should discuss this," said Gloria.

"I know she sees a psychiatrist," I said. "For schizophrenia."

"Just because someone has a diploma hanging on his wall doesn't mean he's qualified to declare her a schizophrenic," said Trapp. "But then, Gloria knows my opinion of the psychiatric profession."

"That was over forty years ago," said Gloria. "And just

because one doctor may have been corrupt, it doesn't mean—"

"It was more than just one doctor," said Trapp.

I was confused. Were they talking about Toni or about her grandmother?

"Toni hears voices," said Trapp. "But who is this Dr. Ellsworth to tell her she's a schizophrenic? Maybe she just perceives better than the rest of us. Maybe the voices she hears are uncommunicated ideas, floating free."

32

A Singing Pig

The sectional tournament was held in a Shriners' meeting hall. I didn't know what a Shriner was, but according to Cliff, they are people who wear funny hats.

There must have been more than sixty bridge tables set up in neat rows. I don't think I saw any Shriners, just a lot of bridge players, and a few of them wore funny hats. Bridge gibberish was coming at me from every corner of the room.

"After going into the tank for ten minutes, he leads a club, giving the declarer a sluff and a ruff! Then, in the post-mortem, he asks me if there was something he could have done differently. 'Yes,' I tell him. 'Play *any other* card.'"

We made our way to the long directors' table. There were three directors, two men and a woman, all wearing matching purple shirts with the ACBL logo printed on the front pocket. Trapp gave me his wallet and I paid for the entry.

"This is Lester Trapp," said Gloria. "I spoke to a Harvey Willfolk about a special table."

One of the male directors looked up for the first time. "What kind of special—is he blind?"

"Very astute," said my uncle.

"I'll take this," said the woman director. "Welcome, Mr. Trapp. We have you in section B, table seven."

She took back the entry form that the other director had handed me and gave me a different one, with 7-B marked on it. "You're his cardturner?"

I said I was.

"You understand that you are just to tell him what cards are in his hand? You are not to tell him what cards have already been played, or in any way suggest what card he should play?"

"Sorry, Trapp," I said. "They won't let me tell you what card to play."

"I'll manage somehow," said my uncle.

People stopped and stared at us as we made our way to our assigned table.

"Can't be any worse than the partner I had this morning," I heard someone say with a laugh.

Just you wait, I thought. *We're going to kick your ass!*

This was the third day of a four-day tournament. At a bridge tournament there are separate events each day, unlike, say, at my sister's soccer tournament, where there's just one winner. Trapp and Gloria would be playing in a two-session pairs game. There had been other events on Thursday and Friday, and there would be something new on Sunday. Judging by the zombielike expressions on most of the faces in the room, I guessed that many of them had played every day, two or three sessions each day.

We settled into 7-B, where two women were already seated East-West. They were well dressed, with brightly colored blouses and linen jackets. Gloria explained our situation to them.

"It's wonderful he's still able to enjoy the game," said East. She had a round face and wore big round glasses.

"You're such a dear to help out your uncle," said West. She also wore glasses, and had one of those jeweled strands that went around her neck, connected to either side of the frames.

They came off all sweet and friendly, but don't let the kindly-old-grandmother act fool you. They smelled blood. What better way to begin a tournament than with a couple of top boards off a blind guy?

Unlike at the club, we didn't shuffle and deal. Instead, we sorted the deck into suits. A caddy came around and passed out *hand records*. There were three caddies, two girls and a boy, all about Leslie's age.

A hand record is a sheet of paper with a bridge diagram on it, indicating which cards should be in which hand. We had boards thirteen and fourteen, and the hand records for those boards. Each of us took a suit; I took the clubs and distributed them as indicated on the hand record.

Naturally we didn't play those two boards. A director, speaking through a microphone, instructed us to pass the boards lower, skipping a table. I took the boards to table five, and we got our two new boards from table nine.

I found out the reason for hand records later. When the session was over, you could pick up a sheet of paper showing the hand records for every single board. If you don't know why bridge players would want this, then you haven't been paying attention. Besides actually playing bridge, their favorite thing to do is to talk about hands already played. That's what their bridge gibberish is all about.

The game got under way. I removed the South hand from board seventeen, then led Trapp to a nearby corner.

"So, you just told him all his cards?" East asked when we returned.

"And he's going to remember them?" asked West.

"You can ask me," my uncle said. "Despite my lack of eyesight, I can hear and speak."

"Pass," said Gloria as she set a green pass card on the table.

"Are we supposed to say our bids out loud?" asked East.

"It would be helpful," said Trapp.

"One heart," she said, but then set the 1♠ card on the table.

Gloria pointed out the discrepancy, and the woman apologized, complaining about how confusing it was to have to say a bid out loud when using bidding boxes. "Do you want to call the director?" she asked.

"Just make the bid you want to make," said Gloria.

"One spade," the woman said, keeping the bidding card on the table.

"Two clubs," said Trapp.

I placed the bid on the table.

The final contract was three no-trump doubled, and Trapp was the declarer. He made it by *squeezing* East.

He didn't actually grab East and squeeze her. Gloria

explained it to me later, at dinner, using the sheet of hand records. For reasons that will soon be clear, it's best for me to explain it to you now.

This was the situation with three cards left to play. Trapp needed to win the rest of the tricks to make his contract.

Dummy
♠ 3
♡ KJ

West
♡ 10
♢ 98

East
♠ Q
♡ Q8

Trapp
♠ J
♡ 2
♣ 2

Trapp had won the previous trick, so he was on-lead. I couldn't see all four hands, of course, just Trapp's and the dummy hand. My guess had been that he would lead the two of hearts, hoping to finesse West's queen. As you can see, that wouldn't have worked, since East was the lady who actually had the queen of hearts.

"Two of clubs," he said, and I set the card on the table.

Nobody else had any clubs, so the lowly deuce of clubs would actually win the trick. Meanwhile, everyone else had to make a discard. West discarded the ♢8, and Trapp told Gloria to play the ♠3, but East was *squeezed*.

Whatever card she discarded would cost a trick. If she threw the ♡8, Trapp would then play the ♡2 and win the last two tricks in the dummy with the king, then the jack of hearts. If instead she threw the ♠Q, Trapp would win the last two tricks with the ♠J in his hand, and then the high heart in dummy. Either way, East was screwed.

That three-card ending didn't just happen. Trapp had planned for it earlier, then carefully set it up that way.

Remember, the same hand will eventually be played at every table across the room. At most tables, the person sitting in Trapp's seat will try a simple *finesse*. That play would have failed in this instance. Instead, Trapp executed a more complicated maneuver known as a *squeeze,* allowing him to make his contract.

"Why are you explaining it to Alton?" Trapp asked Gloria. "He doesn't understand a thing about bridge."

"He knows more than you think," said Gloria.

I remained silent.

Back at the bridge table, Trapp had made his contract, and East and West were arguing.

"What did you double for?" asked West, the round-faced one.

"What does it matter?" asked her partner. "No one else will make three no-trump. If he could have seen the dummy he would have taken the heart finesse like everyone else. We were fixed."

Normally Trapp would just sit back and let the opponents argue, but I think he was offended by her use of the word *fixed*. She had just called him stupid and lucky. Worse, she blamed his supposedly lucky play on his blindness.

"Why would I take the heart finesse when I know you have the queen?" he asked.

West admonished her partner to hold her hand back.

"He can't *see* my cards!" East exclaimed.

"The kid can see," said West. "There's something funny going on between them."

"Now, hold on!" warned Gloria.

"He said he *knew* she had the queen of hearts," said West.

Gloria glared at her. "He knew she had the queen because she opened the bidding, and you had already shown up with the king and jack of diamonds."

"Don't bother," Trapp said to Gloria. "Never try to teach a pig to sing. It just irritates the pig."

"Director!" yelled East, waving her arm in the air.

When a director arrived, East accused Trapp of calling her partner a pig.

"I most certainly did not," said my uncle.

"Now he's lying about it," said West.

"She had accused me of somehow peeking at her partner's hand," said Trapp, "possibly in collusion with Alton. My partner tried to explain my line of play, but I told her not to bother. I knew such an effort would be as useless as trying to teach a pig to sing."

"You heard him!" West exclaimed.

"My partner was not trying to teach you to sing, madam," said Trapp. "Ergo, I did not call you a pig."

131

The director penalized both pairs, East-West for accusing Trapp of cheating and North-South "for calling an opponent—strike that—for *comparing* an opponent to a pig."

Throughout it all, I kept my expression blank, but I had to bite the inside of my cheeks to keep from laughing.

The director told us to go on to the next hand and advised everyone to treat the other players with respect. "This is a zero-tolerance tournament."

"Well, it's very distracting when we have to keep saying every card out loud," complained East.

"I'm sorry my partner's blindness makes life so difficult for you," said Gloria.

33

The Great Bridge Detective

That first pair was the exception. Everyone else was friendly and tended to be very supportive of Trapp, even after he got a good board off them.

Don't get me wrong. Some of our opponents were also very good players. Twice I heard Trapp say "Nicely played," which was about as many times as I'd heard him use that expression in all the times he'd played at the club.

The director watched us for several rounds, and after he left, another director came and took his place. Then the third one came. I don't think they were worried about Trapp's behavior. I think they were fascinated by the blind guy who played so well.

I had no way of actually knowing how well Trapp and Gloria were playing. Unlike at the club, the scores didn't travel with the boards. After each round, a caddy collected all the scores and brought them to the directors' table, where they were entered into a computer. Still, I assumed they were doing well because, well, because they were Trapp and Gloria.

After we played our final board, the results were posted with one round to go, showing everyone's results going into the final round. Despite the penalty, Trapp and Gloria were leading with a 62 percent game.

Around me, players were asking each other what they had done on various boards. They were all trying to figure out if they would move up or down, once the last round was recorded.

I reported back to Trapp and Gloria. They were more concerned about beating the dinner rush at the local restaurants than about sticking around for the final results. Besides, the results weren't final. The event was only half over.

I already told you some of our dinner conversation. The restaurant quickly filled up with bridge players going over the hand records with friends who had played the same boards.

"What'd you do on board five?"

"Four spades, making."

"What was the lead?"

"A low club."

"Well, no wonder. They led the ten of diamonds against me. After that, I had no chance."

"They led the ten of diamonds against me, too," Trapp said quietly, so only Gloria and I could hear.

"Did you make it?" I asked.

"What do you think?" asked Gloria.

———————

Trapp didn't need hand records. He could tell you who held the jack of clubs on board eleven, or how many hearts were in the East hand on board two.

I don't think he purposely set out to memorize every three of spades or seven of clubs. I think it's more like the way you or I memorize song lyrics. You might not think you know all the words to a song, but then you hear the music, and you sing the first line, and that leads to the next line, and before you know it, you've sung the whole song.

That's how it was with Trapp and bridge hands. He'd remember the cards he held, and then the decisions he had to make during the bidding, and the opening lead, and it would all just flow from there.

Gloria described it to me another way. She said that Trapp was like a brilliant detective solving a crime. Each card was a clue: West had the ace of diamonds. East showed up with a singleton club. Trapp wouldn't forget those clues any more than a detective would forget a bloody knife found under a mattress.

34

Director, Please!

We returned to the Shriners' hall. I was incorrect when I said earlier that Trapp and Gloria were in first place. They were leading all the other North-South pairs in their section, section B. That part was still true, although their score had dropped a bit in the last round, to 60.5 percent. To win the event, however, they'd have to have a higher percentage than everyone in the room, including sections A and C, and all the East-West pairs too.

The top twenty-five pairs were posted on the wall. Trapp and Gloria were currently in sixth place. The overall leader was at 66 percent.

We remained at our table, B-7, for the evening session, but the rest of the field was scrambled. Half the pairs who had been North-South for the first session would be East-West for the second session. Some from section B would be in section C, and some from section C would be in section A.

If I were a super-talented author, you'd no doubt feel the suspense as I described the evening session to you, hand after hand, card after card. When I got to the part where Trapp and Gloria were playing against the pair with the 66 percent game, the tension would be so great, wax would ooze out your ears, no matter how many tiny hairs you have in there.

But I'm not.

Besides, I didn't know one pair from another. I couldn't tell you *when* or *if* we played the pair with 66 percent. Trapp and Gloria displayed such a lack of emotion, I couldn't even tell you what the highlights of the session were.

What I did notice, all around me, was people making really dumb mistakes. I'm not talking about subtle errors in bridge strategy. I'm talking major screwups, the kinds of mistakes I'd probably make if I were playing.

One time, somebody failed to follow suit. He had trumped a diamond, and then later discovered he had a diamond mixed in with his hearts. Another time, somebody bid when it wasn't his turn. Somebody else made an insufficient bid. He bid 1♡, not noticing that 2♣ was already on the table.

Each time something like that happened, a person would raise a hand and call out, "Director, please!"

The directors had a very specific rule for each situation. So not only were these mistakes really dumb, I realized, but they all had happened many times before.

Another type of director ruling involved *unauthorized information*. You're not allowed to say anything that might give your partner information about your hand, not even "Oops!" In fact, one time I overheard the director say that a person had conveyed unauthorized information simply because he had hesitated too long during the bidding. The extra-long hesitation told his partner that he was seriously considering making some other bid.

With one round to go, Trapp and Gloria were at 63 percent. This was just for the evening session. The final result would be a combination of both sessions.

We waited for the director to enter all the scores from the last round.

"Shall we go?" said Trapp. "I'm a bit tired."

I couldn't believe it. "Don't you want to find out if you won or not?"

"I'm satisfied with the way I played," he said. "That's all that matters."

"The hell it is!" said Gloria.

They won. Gloria whooped with delight when I reported the final results. They each got 15.5 masterpoints.

Trapp pretended he didn't care, but don't you believe it. I had never seen him happier. He even sang a song on the drive home.

We had been discussing music. I'd never heard of any of the songs he and Gloria mentioned, and they'd never heard of the stuff I listened to. I played three songs for them, and Trapp actually liked two of the three.

"You never heard of 'Bye Bye Blackbird'?" he asked me.

"Nope," I said.

"It's a classic," said Gloria.

"Sorry," I said.

Of course, neither of them owned anything like an iPod, so they sang it for me.

Gloria's voice was surprisingly sweet and melodic. Normally, when she just talked, it was gritty and full of cracks.

> *"Pack up all your cares and woe,*
> *Here I go, singing low,*
> *Bye bye, Blackbird."*

Trapp sang the last verse. Listening to him, you just got a hint of the melody, and had to imagine the rest.

> *"Make my bed and light the light,*
> *I'll be home late tonight,*
> *Blackbird, bye bye."*

35

Toni and Cliff

The next morning (afternoon, technically), I was awakened by a call from Toni.

"Hello," I said, still groggy.

"Alton?"

"Yeah, it's me," I said. My voice sounds deeper and a little scratchy when I first wake up.

"So how'd the tournament go?" she asked.

"Great! We won. We scored above sixty percent both sessions."

"'We'?" Toni asked with a laugh, then admitted she used to feel the same way when she was Trapp's cardturner.

I started to tell her about the women who accused Trapp of cheating, and what he said to them, but Toni interrupted me.

"He already told me all about it," she said. "What they said was much worse than what he said."

She explained that bridge is a highly ethical game. Cheating is so bad that the second-worst thing you can do is to accuse someone of being a cheater.

"You spoke to Trapp?" I asked. *Then why did she call me to ask about the tournament?*

"Can I ask you something?" she asked.

I waited.

"Does Cliff think I'm crazy?"

"Uh . . . no," I said.

I hesitated too long before answering. I think she took it as unauthorized information, but I was just taken aback by her question.

"What did he say? Did he say something?"

"He didn't say anything. I haven't talked to Cliff."

"Really?"

"Really. I didn't get back until late last night and your phone call woke me up."

"Oh, sorry. If he says anything about me, will you tell me?"

"Maybe," I said. "I don't know. So you went to Gilliam's party?"

Now she was the one who hesitated. After a long pause, she finally said, "You didn't miss much."

"Was Katie there?" I asked.

"Who?"

I repeated Katie's name, although Toni's "Who?" had pretty much answered that question.

"There were a lot of people there," she said. "I'm not good at names. Why?" she asked in a teasing, gossipy sort of voice. "Is she someone you *like*?"

I hesitated.

"You don't have to answer that," she said.

"It's complicated," I said.

We hung up shortly thereafter. She apologized for waking me, and I told her I'd been just about to get up anyway.

When Katie and I were still together, she used to ask me those kinds of questions about Cliff too. *What's with your friend Cliff? I don't think he likes me very much. What does he say about me? He hates me, doesn't he?*

I remained sitting up in my bed, trying to decide if I should call Cliff. Who was I kidding? I knew I'd call him, and I knew the call would depress me.

I dialed his number.

"Hey, Alton," he answered.

"So how was Gilliam's party?"

"Oh, kind of a dud."

"So, did you go with Katie?" I asked.

"No, I think things are kind of ratcheting down between Katie and me. Your bridge friend was there, what's her name, Toni?"

As if he didn't know her name!

"There's nothing going on between you two, right?" he asked.

"No," I admitted.

"So, since you're not interested in her, she's free?"

Did you notice that I never said I wasn't interested in her? Still, who was I to say she wasn't free?

"Did you and Toni hook up?" I asked.

"Oh, you know how it is, everyone dancing."

"So, you danced with her?"

"No, she didn't want to dance. We just talked, and maybe kissed a little." Cliff gave a short laugh, then said, "She's cray-zee!"

Toni had no reason to be worried. Cliff made "crazy" sound like a good thing.

"How do you mean?" I asked.

"Oh, you know, just the way she— Okay, here's something. Gilliam's parents own a karaoke machine, only their taste in music is pretty lame."

"Were his parents there?" I asked.

"No, but it was their karaoke machine. So we're all trying to find some song somebody might have heard of. Then suddenly Toni just gets up, turns on the machine, and just starts singing this old-time song. It was like she stepped out of a time machine."

"What was the song?" I asked.

"I don't know! Nobody had ever heard it before. Something about a bird. That's not the point."

"'Bye Bye Blackbird'?" I asked.

There was a long hesitation on the other end. "How did you know?"

I don't know how I knew. I was still trying to figure out how two people could *maybe* kiss.

36

Synchronicity

I looked it up on the Internet. "Bye Bye Blackbird" is a song from 1926.

I had gone my entire life without hearing it, and then on the same night that Gloria and Trapp sang it to me on the car ride home, Toni sang it at a party, quite possibly at the very same time.

Trapp had a word for that: *synchronicity,* he called it. "It's when two related things occur without any apparent cause-and-effect."

We were driving to the bridge studio, and I told him about the coincidence, leaving out the part about Cliff and Toni *maybe* kissing.

He said that synchronicity was different from a mere coincidence. With synchronicity you feel that there's a definite connection. You just don't know what that connection is.

I was reminded of something that had happened to me the year before, quite possibly another moment of synchronicity. I had never told anyone about it, not even Cliff, because it was really no big deal, although it did feel like a big deal at the time.

There was a kid I knew in third grade named Doug Bridges. He lived down the street from us. He only lived there for about a year; then his family moved away.

He was one of those people you know for a short while and then forget about. I hadn't thought about him since the third grade, but then, one day last year, I don't know why, I suddenly thought about him. I had a very vivid memory of my third-grade class going on a field trip to a bakery. Before we got on the bus, our teacher had us pair off. She told everyone to choose a buddy.

Cliff and I were best friends even then, but I noticed Doug, the new kid, standing sadly alone, so I asked Doug to be my buddy. I remembered everyone in my class was given a freshly baked cookie at the bakery. Seven years later, when I suddenly found myself thinking about this incident, my memory was so strong I could smell the bakery and taste the cookie.

That's it. No big deal. I had this memory flash, and most likely would have forgotten all about it, but the next day, my father asked me if I remembered Doug Bridges, who used to live on our street. "He was killed in an automobile accident yesterday."

"Are you certain you didn't remember the bakery incident *after* you'd heard he had died?" Trapp asked me.

I was sure. That's why it had seemed so weird.

"Synchronicity," he agreed. "But just because there is

no apparent cause-and-effect, it doesn't mean that one doesn't exist. We simply may be unable to perceive or comprehend the connection."

"Like when Captain listens to the radio," I said.

"Hah!" he laughed, then said, "Exactly so."

"What about the fact that his last name was Bridges?" I asked.

"What about it?"

"And now I'm taking you to play bridge?"

He said that was a meaningless coincidence. For there to be synchronicity, it must feel like there's some sort of connection just beyond your grasp. "Perhaps," he suggested, "Doug Bridges at the instant of his death somehow thanked all the people who had been kind to him over his lifetime, by reminding them of their good deeds."

I smiled. That was a nice idea, anyway.

Trapp then told me about an incidence of synchronicity that had happened to him more than fifty years ago, when he was in his early twenties. One night, he and a group of friends had been staying up late, "drinking cheap wine, as we contemplated our future."

He had thought of something he had read in a book. "About how the character traits we admire—kindness, generosity, honesty—all lead to failure. And the character traits we supposedly abhor—greed and selfishness and the like—are the character traits of successful people."

He had tried to repeat the quote to his friends, but it didn't come out right. He couldn't quite remember it. He also couldn't remember where he had read it.

It was still bugging him the next day. "I was searching

through my bookcases and all my boxes of books, hoping that if I saw the title it would jar my memory, when suddenly the phone rang, interrupting my search. The call was from a woman I hardly knew, someone who had never called me before. She wanted to know if I owned a copy of *Cannery Row,* by John Steinbeck, and if so, could she borrow it?"

I felt a chill. I already knew what was coming next.

"*Cannery Row* was the book I had been trying to remember."

"And she just called out the blue?" I asked. "Had you ever mentioned the book to her?"

"No. I'd played against her a few times at bridge tournaments. That was it. Her name was Annabel King. Her husband was a senator. He had taken the book from her, because he thought Steinbeck was a Communist."

Trapp had brought his copy of *Cannery Row* to the next tournament, where he and Annabel King agreed to play as partners.

37

Trapp's Closest Living Relatives

The game didn't go too well. I'm back to Trapp and Gloria now, not Trapp and Annabel. Trapp and Annabel won the first time they played together, but on this particular Monday, Trapp and Gloria just barely broke 50 percent.

"I shouldn't have played so soon after the tournament," Trapp said to her after we finished. "I'm still worn out."

Gloria said it had nothing to do with how he had played. "It was just one of those days where the opponents made all the right decisions, and there was nothing we could do about it."

Maybe. It was hard for me to tell if what Gloria said was true, or if she was just being nice. Still, Trapp canceled the rest of his games for the next week and a half. He wanted to rest up for the regional tournament.

I'd be taking him and Gloria there a week from Wednesday. They would play in something called a knockout, which would be an even greater test of his ability and his endurance. It would be a two-day, four-session event, and they'd be competing against only the top players at the tournament.

A knockout is a team event, with four people on each team. I didn't quite understand how that would work. Two old friends would be flying in from Connecticut to join them. I also found out that the regional would be held in a fancy hotel, where we would spend the night, and I'd get to order room service.

Toni called me that night. "Since Trapp won't be playing Thursday, do you want to play with me?"

"You mean bridge?" I asked.

"No, hopscotch."

I knew what she meant, of course. I was just stalling as I tried to figure out how playing bridge with Toni would fit in with me and Cliff, and Cliff and Toni, not to mention Cliff and Katie.

"At the studio?" I asked.

"That's the place," she said.

"Those people there are experts," I pointed out. "I barely know how to bid."

She said she'd e-mail me some simple bidding rules. "C'mon, what's the worst that can happen?"

I agreed to play. I suppose I knew I would the second she asked me. Still, I wondered if I should call Cliff first and get his okay.

Toni's so-called simple bidding rules arrived on my computer the next day. There were eleven pages, single-spaced. Leslie helped me study. We dealt out bridge hands and then figured out how each person would bid, pretending we didn't know which cards were in each of the other hands. We would then play the hands too, to see if we could make our contract.

In my daydreams, I dazzled Toni with my superb bidding and brilliant card play, but my daydreams never went any further than that. I couldn't let them. I was still pretending to myself that I was only interested in bridge, not Toni.

I never called Cliff. I told myself it wasn't necessary, because Toni had probably told him she'd be playing bridge with me. And if she hadn't told him, why should I?

There was something else, too, that kept me from letting my daydreams go too far. It was something that I'd been wondering about for a while, and maybe you have been too.

Were Toni and I cousins? In other words, was Trapp her grandfather? Or, to be more blunt, when Trapp was a young man, did he have sex with Annabel King, the senator's wife, his own wife's sister?

It would explain a lot, like why Trapp's marriage didn't last, and why he was so close to Sophie Castaneda. She was his daughter. It also might have something to do with Annabel going insane.

And so much for my family's being his closest living relatives.

38

Thank You, Partner

I felt energized as I drove to the bridge studio on Thursday. After having turned Trapp's cards for him week after week, hand after hand, card after card, I was excited about getting to turn my own cards for a change. I was also nervous.

I tried to calm myself down as I walked up the concrete stairs of building two. I took a deep breath, then opened the door to the bridge studio.

From across the room, Toni smiled and waved at me. I don't think there's anything better than seeing a pretty girl smile and wave at you, the way her face lights up when she catches your eye. I casually waved back, then made my way to table ten, where she was sitting.

"Hello, partner," she brightly greeted me. "I chose East-West, so we wouldn't have to keep score. I hope that's okay."

"That's fine," I said, sitting across from her, in the East seat.

I told her I'd learned all the rules she sent me. "Leslie helped me study."

"They're not rules," said Toni. "They're guidelines. It's not about memorizing rules. You have to think. *What is my partner trying to tell me? What information does my partner need from me?* We have to let each other know what we've got, so we can figure out what the trump suit should be, and whether we should bid game, or even slam."

"I'm not bidding slam," I said.

"You might," she said. "If it's right."

"I'm not bidding slam," I repeated.

She smiled, then said, "Too bad Trapp doesn't know Leslie. He'd love her."

The director announced we would play nine rounds, three boards per round. "Shuffle and play."

We started with boards twenty-eight, twenty-nine, and thirty. I dealt board thirty, and somehow couldn't seem to give everyone thirteen cards. I had to deal it three times. Then, when I removed my hand from board twenty-eight, I dropped two cards on the table, the king and ten of hearts. You would have thought I'd never done this before.

Technically, our opponents were supposed to call for the director, but the man sitting South told me to just put them back in my hand and not to worry about it. "Pretend you never saw them," he told Toni.

"I'm not used to sitting East," I said. "I usually sit South."

As if that made a difference.

The woman sitting in the North seat told me that the first time she played duplicate bridge, she was so nervous her entire hand just exploded onto the table.

"The day's still young," I said, and everyone laughed. This was my first hand:

♠ KQJ2
♡ AK10953
♢ A
♣ K10

I counted my points using the method Toni had taught me.

A = 4   Void = 3
K = 3   Singleton = 2
Q = 2   Doubleton = 1
J = 1

I had twenty points just counting my high cards, and then three more points for my singleton diamond and doubleton club. Twenty-three points! My hand was shaking. I tried to keep a blank expression.

Toni's rules had a bid for a hand like this. I was supposed to open "Two clubs." A two-club opener doesn't really say anything about the club suit. It just says, "Partner, I've got a really huge hand."

I steadied myself, and was just about to make that bid, but caught myself in time. West was the designated dealer for board twenty-eight. Toni **was first** to bid.

She reached into her bidding box and set the 1♠ bid on the table.

She had an opening hand too. Her bid promised at least five spades. That meant we had nine spades between us, maybe more.

North passed, no surprise there, and it was up to me.

I could still bid 2♣, but I didn't think that was right. None of Toni's bidding rules said what to do if your partner opens the bidding and you have a twenty-three-point hand.

I took a deep breath, reached into my bidding box, and set the 7♠ card on the table.

"Wow, you don't fool around, do you?" North said with a laugh.

I shrugged.

Since Toni was the first to bid spades, she would be declarer and I'd get to be dummy. That was a relief.

North made her opening lead; then I set my hand on my table for all to see.

Toni surveyed my hand. "Thank you, partner," she said, then proceeded to take all thirteen tricks, scoring a grand slam on our very first hand.

39

Two Idiots at Table Seven

I wish I could report that all the hands went like that. It had seemed so easy when I was practicing with Leslie. This person would bid this, then this person would bid that, then he'd play this card and she'd play that card.

It's a lot harder when you can't see all four hands. There are billions of different possible hands, and there was no way Toni's eleven pages of bidding rules could cover every one of them.

When I turned cards for Trapp, I'd been able to guess which card he'd play about half the time. The problem was the other half. Once I played a wrong card, there was no recovering. I went down in every one of my contracts except one, and on that one I didn't bid high enough, so we still got a bad board.

I got worse, not better, as the game progressed. I now knew what Trapp meant when he said he was worn out after a session of bridge. By the time we reached the last round, my brain had turned to mush.

Yet despite all my screwups, whenever I glanced across

the table, I never saw anything but trust in Toni's eyes. She looked at me with absolute confidence, certain that *this time* I would get it right.

Because we were sitting East-West, Toni and I got up and moved to another table after each round. I always sat in the East seat.

Our opponents had all been very nice, maybe too nice. They said how delighted they were to see us playing on our own, without Trapp. I think they meant it, and not just because they were getting good boards off us.

Until we got to table seven.

"Hi," Toni greeted our opponents as we sat down for the final round.

They ignored her. "If you returned a spade we could have beaten it another trick," said the man in the South seat. He had bushy hair and wore steel-rimmed glasses.

"If you wanted me to return a spade you shouldn't have returned a low club," said North, a man with blond hair and skin so pale it was almost transparent. He also wore glasses.

They were maybe forty or forty-five years old, which made them the second-youngest pair in the room.

"Hi," Toni said again.

The bushy-haired man glanced at her, then turned back to his partner and muttered, "I hate playing against beginners."

We began with board ten, and, as usual, I screwed up both the bidding and the play. Only this time it got us a top board!

My final contract was two diamonds, and I was the declarer. I managed to take my eight tricks, but I should have made an overtrick. Every other East-West had bid four

spades and had only taken nine tricks, because of an unlucky lie of the cards. I took fewer tricks than everyone
else, but I was the only one with a positive score.

The blond man glared at me. "How can you only bid
two diamonds?" he demanded. "Your partner opened the
bidding, and you had fifteen points!"

"I didn't think she'd pass," I said in my defense.

He sneered at me, then said, "What an idiot!"

"And then he played it as badly as he bid it," his partner added. "That's why I hate playing against beginners.
They give everyone else tops, and then they fix us."

"You were a beginner once too," Toni pointed out.

He looked down his nose at her and said, "Believe me,
if I played as badly as your partner, I would have quit the
game a long time ago."

Toni was the "idiot" on board eleven. I'm not sure what
she did exactly, but this time our opponents were happy
about it.

"I knew you were stupid," the bushy-haired man said,
laughing at her. "I just didn't know you were *that* stupid!"

Toni turned red. "Well, now you know," she said
quietly. Her cheek was quivering. I was afraid she might
cry.

The men were still laughing as I removed my hand from
board twelve, which thankfully was the last hand of the
day. I sorted my cards. It was a lousy hand. My only high
cards were a king and two jacks.

Toni set the 1♠ card on the table. I probably should
have passed, but I raised to 2♠. The bushy-haired guy bid
3◇; then Toni surprised me by bidding 4♠.

North doubled, snapping the red card on the table with a flourish.

I knew I should have passed the first time!

I passed, South passed, and it was Toni's turn again. She was thinking.

"You can't go back to three spades," said the blond guy, and he and his partner chortled over that one.

Toni didn't seem to notice their laughter. She reached into her bidding box, then gently set her bid on the table. It was the blue card with two Xs.

The men stopped laughing.

It was the first time I had ever seen anyone use the re-double card.

Toni	North	Me	South
1♠	Pass	2♠	3◇
4♠	X	Pass	Pass
XX	Pass	Pass	Pass

North led the ace of diamonds, and I set my pitiful hand on the table. "Sorry," I said. "This is all I got."

"Thank you, partner," said Toni. "The five, please."

I played the five of diamonds, as directed.

There was an intensity in her eyes that I had never seen before. She carefully watched every card the opponents played. Her voice was flat yet authoritative as she dictated what card I was to play from the dummy.

After the first six tricks, she had won four, and the opponents had won two. She could only let them win one more.

"Jack of clubs, please."

I played the card as directed.

My jack won the trick, and Toni won the next trick in her hand.

It was around this point that I noticed the blond guy squirming in his chair. When Toni won the next trick, the bushy-haired guy started squirming too.

North won the next trick, but he wasn't happy about it. He sighed disgustedly, then led a card, and Toni took the last three tricks.

"First she squeezed me out of my exit cards," the blond man griped, "and then she endplayed me."

"Well, you shouldn't have doubled!" accused his partner. "You warned her of the bad spade break."

"I wouldn't have doubled if you hadn't made that lousy three-diamonds call!"

"It got you off to the right lead! We would have set it if you switched to a club at trick two. You needed to break up the endplay."

"Yeah, right! I'm supposed to see that far ahead? On the first two hands she can barely follow suit, and then she suddenly turns into Syd Fox!"

Four spades, doubled and redoubled, was worth 1,080 points. North and South were still arguing as Toni and I got up from the table.

"Wow, you did great!" I said to her, away from the table. "Or I guess I'm supposed to say, 'Nicely played, partner.'"

"I didn't do it alone," said Toni.

I smiled. "That's nice of you to say," I told her, "but all I did was bid two spades. You did the rest. I don't even know what an *endplay* is."

Toni looked down at her shoes. "That's not what I meant," she whispered. "My grandmother told me to re-double. She also told me what cards to play."

She looked back up at me, smiled nervously, then said, "I think those two idiots made her mad."

40

The Subconscious Mind

So that was what Cliff meant when he said Toni was cray-zee. He meant she was crazy! Nutso! Bonkers! Out of her freaking mind!

No, I didn't really think that, but before you start thinking I'm crazy too, I did not believe she had heard the voice of her dead grandmother. I was no expert on schizophrenia, but it was my belief that what Toni had heard was her subconscious mind.

I knew Trapp had been giving her bridge lessons. She also had been his cardturner before me, and had watched him play hundreds of hands. I believed that somewhere, deep down, she had absorbed it all. She knew more than she knew she knew.

When those guys said all those mean things, it was Toni, not her grandmother, who got mad. Her anger formed a connection between her conscious and subconscious minds, a *bridge,* if you will.

I didn't say any of that to Toni. I tried my best not to show any alarm or surprise at her confession.

She was looking at me nervously, anxiously. Her eyes seemed to be pleading with me.

I think I might have said "Oh."

Whatever reaction she wanted from me, she apparently didn't get it. She abruptly left the bridge studio without even waiting for the final score. I think she might have been crying.

For the record, we finished in last place with a 35 percent game. Without her "grandmother's" help, we probably wouldn't have broken 30 percent.

I awoke in the middle of the night, suddenly realizing that I could have made three hearts on board twenty-four if I had played the ten instead of the queen! Toni wasn't the only one with an overactive subconscious mind.

41

Entourage

The regional was a six-day tournament, but we were only going for two days, Wednesday and Thursday. I crammed a change of clothes into my backpack.

It had been almost a week since my game with Toni, and I hadn't talked to her since. I knew she and Cliff had spent some time together, but if she told him about our bridge game, he didn't mention it to me.

"Are you going to have your own room?" my mother asked me.

"I guess so," I said. "Trapp can afford it."

"I'm well aware of what *Uncle Lester* can afford. What about Teodora?"

"What about her?" I asked.

"Is she going to have her own room too, or is she going to be sharing a room with Uncle Lester?"

"She's his nurse," I said. "She needs to be near him."

"That's what worries me," said my mother.

I hadn't told my mother my theory about Sophie being Trapp's daughter.

I parked in Trapp's driveway and loaded his and Teodora's luggage into my car. Teodora kissed me on the cheek and called me her gallant young knight, pronouncing both the *k* and the *n*. Captain barked at me. I think the dog knew from the suitcases that I was taking Trapp away from him for a couple of days.

I would have been happy to pick Gloria up at her condo, but she had told Trapp that was too far out of the way, and insisted on meeting us at a parking lot near the freeway. If I had known that the parking lot would be deserted, and that the restaurant connected to it was boarded up and covered with graffiti, I would have insisted on other arrangements.

I pulled into the parking lot and there was Gloria, standing by her car, wearing every piece of jewelry she owned, purse in one hand, a flowered suitcase by her side.

Don't these people ever watch the news? I wondered.

I made her move her car to a busier parking lot. She called me a worrywart.

"Alton takes such good care of us," said Teodora, sitting behind me. She massaged the back of my neck.

Before you get the wrong idea about Teodora, I just think she's one of those people who seem to overflow with love and warmth. And if my mother was right, and she did share some of her love with my seventy-six-year-old uncle, well, good for him, I thought. Good for both of them!

"Used to be," Trapp said, "when I'd go to a bridge tournament, I'd never stay in a hotel room. I'd just sleep on someone's couch—if I was lucky enough to get the couch! There might be five or six of us bridge bums crashed out on the floor. Now I'm staying in a suite at a four-star hotel—with my *entourage*. You'd think I was a rock star!"

"You are a rock star," said Teodora.

"And everything's booked for Chicago," Trapp added.

"What's Chicago?" I asked.

"My next gig," said Trapp. "Hah!"

"The nationals are in Chicago this year," said Gloria. "And I plan to pay for my own hotel room and airfare."

"Too late," said Trapp. "Mrs. Mahoney has already done it online."

"He flies me to Chicago," said Gloria. "Puts me up in a fancy hotel. Gosh, what will the neighbors think?"

"Ooh-la-la," said Teodora.

"Hah!" laughed Trapp. "What else am I supposed to do with all my money?"

In the back of my mind, I could hear my mother say, *Now's your chance, Alton!* I could almost feel her elbow jabbing me in my side. *Tell him about your father losing his job.*

I ignored my mother's voice. I had my own agenda. "When you used to go to tournaments and sleep on floors," I began, "was that when Annabel was your partner?"

In my rearview mirror I saw Gloria cross her arms back and forth in front of her face, telling me not to go there.

"No, that was before Annabel," said Trapp. "When I was sleeping on floors, Annabel was playing bridge in the White House."

Despite Gloria's gesture, I couldn't let that pass.

"The White House?" I asked.

"Ike was an avid bridge player," he said.

Ike, in case you don't know (I didn't), was the nickname of President Dwight D. Eisenhower. When he ran for president, his campaign slogan was "I like Ike."

"Sounds like a TV sitcom," I said.

"TV was still new then," my uncle said. "I remember we all had such high hopes for it. We thought it would bring culture to the masses. Hah! Little did we know that it would lower everyone's cultural and moral standards."

"I like television," said Teodora.

"It was a different era back then," said Gloria. "Nowadays, everyone walks around in their own little world, plugged into their cell phones or iPods. We used to interact more with each other. We played games like charades, or board games like Scrabble or Monopoly. And of course, the greatest game was bridge."

"Alton likes video games," said my uncle. "He chases little pixels of light."

I ignored the remark. "So you were telling me about Annabel playing bridge in the White House?"

In the rearview mirror, Gloria dragged her finger across her throat, but I pretended not to notice.

42

Annabel and Ike

President Eisenhower had regular bridge games at the White House. To be invited to play was considered a tremendous honor. After Henry King was elected to the Senate, he insisted that his young wife learn to play, just in case such an opportunity arose.

Annabel was only nineteen when her husband was elected senator, and she was thirteen years younger than he was. She had been a competitive diver, and nearly made the 1952 Olympic team. Henry King had watched the Olympic tryouts. He had seen her perfect body turning gracefully through the air. He overwhelmed her with his wealth and power, and they were married the day after her eighteenth birthday.

In Washington, and no longer diving, the obedient wife channeled all her competitive energy into the game of bridge.

"She would play once a week with other congressmen's wives," Trapp said. "They just played a penny a point, but she regularly came home with forty or fifty dollars. One time she won a hundred and seventy-seven, much to her husband's displeasure."

"Why?" I asked. "I thought he wanted her to learn bridge."

"He wanted his wife to fit in with the other genteel and dignified ladies, eat little tea sandwiches, that sort of thing. He didn't want a cardsharp. In fact, he used to tell her to try not to do so well."

Then the big moment came. Eighteen months after he was elected to the Senate, Senator King and his wife were invited to the White House to fill in at bridge.

"This was what he had hoped for," Trapp said, "but it turned out to be the most humiliating experience of his life. And it was only the first of a series of humiliations."

Eisenhower was quick to recognize Annabel's bridge talent and, by comparison, Henry's lack thereof. Every compliment he paid to Annabel was a slap in the face to her husband. The president made jokes at Henry's expense. "Whenever Henry's the declarer, there are two dummies!"

The president, who had been a World War II general, believed that the same qualities that made him a successful leader also made him a good bridge player: judgment, patience, decisiveness, and most importantly, the ability to think clearly and plan ahead.

"Annabel had all those qualities," said Trapp. "Henry King had none of them. In the president's eyes, King wasn't just a bad bridge player, he was an incompetent fool."

But thanks to Annabel, the Kings became regulars at the White House bridge game. "She's smarter than you, Henry, and a hell of a lot better-looking," Eisenhower once said to him, only partially in jest. "Just what do you bring to the equation?"

In the end, Henry King did what once would have been unthinkable to him. He turned down a presidential invitation, making up some excuse about why he couldn't attend the bridge game.

"That's okay, Henry," Ike said to him. "We don't really want you anyway. Just send your charming wife."

That was the first time he hit her.

"But it wasn't the last," Trapp said. "He also forbid her to ever play bridge again."

"You have to understand, Alton," said Gloria, "those were different times. In many ways, a woman was considered the property of her husband."

"Especially if your husband was someone as rich and as powerful as Henry King," said Trapp. "He was also thirteen years older than her, so she felt dominated in that way as well."

"Hold on," I said. "If she never played bridge again, how did you and she become partners?"

"Once bridge gets in your blood, it's hard to quit. She started sneaking out of her house to play in bridge tournaments with one of the other wives from her bridge group. Of course, that woman didn't have anywhere near Annabel's skill."

"Which is why she called you," I realized. "Not just to borrow a book."

"Perhaps," said Trapp. "I didn't know any of this when I first started playing with her. I didn't know that if her husband found out she had been to a bridge tournament, he would beat her. 'I am the King!' that maniac would shout at her. 'It is your duty to serve and protect the King!'"

Annabel showed up at a tournament with a black eye. She laughed it off, claiming she had hit it against the corner of the kitchen cabinet when she had bent down to pick up an almond. On the second day of the tournament she showed up with two black eyes.

"That was when I learned the truth," said Trapp.

"What did you do?" I asked.

"What could I do?" he asked me. "Like Gloria said, those were different times. Police rarely got involved in so-called domestic squabbles. They certainly wouldn't get involved when the alleged wife beater was a very powerful senator from a very prominent family. I asked her to be more careful."

From the backseat, Gloria was once again gesturing for me to put an end to this discussion.

"Would she ever redouble?" I asked.

"What?"

I repeated the question.

"Redouble?" he asked. "What do you even know about redoubling?"

"Nothing," I said. "I've never seen anyone use the redouble card. I was curious if Annabel ever did."

"There's usually no reason to redouble," he said. "You have very little to gain, and a lot to lose."

"So she never did?"

He smiled, thinking about her. "She did it all the time," he admitted. "She'd do it to rattle the opponents. Shake their confidence. But before you ever think about redoubling, you better be able to play the cards as well as Annabel."

In the backseat, Teodora had joined Gloria in her effort to get me to change the subject, but I still had one more question. I needed to be very careful how I asked it. It required finesse.

"When you first met Annabel," I said, "how old was Sophie?"

"Sophie?" he repeated. "She must have been . . . Hah!" he suddenly laughed. "You know why he's asking that, don't you?"

Gloria and Teodora remained silent.

"He thinks I'm Sophie's father. Toni's grandfather. My nephew is accusing me of adultery."

"No, I was just curious," I said lamely. My blind uncle had seen right through me.

"Sophie was three years old when I first played bridge with her mother," he said, answering my question. "Annabel and I were bridge partners; nothing more, nothing less."

43

IMPs

We drove the rest of the way without any more discussion about Annabel. She didn't sound crazy to me, no crazier than any other bridge player. No crazier than I was when I asked if Annabel would ever redouble.

I believed Trapp when he said that she was just his bridge partner, "nothing more, nothing less." And I was glad. It meant Toni and I weren't related.

We were met at the hotel by Arnold and Lucy, friends from Trapp's bridge-bum days.

"We would have flown halfway around the world to be on a team with Trapp," said Arnold.

Lucy hugged my uncle as she gushed about how wonderful it was to see him playing bridge again. Then she got all flustered and apologetic because she had used the word *see*.

"It's all right, Lucy," Trapp assured her. "I'm aware you have the ability to see me, even if I can't see you."

"Well, it's probably just as well you can't see me," Lucy said. "I don't look like myself anymore."

"Have you ever looked like yourself?" he asked her.

Lucy laughed and said, "No," but then changed her mind and said, "Once."

Arnold and Lucy were married, but not to each other. Their spouses were also at the tournament, playing with other partners.

"You should never play bridge with your wife," Arnold told me. "It'll ruin your marriage."

"Even worse, it will ruin your bridge game," said Lucy.

We checked into our rooms. I had my own room, as did Gloria. Trapp and Teodora were sharing a two-room suite, which made sense, I thought, despite what my mother would have thought. We had lunch at the café in the hotel. Hamburgers were thirteen dollars.

Trapp, Gloria, Arnold, and Lucy went over old times, old friends, and old bridge hands too, some from more than forty years ago.

"And then you bid one spade, despite having only three points and only two spades!"

"It kept the opponents out of slam."

Just like Trapp, Arnold and Lucy seemed to be able to remember every hand they'd ever played.

I had thought of bridge as an old person's game, but I realized that hadn't always been true. Fifty years ago they hadn't been much older than Toni and me.

"We're probably boring poor Alton to death," Lucy suddenly said.

"What do you like to do, Alton?" Arnold asked. "When you're not hanging out with an old fart like Trapp?"

Everyone was staring at me. "Um, I don't know," I said. I knew better than to mention video games.

"Is there a girlfriend?" asked Lucy.

"I'm keeping my options open," I said, not wanting to come across as a total loser.

"Well, if I was forty years younger," said Lucy, "and if I lost forty pounds . . ."

For the record, I never described Lucy as overweight. I simply reported what she said. I have been very careful not to refer to any woman as old and fat.

The tournament was held in an area of the hotel called the Grand Ballroom. There must have been at least three hundred tables. Interspersed between the rows were tall poles with letters at the top, *A* through *Q*, indicating the location of the different sections.

At the sectional there had been three sections: A, B, and C. *Q* is the seventeenth letter of the alphabet.

There were two directors' tables, on opposite sides of the Grand Ballroom. One was for the pairs game, the other for the knockouts.

We'd be playing in the knockouts. When we purchased the entry, we had to tell the director the team's total number of masterpoints. Trapp had 11,200. Gloria had 5,050. Arnold had 12,800, and Lucy had 13,500.

Would you believe it? All these bridge geniuses, and none of them could add four numbers in his or her head. They came up with four different totals, and all four were wrong.

"Forty-two thousand, five hundred and fifty," I informed them.

Once all of the teams had turned in their masterpoint totals, the directors separated them into brackets. The sixteen teams with the most masterpoints were placed in the top bracket. The next sixteen were in the second bracket, and so forth.

We were in the top bracket, no surprise there. What did surprise me was that we weren't the team with the most masterpoints. We were actually sixth. There was one team with over 110,000, and another with 87,000.

We got our table assignment. Gloria and Trapp sat North-South at A-5. Two women about my mother's age were already seated in the East and West seats. The teammates of these women, two men, were sitting North-South at B-5, playing against Arnold and Lucy, who were seated East-West.

Gloria explained my role, and the women accepted it without any degree of skepticism or amazement. Their only comment about Trapp's blindness was when East, a woman with auburn hair and a nice smile, suggested he might want to try Braille cards.

"I tried them," my uncle said, which was news to me. "Couldn't get used to it. I don't know what it is. I never could remember my hand. I had to keep running my fingers back over the cards to be sure. But Alton just has to tell me once, and it sticks."

"Do you play bridge, Alton?" the other woman asked me.

"Hah!" laughed Trapp.

"I've played a few times," I said.

My uncle didn't react to that, but I know my answer surprised him.

Once we started playing, everyone was all business. It was clear, even to me, that both women were very strong players. The one who had mentioned Braille cards got a "Nicely played" from Trapp on the very first board.

We would play the entire session against just this one team. The loser would be knocked out, and the winner would get to play in the second round that evening.

After we finished the first six boards, Gloria called for a caddy, who took those boards over to Lucy and Arnold's table. While we waited for the caddy to return, Gloria asked one of the women if she had played in China.

"We both did," the woman admitted.

"I thought so," said Gloria. "Congratulations."

It turned out our opponents had been a part of the U.S. women's team that had won the world championship in China just a few months earlier. Gloria had recognized the auburn-haired one from her picture in a bridge magazine.

"There are bridge magazines?" I asked.

"I'm afraid so," said one of the women.

"So when you're not playing bridge, and not talking about bridge, you're reading about bridge?"

The women laughed.

"Who are your teammates?" asked Trapp.

"You don't need to worry about them," said East. "They're nobody."

"Just our husbands," said West, and they both laughed.

The caddy returned with the six boards that had been played at the other table, numbers seven through twelve. We played them without shuffling.

When we finished those six boards, the two women left

the table, and Arnold and Lucy took their place. We compared results.

The scoring for a team game is done differently than for a pairs game. They used something called International Match Points, but everyone just called them IMPs, as in, "We lost ten IMPs on board one. We won one IMP on board two."

This is the chart they used.

Difference in Points	IMPs
20–40	1
50–80	2
90–120	3
130–160	4
170–210	5
220–260	6
270–310	7
320–360	8
370–420	9
430–490	10
500–590	11
600–740	12
750–890	13
900–1,090	14
1,100–1,290	15
1,300–1,490	16
1,500–1,740	17
1,750–1,990	18
2,000–2,240	19
2,250–2,490	20
2,500–2,990	21
3,000–3,490	22
3,500–3,990	23
4,000 and up	24

On the first board at our table, the opponents got 420 points for making four spades. That was the one where Trapp had said "Nicely played." At the other table, Arnold and Lucy had held the same cards as the women, and they had also bid four spades. But Arnold didn't play it as well and went down one, giving their opponents fifty points.

That gave the other team a total of 470 points on that board (420 + 50), which according to the chart was worth 10 IMPs.

"Sorry, I guess I could have made it," said Arnold.

"No sorrys allowed," said Gloria. "She played it really well."

On board two, our opponents made two hearts at our table, for 110 points. Lucy and Arnold made three hearts, for 140. We did thirty points better, so we got one IMP.

Our best board was board nine. Gloria bid six hearts and made it, for 980 points. At the other table the opponents took the same number of tricks, but they only bid four hearts, for 480 points. We gained 500 points, which was worth 11 IMPs.

Lucy tallied up the results. They beat us 29 to 26.

I was stunned. I'd gotten so used to Trapp and Gloria winning all the time, it never even occurred to me that they could be knocked out in the first round.

"Don't look so upset," said Lucy, fluffing my hair. "The match is only half over. We still have another twelve boards."

Arnold and Lucy went back to the other table, and the two women returned to ours. "Three?" one of the women asked.

Gloria agreed that was the score; then, without further discussion, we started shuffling the boards.

There are some hands where even a great player doesn't have much of an opportunity to shine. He just passes and follows suit and is more or less at the mercy of his opponents. If they bid and play well, all he can do is go on to the next board, and hope that when his teammates play the hand, they make the same good bids and play the hand just as well.

I think that was pretty much how the first half of the match went. In the second half of the match, Trapp had more opportunities.

We won by 26 IMPs.

44

The Milkman's Clothes

Lucy said she knew a great Lebanese restaurant not too far away, but Trapp said he preferred to eat in his room. He was exhausted. "Besides, I'm sure Teodora has prepared some sort of macrobiotic delicacy for me."

"Lebanese food is very healthy," urged Lucy.

"I need to lie down," said Trapp.

"You're coming, aren't you, Alton?" asked Arnold.

"It will be a lot more fun than a boring hotel room," said Lucy.

I had never eaten Lebanese food, but how good could it be if it was so healthy? Besides, I'd always wanted to order room service.

"Not for Alton," said my uncle. "They have video games in the rooms. Hah!"

"Lebanese sounds great," I said.

Hah yourself!

First I had to escort him to his room. "So you've played bridge a few times?" he suddenly asked me in the elevator.

"Twice," I said. "Once at my house, and then Thursday at the bridge studio with Toni."

I waited for some comment, but he said nothing more about it. He didn't even ask how we did. I think maybe he was mulling it all over, letting it sink in.

Teodora opened the door to his suite. "Did you get knocked up?" she asked, taking Trapp from me.

"Knocked out," said Trapp. "No, we're still in it. *Knocked up* means you're pregnant."

Teodora squeezed my arm and said, "Well done, Alton," as if I deserved the credit for the victory.

Knockouts go quicker than pairs games, since you play board after board against the same opponents and don't have to wait for everyone else to finish and then move to a new table. Lucy's husband and Arnold's wife still had three rounds to go in the pairs game when we left for the Lebanese restaurant in Arnold's rental car.

"Is he really going to Chicago?" Lucy asked.

"He booked the rooms," said Gloria.

"You think he's up to it?" asked Arnold.

"To tell you the truth," said Gloria, "I think the nationals are what's keeping him alive."

"He'll win," I said. "You just knocked out two world champions!"

"Their husbands weren't exactly world-champion caliber," said Arnold.

———

The Lebanese restaurant was in an old cement factory that now housed quite a number of upscale shops and restaurants. There were lots of exposed pipes and odd-looking pieces of machinery, but it was all for decoration.

Lucy ordered a bunch of appetizers and salads for the table. It tasted pretty good to me, and everyone seemed to be enjoying the meal, until I ruined it by asking, "So what ever happened to Annabel?"

All I got for an answer were three cold stares.

I knew Gloria didn't want me talking about Annabel in front of Trapp, but he wasn't around now, so I didn't see the harm. I pressed on. "Why has it been so long since Trapp played in a national tournament?" I asked. "Did something happen the last time? Is that why Annabel went insane?"

"Who told you she was insane?" Lucy asked sharply.

Her tone of voice caused me to shrink back. "I don't know," I said. "Just something I heard somewhere."

"What did you hear?" asked Arnold.

"She gave the milkman a thousand dollars for his clothes. And then made him wear her clothes."

Their stares grew colder.

"Maybe I heard wrong," I said. "I don't remember exactly."

"If you don't know what it is you're talking about, then you really shouldn't talk about it, should you?" asked Lucy. Her anger surprised me.

"She did not make the milkman wear her clothes," said Arnold. "Annabel gave him some of Henry's clothes."

"There was nothing untoward about it," said Gloria. "They changed in separate rooms. Annabel put on the milkman's uniform in order to sneak out of her house and play with Trapp in the nationals."

"Her husband kept her locked up like a criminal," said Arnold. "The servants were under strict orders not to let her leave the house."

"I still remember the way she looked," said Lucy, her voice softening. "In those days, people used to dress up for bridge tournaments. Women in dresses. Men in suits and ties. And there was Annabel in those white overalls, with her hair cropped short. She was absolutely radiant! Even without her hair and in those clothes, she was the most beautiful woman in the room."

"That was because she was with Trapp," said Arnold. "Whenever she was with him, her face glowed and her eyes sparkled like diamonds."

"She was in love with him?" I asked.

"And he was even more in love with her," said Lucy.

"But in the car, he said she was just his bridge partner."

"That doesn't mean he wasn't in love with her," said Lucy. "It just means he was a fool."

45

Thugs in Business Suits

The year was 1963. Trapp and Annabel were playing for the national championship. It was a two-day, four-session event. After the first day, half the field was eliminated, leaving only the best of the best.

"All the legends of the game were there," said Arnold. "Goren, Jacoby . . ."

"And Annabel and Trapp had as good a chance of winning as any of them," said Lucy. "They were in fifth place going into the final session."

About an hour into the session, a group of men entered the playing area. "Thugs in business suits," Arnold called them. The men spread out and walked up and down the aisles between the rows of tables. Lucy said there were more than twenty of them, but Arnold said there were only twelve.

Arnold and Lucy had also been playing in the event, but not with each other. Gloria hadn't been there, but she had heard all about it.

One of the thugs spotted Annabel, and then they all converged on the table.

"Two men were holding Annabel," said Lucy, "and the rest formed a wall around her. She was dragged away, kicking and screaming."

Lucy's voice cracked as she spoke. Forty-five years later, the memory still brought tears to her eyes.

"Couldn't anyone stop them?" I asked.

"Your uncle tried," said Arnold. "I drove him to the hospital. He had a busted nose and three broken ribs."

"What about the police?" I asked. "Did they have nine-one-one back then?"

"This was Chicago," said Arnold. "Those men were the police."

That was the last time Lucy or Arnold ever saw Annabel. It wasn't until almost six months later that they learned she had been locked up in an insane asylum.

"The Rolling Brook Sanitarium," said Arnold. "Trapp went there almost every single day, but they wouldn't let him see her. He demanded to speak to her doctor, but they wouldn't let him do that, either, because he wasn't family."

"But then when Nina became involved," said Lucy, "they wouldn't let her talk to Annabel either."

"Who's Nina?" I asked.

"Annabel's sister," said Gloria.

"Trapp and Nina must have filed half a dozen lawsuits on Annabel's behalf," said Arnold, "but the King family controlled the judges, too. The judge said he couldn't do anything without a signed affidavit from Annabel. But how were they supposed to get a signed affidavit if they weren't allowed to see her?"

Not even the other patients were allowed to see her. She was kept isolated for more than two years.

"She wasn't insane when she entered Rolling Brook," said Gloria, "but after two years . . ."

The only way Trapp could find out any information about Annabel was to wait in the parking lot, and then bribe the orderlies and janitors when they got off work. Most had never seen her, but they had heard rumors about her. And they heard her screams.

She wasn't being beaten. Her screams were screams for attention.

At some point, Annabel managed to obtain a bottle of bleach from a janitor's cart.

When Arnold first mentioned the bottle of bleach, I actually felt hopeful. I thought that maybe she threw bleach in a doctor's face, then escaped out a window into Trapp's waiting arms.

I watch too much TV.

She committed suicide by drinking the bleach. It took her several tries, because she kept vomiting it back up.

We walked out of the restaurant. I ran my fingers over the cold, hard bricks of the cement factory.

A heart like a brick, my father had said. Whose heart wouldn't turn cold and hard?

I thought of my mother as a little girl, hearing all those stupid, dirty stories about Annabel King.

I thought of all the stupid things I had said to my uncle.

Did you ever work as a milkman?

When you first met Annabel, how old was her daughter?

I always make the biggest fool of myself just when I think I'm being the most clever.

46

Nixon

In their grief, Trapp and Nina turned to each other.

"They each loved Annabel," said Lucy, "and for a while, they confused that with thinking they loved one another."

We were in the car, driving back to the hotel.

"I was the best man at their wedding," said Arnold, "but I knew the marriage wouldn't last. Everyone put on happy faces, but it was the saddest wedding I'd ever witnessed."

They were divorced within the year. Trapp quit playing bridge and started the Yarborough Investment Group.

"It was just another game to him," said Arnold. "Except, instead of masterpoints, now he was accumulating money. You want to know what he once told me? He said he preferred masterpoints to money because masterpoints were worthless."

Twenty years later, Gloria happened to run into him at a shoe repair shop.

"I needed a strap fixed on my purse. Trapp was worth millions, but he still got his shoes resoled."

She asked him if he would like to play bridge sometime. She mentioned that there was a sectional the following weekend, and she was looking for a partner.

"His face turned white," Gloria told us. "He started trembling."

He told her no, he couldn't, then hurried out of the shop.

"But then at three o'clock in the morning my telephone rang," Gloria said. "It was Trapp. All he said was 'I might be a little rusty.' We played a week later and had a seventy percent game."

Richard Nixon was Eisenhower's vice president. In 1960 he ran for president and lost to John F. Kennedy, and according to Arnold, most people thought that would be the last they'd ever hear of Richard M. Nixon. By 1967, Henry King, who had been in the Senate for more than a decade, was expected to be the next Republican presidential candidate.

But Nixon wasn't finished.

"I'd always hated Nixon," said Arnold. "But one thing I've got to give him credit for: he was good at destroying his enemies. And to him, Henry King was the enemy."

Nixon tried to dig up dirt on Henry King and came across all the court documents Trapp and Nina had filed. That was more than just dirt. He hit a gold mine. He initiated a well-publicized investigation into the care and treatment of the mentally ill, and into the suicide of Annabel King, his "dear friend's wife."

Rolling Brook Sanitarium was shut down, and two of the doctors went to prison.

"What about Henry King?" I asked.

"He and Nixon made some kind of secret deal," said Arnold.

Arnold didn't know what the deal was, but Henry King abruptly resigned his Senate seat and lived the rest of his life in relative seclusion. Nixon was elected president in 1968.

When Sophie King turned eighteen she changed her last name to Finnick (Annabel's maiden name) and never spoke to her father again. She never allowed him to see Toni, his only granddaughter.

47

Teodora's Tea

I almost felt like crying when I knocked on the door to my uncle's suite. I couldn't stop thinking about Annabel, and had to remind myself that her death had occurred more than forty years ago. He had gotten over it, or, if not over it, at least he'd learned to live with it. He certainly didn't need me to open up old wounds. I'd already asked too many stupid questions.

Teodora answered and told me that Trapp was still in the process of waking up, whatever that meant. She told me to go ahead and shovel and she'd take him down in a few minutes.

She must have said shuffle, not shovel.

Lucy and Arnold were sitting East-West at B-2, and Gloria was North at A-2. Before joining her, I decided to research the competition. The lists of teams and matches were posted on the wall beside the directors' table.

I was hoping to play the team with more than 110,000

masterpoints. I was looking forward to knocking out the big shots. Instead, I saw that our next opponents were the lowest-ranked team in our bracket. However, I also saw that they had defeated the team with 87,000 in the afternoon session, so maybe they shouldn't be taken lightly.

I joined Gloria, took the cards out of board seven, and started shoveling. I reported that Trapp was still resting and would be down shortly.

The two men sitting East-West were a lot closer to my age than to Gloria's. They were probably in their late twenties or early thirties. I think West had a tattoo, but it might have just been a birthmark. I could only glimpse a small portion of it, underneath his shirt collar.

"It's got to take its toll," he said. "Memorizing every card."

Fifteen minutes later, Trapp and Teodora still had not come down. At the other table, Lucy and Arnold were already playing.

"I guess you're going to have to fill in, Alton," said Gloria. "Until he gets here."

For a moment I was stunned, or maybe for several moments, but then I thought, *Okay, I can do this*. It probably would only be for one hand, so even if I screwed up, Trapp could overcome it. But just imagine his surprise if I got us a good board.

I'd sat on the sidelines long enough. It was time for me to get into the game!

Gloria laughed. "Don't worry, I'm only kidding," she said.

"You should have seen the look on your face!" laughed West.

I smiled, pretending relief.

A minute later, Trapp and Teodora entered the Grand Ballroom. To save time, I removed the South hand from board seven and met them before they reached the table. "Spades: queen, jack. Hearts: eight, seven, five, three, two. Diamonds: jack, ten—"

"Whoa, slow down," said Trapp. "Let me get my bearings."

Teodora handed me a thermos bottle. "Make sure he drinks this," she told me. "A little bit at a time."

I held the thermos in one hand and the fan of cards in the other, and once again told him his hand. "Spades: queen, jack. Hearts: eight, seven, five, three, two. Diamonds: jack, ten, six . . ."

We started with boards seven through twelve. The other table had one through six.

On board seven, Gloria bid and made four spades, for a score of 620.

"Sorry, I guess my diamond lead gave it to her," said West, the one with the maybe-tattoo.

"You had to lead something," said East. "It was the normal lead."

"I considered the eight of clubs," said West.

"That would have worked."

I tried to get Trapp to drink some of Teodora's tea, but he refused, saying it wasn't necessary since he had been dummy, so he didn't exert any energy. He groaned as he stood up, and I led him away from the table.

Once again he told me to slow down when I recited his

hand. I admit I had been feeling rushed because of our late start, but I don't think I was speaking any faster than normal. Usually he got impatient with me because I didn't go fast enough.

East bid and made three no-trump. Trapp hadn't been dummy, but he still wouldn't drink Teodora's tea.

On board nine, he had me repeat the diamonds.

On board ten, he was down one in four-hearts. Gloria said there was nothing he could have done about it, but he seemed disappointed in himself.

The caddy came by with the six boards from the other table, and we gave her the four boards we had played so far.

When I tried to get him to take a sip of tea, he snapped at me. "You drink it!"

It smelled like rotten cantaloupe.

Some time later, I noticed that Arnold and Lucy had finished. We still had four boards to go. True, they had started before us, but it seemed to me that Trapp was playing extremely slowly. More than once, when it was his turn to play, I'd make my guess as to what card he'd call for, but then I'd wait for what seemed like forever until he finally called a card. It was usually the card I had anticipated, which was either good for me or bad for him.

We finished the first twelve boards. Arnold and Lucy came over and we compared results.

On board seven, Arnold had led the eight of clubs and they set four spades. That gave us 12 IMPs.

Unfortunately, that was our only good board. Lucy totaled it up. At the halfway point we were down by 41 IMPs.

Everyone sat glumly.

"They're very good players," said Arnold.

Gloria nodded.

"It doesn't mean we can't come back," said Lucy.

"Forty-one IMPs isn't impossible," said Arnold. "If they can do it, so can we."

"Forty-one is nothing!" said Gloria. "I was down forty-nine once, and we came back and won by two IMPs."

Arnold then said that he once was behind by 55 IMPs at the halfway point and still won.

"I got you both beat," said Lucy. "I was once ahead by fifty-seven IMPs . . . and lost."

Everyone laughed at that, including me.

"Pour me a cup of tea," said Trapp.

I unscrewed the top of Teodora's thermos and filled the cup. Trapp brought it up to his lips, shuddered, then drank it all down.

"Let's go get 'em!" he said.

48

Quack of Clubs

When the two men returned to our table, there was a slight discrepancy in the score. They thought they were only winning by 38 IMPs. We went over the results, and found the error on board six. Unfortunately, we were right.

They seemed almost apologetic about being so far ahead. Bridge isn't an in-your-face kind of game. There's no dancing in the end zone.

I realized that the fact that they had fewer masterpoints than us didn't mean all that much. They were a lot younger. It takes a long time to accumulate masterpoints. Arnold, Lucy, and Gloria had all been playing for about fifty years. Trapp had only played about thirty, having quit for a while. The team we were up against had probably been playing less than fifteen years, but they had already won enough masterpoints to be in the top bracket. They were, I realized, about the age of Trapp and Annabel the last time they played together.

We started with boards one through six this time. On board one, our opponents tried to stop at two spades, but

Trapp, who had passed throughout, suddenly said, "Three diamonds."

He only had seven points: the ace of hearts and the queen and jack of diamonds. I tried to keep my expression blank as I placed the 3♢ card on the table. West bid three spades, and we set it by one trick. That was fifty points for us. If Trapp had let them play two-spades, they would have scored 110 points.

It was a start.

"Pour me another cup of tea," he said.

On the very next board, he bid six clubs and made it for 1,370.

"Well bid," West said, after the hand was over. "Our teammates will probably be in three no-trump."

"You got to push a little when you're down by forty-one," said Gloria.

"It's not forty-one anymore," said East, a worried expression on his face.

Trapp and Gloria kept on pushing. They made slam on board five, and then doubled the opponents on board six, setting them by two tricks for 500.

The caddy came by with boards seven through twelve just as we finished board six. I poured my uncle another cup of tea.

On board seven, Trapp had almost all black cards: seven spades, headed by the king and queen, and five clubs, headed by the king and jack. His only red card was the three of diamonds.

He was first to bid. "Four spades," he said.

I confidently set the bid on the table, and I was still just as confident when he was doubled. In fact, I was a little disappointed he didn't redouble.

He only took eight tricks. That was worth 500 points to our opponents. However, in the post-mortem, our opponents realized they actually could have made six diamonds for 1,370, so this was still a good board for us.

I looked at the IMPs chart. If Lucy and Arnold had bid six diamonds on the board, we would gain 13 IMPs.

Trapp wasn't happy about it. "I could have held it to down one if I played you for jack-ten doubleton of clubs," he said to the guy with the tattoo.

"It's always easier after you've seen all four hands," the man replied.

It's funny how quickly people forget that Trapp cannot actually see the cards.

I started to give him his hand for board eight, but he was still grumbling about board seven.

"It won't matter if Lucy and Arnold bid the slam," I said.

"Six diamonds is hard to bid," he said. "Everybody's going to open four spades with my hand. It's called a pre-emptive bid. It makes it hard for the opponents to bid, since their very first bid has to be at the five-level."

I think that might have been the first time he ever took the time to explain bridge to me. It felt good.

I started to give him his hand for board eight.

"C'mon, c'mon," he interrupted.

I had been saying his cards too slowly.

We reached board ten. The thermos was empty. I thought about calling Teodora and asking her to bring down more tea, but you weren't allowed to use cell phones in the playing area.

The contract was four hearts. West was declarer, and after the first seven tricks, he'd won five and we'd won two. We needed two more tricks to set the contract.

These were Trapp's remaining cards:

♠ K2
♡
♢ K10
♣ J8

"Two of clubs," said Gloria, placing that card on the table.

West called for dummy's ten of clubs, and then it was Trapp's turn.

He thought awhile. The jack of clubs was my choice, but Trapp was on a roll. If he played the eight, I knew it would be right.

"Queen of clubs," he said.

I didn't know what I was supposed to do, so I didn't do anything. I just sat there.

After a long and uncomfortable moment, Trapp wanted to know what was happening.

"We're still waiting for Alton to play a card," said West.

"Queen of clubs," Trapp repeated.

I felt like I'd been kicked in the gut. I remained motionless.

"I'm sorry, I'm going to have to call the director," said West.

"I think you better," Trapp said, his voice quaking.

East raised his hand. "Director, please!"

"I'm sorry," said West.

"No need to apologize," said Trapp.

The director arrived and the situation was explained to him.

"He instructed Alton to play the queen of clubs," said West.

"And apparently, I do not hold that card," said Trapp.

His voice was without emotion, but I could feel his humiliation.

The director thought a moment. I doubted this situation was anywhere in his rule book.

"Okay," he said at last. "We're going to treat this as unauthorized information." He turned to Gloria. "You now know your partner doesn't hold the queen of clubs. You will have to play the rest of the hand as if you don't have that information. Of course, if you're the one holding the queen, then there is no unauthorized information, but don't say so, one way or the other. Otherwise, you'll be giving unauthorized information to your partner."

He turned to West. "You are permitted to know that South doesn't have the queen of clubs, and if that information helps you, you may use it to your advantage. After the hand is over, call me back if you feel you've been damaged."

He then told me to take Trapp aside and tell him his remaining cards. "But you are not to in any way suggest what card to play, and you are not to tell him what cards have already been played, either by him or by anyone else."

I wanted to scream. I wanted to tell the director that there was nothing I could possibly tell my uncle that he didn't already know. I wanted to tell him that not only did Trapp know every card that was played, he also could tell you every card in everyone's hand.

Except that wasn't the case. Not this time.

I rose from my chair.

Trapp remained seated.

"C'mon," I said.

He didn't move.

I pulled on his arm, but I might just as well have been tugging at a block of cement.

"I'm done," he said.

"You have to finish the match," I said.

"You know how to play," he said. "You finish it."

I looked to Gloria for help. Tears were flowing down her face.

"Call my room," said Trapp. "Have Teodora come and get me."

With an unnaturally controlled voice, Gloria asked our opponents if they had any objections to Alton playing the remaining hands.

"That's not a problem," East said, his voice quiet and sober.

I found a house phone and called Trapp's suite. When Teodora answered, I said, "Trapp needs help." Then I returned to the table and played the jack of clubs.

49

A Monkey and a Typewriter

Supposedly if one million monkeys randomly press the keys on one million typewriters for one million years, one of those monkeys, at some point in time, will type Lincoln's Gettysburg Address.

Who knows? I thought. *Maybe I could be that monkey!*

There were only three boards left, including the one that we were in the middle of playing. All I had to do was choose the right card every single time.

I concentrated on every card that was played. I tried to imagine what bid Trapp would make or what card Trapp would play. I tried to form a bridge between my conscious and subconscious minds.

When we finished, Gloria said I had done "very well." East and West complimented me too, not so much for my card-playing skill as for my composure.

Arnold and Lucy returned to the table. Gloria told them what had happened, but they already knew most of it, having heard the commotion, and having seen Teodora come and get Trapp. They also had seen me sitting in the South seat, alone.

"Alton did just fine," said Gloria.

What happened to "very well"? I wondered.

Lucy and Arnold didn't look too optimistic. "Let's add it up," said Lucy.

We lost the match by 24 IMPs. My only consolation was that if we didn't count the last three boards, we would have lost by 5.

We didn't even stay the night in the hotel. When Gloria and I got off the elevator on the tenth floor, Teodora was there to meet us. "Trapp wants to go home."

"Now?" exclaimed Gloria. "It's ten-thirty at night. We've already paid for the rooms. Why don't we just wait and see how he feels in the morning? Maybe a single-session pairs game will give him back his confidence."

Trapp appeared in the doorway. "Pack your bags. We're leaving."

Twenty minutes later, we were on the highway, with Trapp snoring in the backseat next to Teodora, and Gloria up front with me. "Don't you worry, Alton," said Teodora. "He will be himself again."

"It makes no difference to me," I said, angrily staring at the road.

He had never even asked about the remainder of the match. It had never occurred to him that I might have played well enough for us to win.

It wasn't impossible that I could have played the right card at the right time. I wasn't just your random monkey. I had played the game before, and I had watched him play hundreds of hands. I knew what it meant to take a finesse and to pull trump.

You begin each hand with thirteen cards, but I figured my odds were much better than thirteen to one on any given card. For one thing, you have to follow suit. So if someone led a spade and I only had three spades in my hand, I had a one in three chance of getting it right.

He could have at least asked!

All of my passengers had fallen asleep. I turned on the radio to keep myself awake, but not loud enough to wake them.

Bidding had been more of a challenge for me, but there, too, it wasn't as if I had to choose between all thirty-eight possible bids. Usually I had two, maybe three reasonable choices.

I decided I didn't believe that thing about monkeys and typewriters. If Lincoln's Gettysburg Address could be typed solely by accident, then that would mean it would be almost typed millions of times, with maybe just a couple of words wrong. *Four score and six years ago. A government of the people, by the people, and smell the eggplant.* It would also mean that those monkeys would randomly type millions of other works too, including a page out of the phone book with every name in alphabetical order and every phone number correct.

Gloria was snoring too, and then Teodora started. The inside of my car sounded like a factory.

I turned the radio up loud.

50

Ducking Smoothly

I got back home sometime after four a.m. I must have woken up Leslie, because she was waiting for me when I came out of the bathroom.

"Why are you home?" she asked, her eyes more shut than open.

I gave her the short version. "We lost."

"I thought Trapp never loses," she said.

I had thought the same thing. "Don't be stupid," I said.

"Does that mean you're not going to the nationals?" she asked.

"No. I mean yes. I don't know."

I can't deal with double negatives at four-thirty in the morning.

Mrs. Mahoney called the next day (the same day, technically) and said that Mr. Trapp would not be needing my services for two weeks. He had to save his strength, and wouldn't play again until the nationals.

I took that as good news. At least he still planned to play for the championship.

By the way, speaking of my services, he never paid me for the regional. I was supposed to get three hundred dollars. Four sessions at seventy-five a session.

Not that I'm complaining. It was just a thought that crossed my mind, so I reported it to you. *Yes,* I realize he bought me a car! *No,* I wasn't planning to sue him! Sorry, I never should have mentioned it.

Teodora had Trapp on a liquid diet, designed to rid his system of toxins and contaminants. My mother called it "cleaning the plumbing." Or maybe those were Mrs. Mahoney's words. She told my mother and my mother told me that Uncle Lester was having "bathroom issues." I could describe these issues to you more fully—my mother was very descriptive—but I think we've already entered the zone of Too Much Information.

My parents must have thought these bathroom issues were serious, because they asked me yet again if I had spoken to Uncle Lester about his will.

I lied. "He said we'll be well taken care of," I told them, hoping this would put an end to their nagging.

"'Well taken care of'?" my father repeated. "What does that mean?"

"I guess we'll find out when he's dead," I said.

"Don't be crude," said my mother.

———————

Monday, five days after the regional, I was staring at my phone in my hand, thinking about calling Toni. Since Trapp wouldn't be playing on Thursday, I wondered if she might want to play with me again. I was also wondering if I should call Cliff first, but I didn't think I had to. Toni and I were just bridge partners, I told myself. *Nothing more, nothing less.*

The phone went off in my hand. I brought it to my ear without waiting for the name to appear on caller ID. "Hello?"

"Hi!" said the voice on the other end.

It's funny how many changes you can go through in the half second it takes for someone to say hi.

It was a girl's *hi*, high-pitched and full of energy. My heart jumped as I initially thought, *Toni!* Then, in that same half second, my brain registered the voice. My heart still fluttered around a bit as I realized who it was, but I think that was mostly out of habit.

"Hi, Katie," I said.

"So whatcha been up to?" she asked me.

"Oh, you know, the usual," I said. "Playing bridge with old people."

She laughed, or at least pretended to. My statement was probably total nonsense to her. I doubted Cliff had told her about my uncle or how I was spending the summer. I doubted she and Cliff ever talked about me at all.

"So how was the movie?" she asked.

I didn't hesitate. I certainly didn't ask, *What movie?*

"It was pretty good," I said. "Kind of stupid, but I liked it." I figured that would cover most movies.

"Cliff didn't like it."

"Yeah, well . . ."

"He likes things that are deep," said Katie. "You and I are more shallow." She quickly added that she didn't mean that in a bad way. "Cliff's just very intense. You're more *whatever*."

"Whatever," I said.

Katie laughed. "Can I ask you something?"

"You just did," I pointed out.

She ignored my not-so-clever remark. "I want you to be completely honest," she said. "You owe me that."

I didn't see how I owed her anything, but didn't argue the point.

"Is Cliff seeing someone else?"

Again, I didn't hesitate. "Of course not, Katie," I assured her. "Why would you think that?"

"Oh, I don't know."

When you're playing bridge, the slightest hesitation can give away your position. Let's say the declarer leads a jack and you have the queen. If you think awhile and then play a low card, the declarer will know you have the queen. But if you *duck smoothly,* he might think your partner has the queen.

When Katie asked me about the movie, and about whether Cliff was seeing anyone, I ducked smoothly.

"We used to have fun, didn't we?" she asked, changing the subject.

"Yep."

"How did we let ourselves drift apart?"

I stared at the phone a moment, then brought it back to my ear. "I don't know," I said. "These things happen."

"We should get together again sometime."

"I'm not sure that's such a good idea," I said. "Cliff gets jealous easily."

"Really?" she asked, her voice brightening. "I guess you're right. You're such a good friend, Alton."

After hanging up with Katie, I lay on my bed and stared at the ceiling. Maybe I was a good friend, maybe I wasn't. I would have been a better friend if I'd stopped thinking so much about Toni.

Even when I lied to Katie, I realized, that was just as much for my benefit as it was to protect Cliff. I definitely wanted to keep Cliff and Katie together.

There was a depth of soul in Toni that Katie lacked. Although I guess my own depth of soul is questionable, since I was the one who had fallen so hard for Katie not that long ago.

I heard a knock, then sat up as my mother walked into my room. "I just got off the phone with Mrs. Mahoney," she said, her voice trembling just a bit.

She stared vacantly, then came over and touched my face with her hand. "Uncle Lester has passed away."

She sat down on the bed beside me.

51

A Very Scared Little Girl

You probably saw that coming. I don't know how many times I've mentioned Trapp's will and told you how sick he was. Yet I was stunned. I just couldn't believe it. What about the nationals?

There's a different kind of will, the will to live. Gloria was probably right when she said the nationals had been keeping Trapp alive. Bridge had more to do with Trapp's recovery than any of Teodora's herbs or crystals. But then, when he couldn't remember whether he held a jack or a queen, his will was broken. And so he passed away.

That was my theory, anyway, but what did I know? No more than Captain, probably less. I wondered what would happen to Captain.

"Passed away" seemed like an appropriate way of putting it. Over the next few days, I had this recurring image of Trapp sitting at the bridge table. He reaches into the bidding box, removes a pass card, and places it on the table. Then he slowly vanishes.

Leslie cried. Even though she'd never met our uncle, except as an infant, her tears did not surprise me. I had no doubt she loved him.

My mother cried too. That was a little harder for me to take. Maybe she confused her love for his money with a love for him.

Or maybe I was the one who had it confused. Maybe she really did love him, or had tried to love him, but he wouldn't let her. Maybe she was crying because she always called him, never the other way around. Maybe she was crying because he never accepted even one dinner invitation.

Maybe, since she couldn't have his love, she focused on his money.

I didn't cry. I just felt numb.

I thought about all the times I had told him I loved him and that he was my favorite uncle. No doubt those words were just as empty to him as they were to me. They wouldn't be empty now.

I went over to Cliff's one night and we played video games, but I kept hearing Trapp's voice inside my head. *Chasing pixels of light. Like lab rats pushing buttons.*

I told Cliff about Katie's phone call, and how I had come through for him, but he just shrugged and said, "Katie can get annoying, can't she? I can see why you dumped her."

We both knew it was the other way around. Maybe

he was trying to make me feel better. Or maybe he was trying to make himself feel better for stealing her away from me.

There was no funeral or religious service. A memorial gathering was held at the Castaneda house. People were invited to "celebrate the life of Lester Trapp."

Toni and her mother met us at the door. Toni's mother and my mother hugged each other. Both women were sobbing. Toni and I looked awkwardly at each other.

Toni hugged Leslie first, which I suppose made everything legit; then she hugged me.

"He would have won," she whispered.

"I know," I said.

I could feel her tear on my cheek. I have to admit I also felt a little guilty. She was hugging me for one reason, and I was liking it for another.

Captain was there, and for the first time, didn't bark at me. He let me reach down and pet him as he looked at me with sad eyes.

I heard my name called, turned to see Lucy coming at me from across the room, and soon found myself engulfed in her hug. "We were all together just last week," she said, as if she and I were old friends.

Everyone gathered in the family room, where thirty or so folding chairs had been placed around the furniture. All my relatives were there, and I recognized a number of bridge players from the studio, including Gloria and Wallace. I also saw the woman who owned the car dealership.

Oddly, the folding chairs filled up first. Maybe people didn't think they should be too comfortable at a time like this. Toni, Leslie, and I sat on the couch, with me in the middle. Lucy and her husband were also on the couch, so it was a tight fit.

When everyone was settled in the seats, Sophie got up to speak. "I ran away from home when I was fifteen years old," she began. "I think people saw me as some kind of rebel, or maybe a carefree flower child, but on the inside I was still a very scared little girl. I didn't know Lester Trapp. I had only seen his name on the court documents that Nixon brought.

"It took me six months to find him," she continued. "We didn't have Google back then." She smiled, and several people laughed. Then Sophie wiped her eyes on a tissue. Her voice quaked as she continued. "I remember it was the middle of February when I knocked on the door to his house. I must have looked like a tramp, all bundled up, wearing every piece of clothing I owned. It was sleeting. Trapp opened the door and looked at me shivering on his porch.

"'I'm Sophie,' I told him. 'Annabel's daughter.'"

She wiped her eyes again, then blew her nose. It took her a moment before she continued.

"He took me in without asking any questions. He bought me new clothes, and quickly became like a father to me, the way a father is supposed to be, the father I never had. He told me about my mother, my real mother. I knew it was painful for him to talk about her, but those stories helped fill a void inside of me. I found out who I was. I loved my mother, and through his stories, somehow felt loved by her."

There was no stopping her tears now. Toni was also crying, and on the other side of me, so was Leslie.

"I think his only disappointment," Sophie said, laughing through her tears, "was that I never learned to play bridge."

She was unable to continue. She sat back down, and other people stood up and talked about Lester Trapp. I found out that Trapp's body had been cremated. Toni's father read aloud from Trapp's written request regarding the disposal of his remains. "Throughout my lifetime, my body has been nothing but a detriment and a constant disappointment to me. To it, I say, 'Good riddance!'"

This was met with laughter, but I doubt anyone really thought it was funny. When you're at an event like this, even though you're supposed to be thinking about the departed, you can't help but think about your own body and your own ultimate death. That's how it was with me, anyway, and I imagine it was even more so for the people in the room who were a lot closer to death than I was, statistically, although I was still on the lookout for falling pianos. The other thing I was thinking about when I was supposed to be thinking about Lester Trapp was that my leg was touching Toni's.

More people got up to speak. Nina, Trapp's ex-wife, had flown in from Indiana with her husband. She said that after their divorce, she and Trapp had retained a deep respect and affection for each other, and that he had always been there for her when she needed him. Her only reference to her sister was "the tragedy that brought Trapp and me together."

I felt like I should get up and say something too. I wished I had written something down. I'm not very good at speaking in front of people, and I was afraid that whatever I tried to say wouldn't make any sense, or else would sound childish. The only thing I could think of was that he had bought me a car, but that had nothing to do with how I felt about him, so I kept my mouth shut.

Teodora was the last one to speak. She said that at her first meeting with Lester Trapp, she was overwhelmed by his great and powerful aura; however, it sounded like she had said "his great and powerful odor." As she went on and on about Trapp's extraordinary "odor," I heard muffled laughter and saw a lot of confused looks. Soon the word *aura* was being whispered around the room.

52

Deborah in the Closet

A vegetarian buffet was served, and the gathering split up into groups. Family and non-bridge-playing friends ate in the dining room and kitchen, while the bridge players converged on the patio. Leslie, Toni, and I took our plates to the patio.

We heard a lot more stories about Trapp. They all began with something like "He was playing in four spades . . ." and ended with something like ". . . and he won the last trick with the three of clubs!" which caused everyone to erupt with laughter. Leslie would look to me for an explanation, but I didn't understand much more than she did.

Still, I enjoyed the stories. It was nice hearing everyone talk about Trapp. I was reminded of something he'd told me. His body might be gone, but the idea of Lester Trapp was still alive.

Wallace told about the time that Trapp was declarer in a five-diamond contract, without a diamond in his hand. "We had a slight misunderstanding during the bidding."

Even I laughed at that.

"But when I passed his five-diamond bid," Wallace said, "you would not have known anything was wrong from looking at him. The opening lead was made, I set down the dummy, and he simply said, 'Thank you, partner,' as if he were in a perfectly normal contract. As I watched him play the hand, I kept wondering, *Why isn't he pulling trump?* Finally, an opponent led a diamond, and he discarded a spade. Only then did I realize that we might not be in the best contract.

"'No diamonds, partner?' I asked. He glared back at me. The thing is, he managed to hold it to down two. We lost eleven IMPs on the board, but if he had been down three, we would have lost by thirteen. We won the match by one IMP."

"Lucky he wasn't doubled," said Leslie, surprising everyone, I think, with her bridge knowledge.

"No, he would have been happy to have been doubled," explained the woman who sold me my car. "Then he would have gotten another chance to bid."

"I have a story," I said, suddenly finding my courage.

I told about my first day as Trapp's cardturner, and how he had called me a moron and imbecile when I first tried to give him his hand. "I didn't know what I did wrong, but you should have heard him scream at me!"

"We did," said someone I recognized from the club.

I then told about the car ride home and those thirteen letters, *"G-b-c-d-i-o-a-o-r-y-t-g-l."* I asked if anyone could repeat them, but nobody volunteered.

"Then he gave me the same letters in a different order. *G-i-r-l, b-o-y, c-a-t, d-o-g.*"

By the time I got to *cat*, several of them were saying the letters right with me.

"Thirteen letters," said Arnold. "The number of cards in a bridge hand."

"Divided into four suits," said Wallace.

Toni smiled at me as if to say, "You did good."

By the way, if you're wondering how I could have recited those letters out of order, I used a little trick, which I think might be the same trick Trapp used. I began with the first letter of *girl*, then the first letter of *boy*, then *cat*, then *dog*; then the second letter of each word, and so forth.

That is the way I wrote it in chapter ten of this book, but that was just a guess. I can't say for certain in what order Trapp gave me those letters.

Arnold's wife, Deborah, had the best Trapp story. The story took place before she and Arnold were married.

Trapp was living in an apartment in Norwalk, Connecticut, at the time. There was a regional in Bridgeport, not too far away, and Trapp had let Deborah crash on his sofa for the tournament.

"It was my first day there," Deborah said. "He was playing in a pairs game and I was in a knockout, so I got back to the apartment before he did. There was only one bathroom, and being the good guest, I took my shower before he came home. It wasn't until after I stepped out of the shower that I noticed there weren't any towels."

"Typical," said Lucy.

"So, very wet and very naked, I peeked out the bathroom door, to make sure the coast was clear, then ran into the hall and quickly tried to find a linen closet."

"Uh-oh," said Leslie.

"Uh-oh is right," said Deborah. "I suddenly heard the front door start to open."

Leslie gasped.

"I ducked into some sort of utility closet," said Deborah. "A second later I hear Trapp just outside my door, muttering to himself about some stupid bridge hand. 'If I try to pull trump they'll tap me in hearts. But if I don't pull trump they'll ruff clubs.' This goes on for I don't know how long. I'm in there, freezing my"—she looked at Leslie—"freezing my nose off, and he's right outside muttering to himself."

"Wasn't there anything in the closet you could use to cover yourself up?" asked Leslie.

"There was a vacuum cleaner," said Deborah, "but I couldn't figure out how that would help me. I also noticed some rolls of toilet paper, and actually thought about trying to wrap myself, but I figured that would be more embarrassing than being naked. Finally I just decided that the best defense was a good offense. I stepped out of the closet, in all my glory, and demanded, 'Where do you keep the damn towels!'"

Leslie covered her mouth with her hand.

"Trapp looked up at me for no more than half a second; then he handed me this torn envelope with a bridge diagram scrawled on it and asked, 'How would you play four spades after the lead of the three of clubs?'"

53

A Fresh Start

I have a confession to make: before leaving my uncle's memorial, I asked Toni if she wanted to play bridge sometime, "as a tribute to Trapp."

"He'd like that," she agreed, wiping away a tear.

So, does that make me a rotten human being? Was I just exploiting my uncle's death to pick up a girl?

I don't *think* I was doing that. I *think* I really did think that playing bridge with Toni would be a fitting tribute to Trapp.

If I really was just trying to make a move on Toni, then it was doubly rotten. Not only was I exploiting my uncle's death, I was betraying my best friend.

I was pretty certain that there was something going on between Cliff and Toni, although it's hard to tell with Cliff. He isn't the kind of guy who brags about girls. Not like Gilliam, for example. Whenever Gilliam talks about a girl, you can only believe about one-tenth of what he tells you. Cliff is just the opposite. He has a way of saying very little but somehow implying a lot. You always wonder what good stuff he left out.

Anyway, Toni and I agreed to play on Thursday, her usual day with Trapp. She e-mailed me eight more pages of bidding instructions, and I was in my room, going over them with Leslie, and trying not to think about Cliff, when my parents entered.

"Ed Johnson just called," said my father.

Don't bother flipping back through the pages trying to find that name. I didn't know who Ed Johnson was either. It turned out he was Uncle Lester's lawyer, the one who helped prepare his last will and testament.

My mother summed up our inheritance in three words. "We got squat!"

"He gave it all to charity," said my father. "Diabetes research, I can understand that. But cancer research? He didn't even have cancer!"

"So the lawyer just called you up to say you weren't getting anything?" asked Leslie. "That doesn't make sense."

"Well, it wasn't exactly nothing," my mother admitted. "We got the same as every other relative. What did Mr. Johnson call it? A fresh start."

All my parents' debts would be paid off, including credit cards, car loans, and even the mortgage on our house. In addition, all of my and Leslie's future college expenses, including room and board, would be paid for.

"If we had *known*," my father said, "if you had talked to him like you were supposed to do, then we could have borrowed more money."

I didn't know a lot about my parents' finances, but it

was my guess that their credit cards were already maxed out.

"Can't you borrow the money now?" Leslie asked.

"No, it's whatever our debts were at the time of his death," my mother explained. "We have to provide documentation."

"What about the pool?" Leslie asked.

The estate would pay for the amount we owed for the work already done, but not to complete the job.

My father complained that some of our other relatives lived in bigger, more expensive houses, with bigger mortgages, and that others had more kids who would go to college.

I remembered something Trapp had told me once about his bridge-bum days. Even though he had had very little money, those days were the happiest of his life.

He told me that the secret of success was to never spend more than you had. "Don't use credit cards. Don't owe anyone money." Once you go into debt, he had said, you lose your freedom.

Trapp's donations to various charities included a huge chunk of change for animal welfare groups and another for Seeing Eye dogs. He also set up a fund to teach bridge in schools. The fund would pay for a bridge teacher for any school that wanted to start a bridge club.

"But don't think all the time you spent with him was for naught," my mother said sarcastically. "He also left something just for you, Alton. A book!"

I didn't think my time with him had been for naught. Like my mother had once said, it was for the joy of spending time with my favorite uncle. My only regret was that it didn't last longer, at least until after the nationals.

The book arrived by special courier the following day. Maybe, like me, you thought it would be a bridge book. I was wrong. It was his 1945 hardbound copy of *Cannery Row*.

The dust jacket was torn and felt brittle when I rubbed my fingers over it. It was blue-black with a dreamlike oval picture of an industrial waterfront. The title was written in yellow script above the picture, and the author's name, John Steinbeck, also in yellow, was printed below.

Trapp and Annabel had each held the book I was holding. I opened it and started reading the same pages they had read.

54

Transfer Bids

Of all the bids Toni e-mailed to me, the most confusing was something called a *Jacoby transfer bid*.

It works like this: if your partner opens one no-trump and you have five or more cards in a major suit (hearts or spades), you don't bid that suit. Instead, you bid the suit ranked just below it.

So if your partner opens one no-trump and you have five hearts, you bid two diamonds. Your partner is now supposed to bid two hearts. That's why it's called a transfer bid. You're transferring the bid to your partner.

If you mess up and bid two hearts by mistake, there's no recovering. Your partner will think you are transferring to spades.

A *Jacoby transfer bid* is tricky because you bid a different suit than the one you mean. If you bid diamonds, it means you have hearts. If you bid hearts, it means you have spades.

I was beginning to understand how Trapp and Wallace had ended up in five diamonds that time when Trapp was void in diamonds. Expert partnerships use all kinds of complicated bidding systems. Like trapeze acrobats without a net, they need to be perfectly in sync or face disaster.

I picked Toni up at her house. As we drove to the bridge studio she asked me if I understood transfer bids.

"No problem," I assured her.

She seemed doubtful. "If you forget, that's okay," she said. "It's just one board. Trapp always said the best way to learn a new bidding system is to screw it up a few times."

I was actually encouraged by her lack of confidence in me. If she was willing to let me screw it up until I got it right, then maybe she didn't see this as just a onetime thing.

"So how'd you like the movie?" I asked.

"What movie?"

"I heard you and Cliff went to a movie."

"No," she said. "Who told you that?"

I considered mentioning Katie but decided against it.

"I think it might have been last week," I said.

"We never went to a movie," Toni said, and for a

moment I grew hopeful that maybe I had been wrong about Cliff and Toni. But just for a moment.

"We went to a party at the country club," she said, "if that's what you're thinking about."

"I guess that's it," I said.

"It was so lame!" she added. "I had to wear this stupid poodle skirt, and every song sounded like 'Rock Around the Clock.' I don't get why people think the fifties were so great."

"I know what you mean," I agreed, once again allowing myself some hope.

"Cliff hated it too," said Toni. "So we left and ended up just taking a walk around the golf course. That was really nice. There was a full moon, and there were like all these scary shadows everywhere."

I could imagine. I could imagine way too much. I tried to get my mind back on bridge. *Two diamonds is a transfer to hearts. Two hearts is a transfer to spades.*

At the bridge studio, we asked for table three, North-South. Trapp's table.

I sat in my usual spot, only this time I had no chair to my left and slightly behind me.

"Feels weird, doesn't it?" asked Toni.

"Very," I agreed.

Two women joined us, taking the East-West seats. They smiled sadly at me, and said how sorry they were to hear about my uncle. I thanked them. They tried to engage me in conversation about him, but I just gave one-word answers to their questions. I was glad when the game got started.

We began with board five. I opened one spade, and the next thing I knew I was the declarer in a four-spade contract. I went down one trick, because I didn't realize my ten of diamonds was good. I knew the ace, king, and jack were gone, but I didn't remember seeing the queen.

"Sorry, partner," I said, "I guess my game's a little off today."

"No sorrys allowed," said Toni.

In the back of my mind I heard Trapp ask, "And when has your game ever been on?"

These were my cards for board six:

♠ 87
♡ J106432
◊ 109
♣ 853

Toni opened one no-trump, East passed, and I had to make a decision. Do I pass or bid two hearts?

My hand was totally useless unless hearts were trump. But if I bid two hearts, then I'd have to take eight tricks. If I passed one no-trump, Toni would be the declarer, and she would only have to take seven tricks.

Still, a heart contract seemed right, so I reached for the 2♡ bid.

I suddenly heard Leslie's voice screaming at me inside my head. "Stop! Two hearts is a transfer to spades. You have to bid two diamonds!"

I caught myself just in time. I set the 2◊ bid on the table

and hoped that was right. I actually felt my heart pound as I waited to see what Toni would do.

West passed. Toni didn't even hesitate. Out came the 2♡ bid.

> I came *that* close to screwing up the Jacoby transfer bid. At the last second, I heard Leslie's voice in the back of my mind, screaming at me to remember.

Everyone passed, East made her opening lead, and I tabled the dummy.

Toni looked at my cards and smiled. "Thank you, partner," she said, sounding as if she meant it.

Would you believe it? She actually made an overtrick.

I felt great. It was like an assist in basketball. I passed Toni the ball, and she slam-dunked it.

55

Post-mortem

The round was called. The boards were passed to the next lower table, and the people moved up a table. Our new East-West opponents told me how sorry they were to hear about my uncle.

I thanked them and quickly removed the cards from the South slot.

♠ Q109765432
♡
♢ 432
♣ 8

My hand was worth seven points: two for the ♠Q, three for the heart void, and two for the singleton club.

East passed, and I was about to do the same when I heard Trapp say, "Four spades."

I stopped in midreach.

I need to explain something here. Earlier, when I told you I heard Leslie screaming at me to bid two diamonds, that was only because she had helped me study. I associated her voice with the bids. And before that, when I told you I heard Trapp ask, "And when has your game ever been on?", well, that was my attempt at being clever in a self-deprecating sort of way.

This was different. I heard Trapp say "Four spades." It was as if he were sitting to my left, slightly behind me. Maybe *heard* is the wrong word. I *perceived* it.

One thing I had learned as his cardturner was to never let my emotions show. My heart might have stopped for a few seconds, and my brain was doing backflips, but I simply took a breath, then reached into the bidding box, removed the 4♠ card, and set it on the table.

The guy on my left looked at me like I was crazy. I couldn't have agreed more.

He doubled.

Toni thought awhile, and for a second I was afraid she was going to redouble, but she just passed, as did everyone else.

East	Me	West	Toni
Pass	4♠?	X!	Pass
Pass	Pass		

The opening lead was the ace of hearts. I tried to gather my thoughts and concentrate on the bridge game.

As Toni set down the dummy, I hoped she'd have the ace or king of spades, preferably both.

She had neither. She was void in spades.

Dummy
♠
♡ J97643
♢ K87
♣ AQ62

Opening lead: ♡ A

My Pitiful Hand
♠ Q109765432
♡
♢ 432
♣ 8

"Thank you, partner," I managed.

I told Toni to play the ♡3, and then I trumped it in my hand with the ♠2, winning the trick.

Now what? I thought.

"Queen of spades," said Trapp.

That would have been my last choice. The queen of spades was sure to lose to the ace or king. I would be throwing away the only high card in my hand.

I led the ♠Q. Sure enough, West played the ♠K.

I won't go through the rest of the hand. Maybe you can figure out how to take ten tricks. I did, apparently.

Four spades, doubled, was worth 790 for us.

"I guess I shouldn't have doubled," grumbled West. "All I had was a twenty-three-point hand, including the ace and king of trump!"

Trapp told me what card to play, and I played it. I'd done it a thousand times before.

56

Welcome to My World

Toni and I came in first place with a 70 percent game. You'd think we would have been all excited, but Toni and I barely said a word to each other the whole time. I mostly felt overwhelmed, and more than a little scared. I got more and more scared as we continued to get one top board after another.

Throughout it all, Toni remained grim-faced. I knew Trapp and Gloria never acted too gleeful when they got a top board. It's considered rude, since it means your opponents just got a bottom board. But Toni took it to the other extreme. As she recorded our scores, she seemed angry.

We walked silently out to my car. I turned on the engine while Toni stared straight ahead.

"You played really good," she finally said. "I just wish . . ."

"What?" I asked.

"All I wanted to do was play bridge. Is that asking too much?"

"Are you mad at me?"

"No, not at you. At her!"

I didn't have to ask who "her" was. Trapp couldn't get a 70 percent game all by himself.

"Well, at least you had a good partner," she said bitterly. "I guess you can win as long as you're not stuck with me!"

I stared at the road.

"I know you don't believe it's my grandmother," she said. "You think I'm crazy. You think it's my subconscious or something psychological."

"I believe you," I said.

The traffic light ahead of me turned yellow. I sped up, thinking I could make it, and then changed my mind and had to slam on the brakes at the last second.

"Sorry," I said.

"It's not your fault," said Toni, thinking my "sorry" had been about the bridge game. "She just took over."

I wanted to tell her about hearing Trapp, but oddly, I didn't think she'd believe me. I was afraid she'd think I was just trying to make her feel better, or worse, mocking her.

"Turn left," said Trapp.

That wasn't the way to Toni's house.

"Maybe you're right," said Toni. "Maybe I should start taking my meds."

I had never said that.

"Left," Trapp repeated.

I put on my left-turn signal.

It occurred to me that my dead uncle might be telling

me to turn in order to protect me. Maybe he somehow knew if I continued heading the way I was going, I'd get in some horrible accident. No doubt involving a piano truck.

The light changed to green and I turned left.

"Where are you going?" Toni asked.

"Shortcut," I said.

At the next stop sign Trapp told me to turn left again.

"Are you sure this is the right way?" Toni asked.

I didn't answer.

"Are you kidnapping me?" she asked.

There was a turnout on the side of the road. I pulled into it.

"What's wrong?" she asked.

I took a breath and looked her straight in the eye. "I think maybe I should be the one taking your meds," I said.

She stared back.

"I wasn't Annabel's partner today," I said, and was surprised by the trembling in my voice. "Trapp was." I felt my eyes start to water. "I just turned the cards for him, like always."

"Oh, God," Toni whispered.

I was crying. It was as if all the emotions that I'd kept bottled up at the bridge studio were leaking out of me.

"And now he's giving me driving directions," I said through my tears. "I don't know where we're going."

My hands were very cold. I hadn't noticed until I felt Toni's warm hands wrap around them.

"Welcome to my world," she said.

57

Ninety-three, Ninety-one

I took a few deep breaths, gathered myself together, and pulled back onto the road. I offered to ignore Trapp's driving directions and just take Toni directly home, but she said she was willing to go "wherever the wind took us."

At the signal he told me to turn right.

Toni remained silent, lost in her own thoughts, but then she suddenly laughed and said, "I guess I should have figured it out when you kept making your contracts!" Then she said she was sorry, and gave my wrist a pat.

"No, I know," I assured her.

When we reached Cross Canyon Boulevard, our destination became clear to me. "We're going to his house," I informed my passenger.

I received no more instructions for the remainder of the trip. A short while later, I pulled into his driveway, and Toni and I climbed out of the car.

When I was six, my uncle's house had seemed like a castle to me. As I stared at it now, with its massive stone walls and bolted shutters, it seemed that way again.

"Now what?" Toni asked.

I had no clue. "Do you know who owns this house now?" I asked.

"I think it's in probate."

"What does that mean?"

Toni shrugged as she blew a stream of air out of the corner of her mouth. "It's just a word I've heard a lot," she admitted.

We slowly approached the front door. She took hold of my arm and whispered, "What if Trapp and Annabel are in there?"

I froze.

"I'm kidding," Toni said with a laugh, then added, "I think."

I tried the door, but it was locked. I was about to ring the doorbell but changed my mind. It seemed more appropriate to use the goat's-head knocker.

We took a few steps back and waited. Nothing happened. I rang the doorbell. Still nothing.

"Has Annabel said anything to you about this?" I asked.

"This is your hallucination, not mine," Toni replied, smiling.

I backed away from the door. A stone wall surrounded the house. If I could climb it, I thought, I could try the back door, or maybe I'd find a secret entrance.

"Ninety-three, ninety-one," said Trapp.

"Ninety-three, ninety-one," I repeated.

"What?" asked Toni.

"He just said, 'Ninety-three, ninety-one.'"

Neither of us could remember Trapp's address. I had used it the first time to get to his house, but that had been over a month ago. There were no numbers posted by the door.

I walked the length of his driveway to the mailbox. It was numbered 621.

It occurred to me that maybe I wasn't supposed to go to his house after all. I hadn't perceived any more driving instructions from him since I'd turned onto Cross Canyon Boulevard. I had just assumed this was the destination.

I looked around. There were only a few other houses on the street. It seemed pretty doubtful that Trapp's address could be 621 and another could be 9391.

I got an idea. I went to my car and retrieved my cell phone. I pressed 9-3-9-1, then Send.

Nothing.

Toni came up beside me. "Do you know the right area code?" she asked.

I hung up.

"What would you have done if he'd answered?" she asked.

"You're really enjoying this, aren't you?" I asked.

She smiled. "For once in my life, I'm not the one who's crazy!"

I returned to the front door and tried it again.

"Is it still locked?" Toni asked from the driveway.

"You got any better ideas?"

A look of realization crossed her face. She hurried to the garage.

A keypad was attached to the side wall. By the time I got there she had already entered the first two numbers. I watched as she pressed the nine and then the one.

Nothing.

"They probably turned off the electricity," I said.

She pressed the star key. I heard the low rumble of a motor, and then the garage door slowly rose.

There was no way my subconscious mind would have known the code to his garage door opener—at least, none that my conscious mind could think of.

The only vehicles in the garage were a rusted tandem bicycle and a wheelbarrow with a flat tire. There were also a refrigerator, some garden tools, a croquet set, and at least forty boxes, stacked three rows deep along the right-side wall.

At the rear of the garage was a door leading into the main part of the house. It was also locked.

"We might as well start on the boxes," I said.

I dragged one away from the wall and ripped off the packing tape. Inside were various office products, including a container of paper clips, a stapler, and one of those contraptions with swinging silver balls that bang against each other.

"Canned peas," said Trapp.

Toni was going through a different box. "What are we looking for?" she asked.

"A can of peas," I answered, as if that were a perfectly normal reply.

She eyed me dubiously.

58

In the Pantry

About a half hour later we had gone through about a quarter of the boxes. If you're wondering what I was thinking, I wasn't. I was trying very hard not to think. So far, the closest thing I had found to a can of peas was an old vinyl record album by a band called Canned Heat.

Toni had temporarily given up on the boxes and was checking the refrigerator.

"You don't refrigerate a can of peas," I pointed out.

"No, you stick it in a box and hide it in the garage," she replied. "Just what are we supposed to do with this can of peas, anyway?"

I had no clue. Use it to smash a window so we could get inside the damn house? I guess I assumed it all would explain itself when we found the peas. Actually, I was beginning to doubt I'd heard Trapp correctly, but I didn't dare say that to Toni.

"Eureka!" she suddenly shouted.

I turned. In her hand she held not a can of peas, but a key.

"It was in the bike pouch," she said proudly.

I followed her to the rear of the garage. "You do it," she said, and handed the key to me.

It took a little jiggling, but I managed to insert the key into the lock. I tried turning it. At first it seemed stuck, but then the lock gave way and the door opened.

Toni held on to my forearm, in the same way Trapp used to, and we stepped inside.

We entered the laundry room, took a brief look around, then continued on to the kitchen, which was the more logical place to find peas, not that logic was playing too big a role in any of this. Pots and pans of all sizes hung from an iron rack. Knives stuck out of a butcher-block table.

We tried various cabinets and found dishes, glasses, and a bunch of coffee mugs that Trapp had evidently won at bridge tournaments. I opened a door and found a walk-in pantry filled with shelves of canned food.

"Eureka!" I said.

There were cans of tomato sauce, cans of fruit, cans of soup, but no peas. My "Eureka!" had been premature.

"Teodora only wanted him to eat fresh vegetables," said Toni, who joined me in the pantry. She pronounced Teodora's name the way Teodora said it, "Day-o-daughter."

Toni's voice was equally *alluring*.

"Okay, maybe he had a special craving for canned peas," I said, "but he had to keep them hidden from Teodora. So all we have to do is find his secret hiding place, and then . . ."

"Yes?" Toni asked eagerly.

I had no idea.

Toni smiled at me. "We don't know what the hell we're doing, do we?" she asked.

Her eyes were shining. I was reminded of Arnold's description of Annabel.

Her eyes sparkled like diamonds.

"Not a clue," I admitted.

She didn't seem to mind. For a moment we just stood there, looking into each other's eyes. I took hold of her hands and felt her fingers wrap around mine. I no longer gave a damn about canned peas!

I became aware of the sound of birds chirping, quietly at first, then louder, with squawks and caws.

"My phone!" Toni exclaimed. She pulled her hands away and fished her phone out of a pocket.

The birds had been her ringtone. "Hello?" she said. "Oh, hi. No, I just . . ." Her voice softened as she stepped out of the pantry. "I've been thinking about you, too."

I slipped past her and on out of the kitchen to give her privacy. I found myself in the entry hall, at the place where Trapp had lain on the floor with the candle burning in his ear, sucking out his earwax.

I heard Toni say "That sounds great!" Then, "No, I better meet you there." She spoke in short bursts. "I'm not at home." "I'm at the mall." "With my mom." "She can take me." She stepped out into the hall. "Let me get a pencil."

I went through an archway into an office. The walls were lined with built-in bookshelves that were still crammed with books. There were two desks, an old rolltop and a more modern one with a computer.

I opened the rolltop, found a pen, and handed it to Toni, who had followed me into the office.

She giggled at something Cliff said—I assumed it was Cliff—and then she pantomimed the act of writing. She was asking me for a piece of paper.

There was a stack of papers on the computer desk, but I didn't know if they might be important. When I looked at the top page, I was surprised to see my name on it.

Toni reached out impatiently.

It was the e-mail confirmation of my flight to Chicago. Trapp's, Teodora's, and Gloria's were also there, as well as all of our hotel reservations.

Toni saw the look on my face. With the phone at her ear, she read the e-mails, then abruptly said, "I gotta go. I'll meet you there in twenty minutes. No, everything's fine. Bye."

She hung up. We looked at each other for what seemed like a long time.

"That's why he brought me here," I said at last.

"But what about the can of peas?" asked Toni.

"Who the hell knows?"

She thought awhile, then very quietly said, "Okay."

"You sure?" I asked.

"If you're sure, I'm sure," said Toni.

"I'm sure," I said. I wasn't sure at all.

I looked back at my plane reservation. I felt a shiver run through me as I spoke my next words. "Trapp and Annabel are going to play for the national championship."

"And this time, they'll win," said Toni.

A few minutes later I was driving her to a bookstore café for her rendezvous with Cliff. I agreed to let her off a block away so he wouldn't see my car.

I tried not to think back to Toni and me in the pantry, and what might have happened if Cliff hadn't called when he did. I just had to push those thoughts out of my mind. We had more important things to focus on, and after all, she was my best friend's girlfriend.

"It was lucky he called," Toni said quietly, almost as if she'd been reading my mind. "Or we might not have found those e-mails."

I didn't respond. I didn't know if Cliff's call had been good luck, bad luck, or synchronicity.

"I'm sorry," she said. She hesitantly touched my sleeve, then quickly withdrew her hand.

59

Looking at Colleges

Over the next week and a half, Toni and I talked on the phone at least once a day as we got ready for the nationals. The hotel rooms were all paid for, since Trapp, or more likely Mrs. Mahoney, had used an online travel service. We had four rooms: mine, Trapp's, Teodora's, and Gloria's, although I wasn't completely sure Gloria's would be available. It was possible she still might be planning to go to the nationals.

We figured that as long as they didn't ask for ID, Toni could pretend to be Teodora. If that didn't work, then she could share my room.

Just so you know, it was Toni who mentioned we could share the room, not me.

As for the airline tickets, I could use mine, but Toni would have to purchase a new one, since airlines definitely required identification. We split the cost of a standby ticket, knowing for a fact there would be a seat available.

Toni went to the American Contract Bridge League's Web site and bought a membership under the name

Annabel Finnick. I could still use Trapp's ACBL number, but I got a membership in my own name, just in case. Toni already had her own ACBL number.

The truth is, we still didn't know what the hell we were doing. We were simply going through the motions. We had a list of things to do, and we were doing them, but neither of us believed we would actually be flying off to Chicago to play in the nationals.

"Are we really going to do this?" Toni would ask me during one of our frequent phone calls.

I'd say, "Yeah, we really are," but then a few minutes later I would ask her the same thing. "We're really going to do this?"

"I think so," Toni would reply.

Maybe we would have felt more confident if there had been a can of peas sitting on top of these travel documents, like a paperweight. I hadn't perceived a word from Trapp since that day. Toni hadn't heard from Annabel either. A sign of encouragement would have been nice. Was that too much to ask?

If you're wondering how my parents reacted when I told them that I'd be going to Chicago with Toni Castaneda for three days, and maybe sharing a hotel room with her, then you're even crazier than I was beginning to think I was. I told them that Cliff and I would be driving up north to look at colleges.

They were all for that, since Trapp's estate was now footing the bill. Basically, they urged me to find the most expensive college that would admit a dolt like me. They told me to save my gas receipts.

I did learn that Trapp's house now belonged to Mrs. Mahoney. She returned from visiting her sister, and discovered that someone had been snooping around inside.

"Nothing was stolen, as far as she could tell," said my mother. "But boxes were strewn all over the garage, and every kitchen cabinet was open."

"That's scary," I said.

I told Leslie the truth. I thought someone ought to know, just in case the plane crashed or something. I told her everything, including hearing Trapp's voice.

She didn't doubt me for a second.

"Does he sound happy?" she asked me.

I explained that all I ever got from him were short two- or three-word phrases. *Nine of clubs. Two hearts. Turn right. Canned peas.* "Who knows if the concept of happiness is even relevant?" I asked.

That might seem like too philosophical a question for an eleven-year-old, but Leslie is a lot smarter than most people realize. I think most eleven-year-olds understand a lot more than we give them credit for.

Actually, I didn't tell Leslie *everything*. I didn't mention the pantry.

Leslie also helped me study my new batch of bidding conventions, and this time it wasn't just eleven pages. Toni e-mailed me sixty-one pages I had to learn for the nationals.

If you're wondering why I had to learn all the bidding conventions, since supposedly Trapp would be telling me what to bid, there were two reasons. Back at the bridge studio, there had been times when I'd had trouble perceiving him. If that happened during the national tournament, I'd have to be able to make the bid myself, without *undue hesitation*. Also, partners are not allowed to have any secret bidding agreements. The opponents would be allowed to ask me what a bid meant. I had to be prepared to answer.

Fortunately, all the bidding conventions used by Trapp and Annabel are pretty well known. They all have names. So if somebody asked me about a bid, I could just say "Roman key-card" or "Reverse Drury," and even if I didn't know what any of that meant, the opponents would.

"When you get back from Chicago," Leslie asked, "will you take me to the bridge studio sometime?"

I promised I would.

Two days before our supposed college tour, I still hadn't told Cliff anything about it. I obviously needed to tell him something, since he was part of my alibi, but how do you tell your best friend you're going to spend three nights in a hotel with his girlfriend?

"You don't have to worry about Cliff," Toni assured me. "I'll explain everything to him, in my own way."

I didn't ask for further detail. I didn't like thinking about the two of them together, or how she might *gently* break the news. Still, it would have helped to know what she told him. As it was, I stayed clear of Cliff, afraid I might say the wrong thing.

The night before we were to leave for Chicago, I was unable to fall asleep. I tossed and turned all night. At about three in the morning, I turned on the light and finished reading *Cannery Row,* the book that had brought Trapp and Annabel together. I found the quote that Trapp had told me about.

> "It has always seemed strange to me," said Doc. "The things we admire in men, kindness and generosity, openness, honesty, understanding and feeling are the concomitants of failure in our system. And those traits we detest, sharpness, greed, acquisitiveness, meanness, egotism and self-interest are the traits of success."

60

Not a Wet Sock

We had a 10:05 a.m. flight. I picked Toni up at seven-thirty. She had baked some cranberry-walnut muffins, using her grandmother's recipe.

I ate a muffin on the way to the airport. It was hard and dry. Annabel was a better bridge player than muffin maker. Or maybe it was Toni who couldn't follow directions, but then again, who was I to complain? It wasn't as if I had baked any muffins for her.

We had no surprises at the airport. Toni had no problem using her standby ticket, and the seat next to mine was vacant, as we'd known it would be.

"So what did you tell Cliff?" I asked as we taxied to the runway.

"About what?"

"You, me, Chicago."

"I didn't tell him anything."

"What do you mean, you didn't tell him anything?

249

My parents think he's with me checking out colleges."

"Here, have another muffin."

A moment later we were off the ground.

Cliff is smart, I realized. He's probably smarter than me, and definitely a quicker thinker. If my mother happened to run into him, I felt pretty certain that he'd figure it out and duck smoothly, like I had done on the phone with Katie. After all, he wouldn't know I was with Toni. I was fairly confident he'd come up with some good reason why, at the last minute, he hadn't been able to go with me to look at colleges.

Toni and I mostly spoke bridge gibberish from takeoff to touchdown as we went over the sixty-one pages of notes, eighty-one pages if you include her previous e-mails. There were three seats in our row. I had the aisle, Toni was in the center, and next to her was a man with a computer who glared at us from time to time because our constant yammering kept him from doing his work.

Our only luggage was carry-on. We were both feeling pretty excited when we deplaned and went looking for the shuttle bus to the hotel.

"Can you believe we're here?" she asked me.

"No," I said. "I just hope Trapp and Annabel made it too."

Every single person on the shuttle bus was a bridge

player. They were going over their bidding systems, or discussing bridge hands, or just talking about the tournament in general. It felt exciting to be a part of it.

The hotel was abuzz with bridge gibberish as well. It was like some kind of scary sci-fi movie where everywhere you turned, people were muttering weird sentences.

". . . MUD from three small."

". . . upside-down count and attitude."

"She was squeezed in the black suits."

I didn't know which was scarier, so many people speaking bridge gibberish or the fact that I understood most of what they were saying!

I had no problem checking into my room, and when Toni used Teodora's name, the clerk didn't ask for any ID. He did ask her when she expected a Mr. Lester Trapp to arrive.

"Sometime soon," said Toni.

I hoped so.

A problem arose, however, when he asked us for credit cards. I didn't have one. Toni did, but it was in her real name.

"The rooms are already paid for," I pointed out.

The clerk said he needed to have a credit card on file for incidentals, in case we charged a meal to our room, or made a telephone call, or watched an on-demand movie.

"We won't do any of that," said Toni. "We'll be playing bridge."

"And we both have cell phones," I added, showing him my phone.

Toni showed him her phone too.

In the end we each left one hundred dollars cash as a deposit, which we'd get back when we checked out.

We were lucky, I think, that the hotel was crowded and there were a lot of people waiting to check in. Otherwise he might have given us a harder time.

Our rooms were on the twenty-seventh floor. Toni turned right when we exited the elevator, and I turned left. We agreed to meet in an hour, after we'd had time to unpack and freshen up.

It took me all of three minutes to unpack, and as far as freshening up goes, I took a leak and stuck my hands under the faucet. The hotel soap was too much of a bother to unwrap.

I turned on the TV, but I felt too restless to sit and watch anything. The National Pairs Championship wouldn't start until the next day, but I decided I'd go down and check out the playing area.

I called Toni's room first, to let her know where I'd be.

"I'll go with you," she said. "I'm going crazy just sitting here!"

If you've been wondering whether I was disappointed that Toni and I didn't have to share a room, I don't think so. I think if we'd shared a room, it would have been really awkward, and we would have needed to get out to escape from each other. Coming from different rooms, we weren't escaping from each other but seeking each other out.

I had also decided it was good that Toni hadn't told Cliff

about this. She obviously didn't want him to be jealous.

Based on my very limited experience, if someone is feeling jealous, it is because he has a damn good reason. Before Katie and I broke up, I could sense a certain vibe between her and Cliff. The way they looked at each other. The way she laughed when he teased her.

Don't get me wrong. Cliff wasn't coming on to her. He was just being the boyfriend's best friend, making conversation, kidding around. Still, I felt jealous, and well, you know how that turned out.

Put another way, if Toni had thought it was no big deal to tell Cliff that she was going to Chicago with me, then I was about as much of a threat as a wet sock.

When I turned the corner, I saw Toni waving at me from the elevator. I think I've already told you how it made me feel to see her smile and wave at me. You can have your sunsets and waterfalls. If a piano were to suddenly fall on my head, that's the image I'd want forever engraved in my mind.

61

They Need Us

The playing area was not just one room. There were two giant ballrooms and seven or eight smaller rooms, all filled with rows and rows of people playing bridge. And that, I found out, was just on one floor. Toni and I took an escalator down a level and found the identical setup on the floor below.

It was only a little after four o'clock, so they were still in the middle of the afternoon session. Pairs, knockouts, and something called *board-a-match* were all taking place in different parts of the hotel. I was surprised by how many younger players were there. Many weren't much older than Toni and I. I even saw several kids who looked about Leslie's age, playing with a parent or grandparent.

One of the downstairs ballrooms was designated as the novice area. It was for players with fewer than 200 masterpoints. Just outside that room was a sign announcing various guest lecturers, including Syd Fox.

"That's the guy!" I exclaimed.

The name meant nothing to Toni.

"Remember when we played against those jerks, when Annabel redoubled?" I reminded her. "As we were leaving the table one of the idiots complained that you had suddenly turned into Syd Fox."

We decided we'd go to Syd Fox's lecture, which was at six-fifteen, and then we'd play in the seven o'clock session. Just us, with no help from Trapp or Annabel.

We found a hole-in-the-wall sandwich shop two blocks from the hotel and grabbed a quick dinner. My sandwich had sausage and peppers on it, and Toni ordered one with fresh mozzarella, tomatoes, and basil.

I only mention what we ate because we both said our sandwiches were "amazing." That's pretty funny if you think about it. We were about to enter a national championship, turning cards for Trapp and Annabel, but our sandwiches were "amazing"!

One of the legs on our table was shorter than the other three, so the table kept wobbling as we ate. "How long has Annabel been talking to you?" I asked.

"Always," said Toni. "As long as I can remember."

I told Toni about the time I'd first met her, at Trapp's sixty-fifth birthday party, when she ran up to me and shouted, "Shut up! Leave me alone!"

She didn't remember, and felt embarrassed about it. "I'm really sorry," she said.

"I didn't mind," I assured her. "I thought you were funny."

She reached across the table and put her hand on mine. "You know I wasn't talking to you, right?"

"I know that now," I said.

255

It wasn't surprising that she didn't remember. It had been a big deal to me because it was the only time I'd been to my mysterious uncle Lester's house, and then I met this girl who acted so strange. She had been to Trapp's house many times. To her, it was just another day.

"I do remember that there were times I wished she'd go away and never talk to me again," Toni admitted. "I wanted so much to just be normal. Everybody kept telling me there was something wrong with me. I had to go to a psychiatrist. And then I was supposed to take these pills, but Annabel would say, 'Don't take the pills, Toni.'"

"But most of the time, I was glad she was there," Toni added. "It was like having a fairy godmother. I loved her. I still do."

"Do your parents know you talk to Annabel?" I asked.

"No, not really," Toni said. "My mother just thinks I have special insight. But then again, they do send me to a shrink."

I asked her if that was why she was homeschooled, too, but she said she didn't think so.

"My parents don't believe in what they call 'institutionalized education.' Something about fitting square pegs into round holes. It's not like they keep me locked up in a padded cell or something. I have friends."

"No, I know," I said. "You quilt together."

"You think that's funny, don't you?"

"No," I lied.

"Yes, you do."

"No, really," I said. "So what do you suppose they're doing right now?"

"Who?" asked Toni.

"Trapp and Annabel," I said. "You think they're going over their bidding systems, like everyone else around here?"

"They're not *doing* anything," said Toni. "They need us."

Syd Fox was about sixty-five years old, with wild Albert Einstein hair, and he wore glasses with heavy black frames. Behind those glasses, you could catch a mischievous, almost childish gleam in his eye.

His lecture was surprisingly entertaining. You were supposedly playing bridge with some king. Fox used a whiteboard, where he'd put up different card combinations. He'd show you what cards were in dummy and what cards were in the declarer's hand, and then tell you how many tricks you needed to take.

If you succeeded, the king would let you marry the princess, or prince, depending. But if you failed, the royal executioner would chop off your head.

Here was one:

Dummy
♡ AJ93

West   East

You
♡ K852

You had to choose a line of play that was guaranteed to win three heart tricks no matter how the remaining hearts were divided between East and West.

Syd Fox called on several people. I was afraid to raise my hand, and just whispered my answer to Toni.

The first two people got it wrong and had their heads chopped off. One of them had given my answer.

"Too bad, you're dead," Toni said to me.

A woman finally got it right. She said she'd lead dummy's ace. Next she'd lead dummy's three, and if East played low, she'd play the eight.

"Congratulations," Syd Fox told her. "You may marry the prince."

"I'll take the princess, if you don't mind," the woman said, and everyone laughed.

He gave us four different diagrams. I lost my head on each of the first three, but on the fourth one, I got to marry the princess.

Toni smiled at me.

Going back to what I said earlier, I don't think she would have dared to smile at me like that if we'd been sharing the same room.

62

Twenty-five Percent Slam

Syd Fox's lecture got us fired up and ready to play, and no novice game for us! We wanted to take on the big boys.

We entered something called a *side game*. The main pairs game was a two-session event that had started in the afternoon. The side game was only one session. It was mainly for those who had been knocked out of a KO in the afternoon, or for people like Toni and me, who had only just arrived.

We were in one of the large ballrooms on the lower level. There were several different events taking place in there. We used our real names and ACBL numbers. Our table assignment was KK-8, North-South. The two Ks are not a typo. There were a lot more than twenty-six sections in the tournament, so they had to double up on letters. Somewhere else in the hotel, another pair was sitting North-South at table K-8 with only one *K*.

Two women sat in the East-West seats. West stared at me a moment, then said, "Alton, right?"

I was shocked.

She and her partner introduced themselves as Lydia and Renee.

I didn't introduce Toni to them. She'd be using three different names at the tournament, Toni, Annabel, and Teodora, and I didn't want to have to remember which people knew her by which name.

"We met Alton at a sectional," Lydia told Toni. "He was helping his blind uncle." She turned to me. "Is he here?"

I hesitated. "I think he's coming later," I said.

"He's an amazing player," said Lydia. "And I'd say that even if he wasn't blind."

"I didn't know you played too," said Renee.

"I'm just learning," I said.

"So am I," said Renee. "And I've been playing for twenty-five years."

"The time you quit learning is the time to quit playing," said Lydia.

Okay, I realize you didn't come all the way to Chicago to watch Toni and me play in a side game. That would be like a sports reporter who's supposed to be covering the Super Bowl going on and on about the pregame charity touch-football match between the players' wives. It was bad enough I made you sit through Syd Fox's lecture.

The thing of it is, Toni and I played great! We used a lot of the new bids I had learned, but it was more than just that. I no longer thought of bidding as a bunch of rules to be memorized. It was a conversation. I imagine it's like learning a foreign language. After a while you stop translating every word in your head and start thinking in that language. This was a language based on symbols and logic instead of words and phrases. Every bid Toni made, and even the bids she didn't make, like the dog that didn't bark, gave me information about her hand.

Syd Fox's lecture helped too. None of those exact card combinations came up, but he had gotten me thinking along the right lines, and I made all but one of my contracts. When the scores were posted with one round to go, Richards and Castaneda were in fifth place with a 53 percent game.

Toni was worried about our last round, however. "They bid that lucky slam against us," she griped. "I bet no one else bid it."

It turned out she was right. When the final results were posted we had fallen to 49 percent.

She complained all the way to the elevator, using language I usually hear from Cliff. "All because of that *spade slam!*" (Adjective deleted.) "It took two *finesses!* (The same adjective deleted.) "A twenty-five percent slam! If you'd had the king of spades, or if I'd had the queen of clubs, instead of the other way around, we would have set it. Switch our hands and he would have been down two."

I looked at the hand record. "How could East jump to three spades on that garbage? He has nine points, and flat distribution."

"We were fixed," said Toni.

I laughed.

"What's so funny?" she demanded.

"Listen to us. We sound like everybody else."

She smiled. "Yeah. isn't it great?"

Do you know that thing about how nobody ever talks on elevators? Not true when it comes to bridge players. Mostly, they complained about their partners.

"We pushed them into an unmakeable contract," complained a short round man, "but my partner *sacrifices* at five hearts, because, *she says,* she had no defense. She had the ace and king of clubs!"

No doubt his partner was on another elevator complaining about him.

63

A Long Hesitation

I hope you don't think this is too personal, but I don't like firm pillows. My pillow at home barely has any oomph to it.

It wasn't just the hotel pillow that kept me awake all night. My mind was racing around in circles. It occasionally stopped at new places, but mostly kept returning to the same old ones, again and again and again. I worried that Trapp wouldn't show up the next day. I replayed bridge hands from the side game. I relived the unlucky six-spade hand, and how it kept us from breaking fifty percent.

My brain would not shut up!

There was one place in particular where my mind kept returning, more than any other. It was the moment right after Toni and I exited the elevator.

We just stood there in the hallway as if waiting for something. Finally, after a long hesitation, Toni said, "Well, good night."

There was another long hesitation; then I said, "Night."

If we had hesitated that much during a bridge hand, our opponents would have called the director.

All night, as I flopped around in my too-soft bed, on my too-hard pillow, I kept coming up with different charming and witty things I should have said. Whole conversations unfolded. I would say . . . then she would say, then I would say, and then, and then, and then. . . .

Something had almost happened between us in the pantry at Trapp's house. We both knew it. *But it didn't,* I reminded myself. *And it can't.*

If she had never met Cliff, then maybe, probably, things would have been different between us, but she had. He was the one with whom she took moonlight walks on the golf course, not me.

Toni and I were bridge partners; nothing more, nothing less.

I wondered if she was lying awake thinking about me. I wondered if she was wondering whether I was wondering about her.

Shut up, brain!

I must have fallen asleep, because her telephone call woke me up. I glanced at the clock. It was 10:43.

I said hello in my deep and scratchy just-woke-up voice.

"I'm sorry, did I wake you?" she asked.

"No, I've been up for a while," I lied. "I was just lying in bed thinking."

"I'm starving!" said Toni.

She had just gotten back from swimming laps in the hotel pool and wanted to meet for breakfast. She sounded alert and invigorated.

I groaned as I got out of bed. I hadn't gotten any sleep for two nights in a row, and the pillow had given me a stiff neck. I took a quick shower, got dressed, and met her by the elevator.

"You look awful," she said.

I thanked her for her kind words.

We ate breakfast at the same sandwich shop where we had eaten dinner. The food was still amazing.

I asked her if she had heard anything from Annabel. She hadn't.

"What if they don't come?" I asked. "I mean, we never did find the can of peas."

"So what?" she said. "If they don't, they don't. We'll still have fun. You played great last night. We would have come in fourth if it wasn't for that stupid six-spade bid."

She was still angry about it.

She told me she had checked the scores this morning after her swim. Our opponents had been the only pair stupid and lucky enough to bid six spades. She figured out that if they hadn't bid the slam, we would have come in fourth, and earned .8 masterpoints. And if we had set six spades, which would have happened if either she held the queen of clubs or I held the king of spades, we would have come in third and earned almost 1.5 gold masterpoints.

Yes, these imaginary masterpoints are colored. At bridge clubs, you win black points. At sectionals, you win silver points. At regionals, they're gold or red, depending on whether you come in first. Gold is better. At nationals, you also win gold masterpoints, except for the major national championship events, where the points are platinum.

I almost laughed when Toni explained this to me. It was like when my third-grade teacher used to give us gold stars for doing our homework. But at least back then I could actually see the gold star.

I found it funny that grown-up people cared so much about earning these imaginary masterpoints, and even funnier that they cared what color they were.

But you know what? I'm no different. I was disappointed when I realized how close I had come to winning my first masterpoint. I was doubly disappointed when I learned it would have been gold!

64

The First Hand

Game time was one o'clock, but we didn't actually get started until almost twenty-five after. The line to buy the entry was almost as bad as the lines at Disneyland.

We were in the large ballroom on the upper floor. There were sixteen sections, A through P, with thirteen tables in each section. We'd be competing against the top players from the United States and around the world. It would be a two-day, four-session event. Only those who finished above 50 percent after the first day would continue for the second day.

Our table assignment was G-10, East-West. The sections all had single letters for this event. This was the real deal!

We put the names Annabel Finnick and Lester Trapp on our entry form. We put Annabel's name first, since it was less likely to be recognized. Even if there were people here who might have known her fifty years ago, they would have known her as Annabel King.

The boards had been predealt. There were tiny bar codes on each card. A special card-dealing machine had dealt according to specific hand records. In every section in the room, the person sitting at table ten West was looking at the same thirteen cards I was looking at.

♠ AQ6
♡ KQ1085
◇ AK96
♣ J

It was a good hand. I counted twenty-one points, although I wasn't sure I could count three points for the jack of clubs—one for the jack, and another two because it was a singleton.

I still hadn't heard from Trapp.

My hand was clearly a one-heart opener, but first I had to wait for South, the designated dealer, to bid. She was an Asian woman who wore very tiny glasses. She reached into her bidding box, then set her bid on the table.

1♡

I tried to maintain a blank expression as I stared at it. That was the bid I was going to make.

My mind started racing. What was I supposed to do? Should I bid two hearts? Double? One no-trump? My second-best suit was diamonds. Should I bid two diamonds?

"Pass," said my favorite uncle.

I reached into my box and calmly set a green pass card on the table.

65

The Donkey Hand

North and East also passed, and so, for the very first hand of the tournament, the contract was just one heart. The declarer only needed to take seven tricks, but Trapp and Annabel set it by three tricks! That gave us a score of 300. I wondered what the results had been at all the other table tens in the room.

Toni told me later that when you pass with a good hand because you expect to set the opponents, it's called a trap pass. Not exactly synchronicity, but close.

We played two boards per round. After each round, Toni and I moved up a table. There were no skips.

Most of the time I had no problem hearing my uncle, but occasionally he was fuzzy. I didn't know if the problem was on my end or his. Maybe it had something to do with my stiff neck, and not being able to hold my head at the necessary angle, or maybe the reception was just worse at some tables than at others.

Even if it was fuzzy, I usually could figure out what he

was trying to tell me. After all, I did almost earn my first gold masterpoint.

There was only one really bad screwup. I clearly heard him say "Ace of spades," which, I admit, seemed odd at the time, since Toni had played the king of spades; however, I had seen him make a similar play before.

"Eight, not ace, *eight*!" he said as I set the card on the table, but by then it was too late.

Since I had won the trick, it was my turn to lead. I waited, but got nothing from him. I don't think this was due to a problem with communication or perception. I think he was pouting.

I chose the card myself. It probably didn't matter anymore what card I played since we'd already be getting a bottom board.

I didn't hear from him again until two cards later. His voice was loud and clear. He called me a donkey.

After the session was over, we could see where we stood with two rounds to go. There were too many players, and not enough time, for the directors to post the usual one-round-to-go results. After eleven rounds, Annabel Finnick and Lester Trapp were in fourth place in section G, East-West, with a 55 percent game. It felt strange to see their names.

I wasn't too worried that somebody might notice their names. The only people who would check these particular results were the other twelve East-West pairs in section G. Besides, people tended only to look for their own names.

Toni and I stuck around another twenty minutes for the final results. Finnick and Trapp remained at 55 percent, and fourth in their section. For this, they earned .7 platinum points. I wondered how much the donkey hand had cost them.

66

The Beer Card

There must be at least fifty thousand restaurants in Chicago. Toni and I ate dinner at the same sandwich shop.

I ordered a vegetarian sandwich this time. Toni never seemed to have any difficulty hearing Annabel. Maybe meat clogged my receptors.

I told her about the donkey hand. She didn't think it was my fault. She said there were lots of times when it's right to overtake your partner's king with your ace. "You might need to unblock, or it might be necessary that you be on-lead. You had no way of knowing."

Maybe, maybe not.

Toni told me about a play made by Annabel. She got a pen out of her purse and drew a bridge diagram on a napkin.

The contract had been 3NT.

Dummy

♠ AQ7

Trapp (me)   Annabel (Toni)

♠ K5

♢ 7

Declarer

(plays the ♣9)

The declarer led the ♣9, and nobody else had any clubs left. Trapp discarded a diamond, and the dummy got rid of the ♠7. Annabel still had to play.

"If you were Annabel, what would you discard?" Toni asked me.

I looked at the diagram. "Do you know if the declarer had any diamonds left?" I asked.

"He only had spades," said Toni.

I wasn't very good at reading bridge diagrams. I wished I could see the real cards. Still, it seemed pretty obvious that Annabel should discard the ♢7. She needed to save the ♠5 in order to protect her ♠K. Otherwise, on the next trick, the declarer could tell dummy to play the ace, and Annabel would have to play her king.

"So what happened?" I asked Toni.

"Well, on the next trick, the declarer tried the finesse," she said. "He played the queen of spades. Annabel won that trick with her king of spades, and then she won the last trick with her seven of diamonds, setting the contract."

(She had discarded the ♠5!)

In bridge, as in life, Annabel did not consider it her duty to serve and protect the king.

> Annabel made a risky defensive play and won two tricks instead of just one. She won the last trick with the ◇ 7.

"The seven of diamonds is the beer card," Toni told me. "If you win the final trick with the seven of diamonds and it sets the contract, your partner is supposed to buy you a beer."

"You're making that up!"

"Swear to God," she promised, crossing her heart.

"Wait a sec," I said. "Let me get this straight. Besides trying to win against the best players in the world, Annabel also managed her cards so she'd win the last trick with the seven of diamonds, *just for kicks?*"

Toni smiled.

"Well, wherever she is," I said, "I hope she's enjoying her beer. Or I guess I should say, I hope the *idea* of beer is being enjoyed by the *idea* of Annabel."

Toni looked confused, but not half as confused as I was.

I raised my cup in the air. I was drinking a mango smoothie. "To Annabel!" I said.

Toni raised her bubble tea. "To Annabel!" she repeated.

We clinked our cups together.

Paper cups don't actually clink, but it was the idea that counted.

67

A Message from Afar

The top hundred pairs were posted on the wall just inside the door to the playing area. I had to wait for several people to move before I could get a look. Finnick and Trapp were currently in seventy-eighth place.

"Alton?"

I turned around to see Deborah, Arnold's wife. "What are you doing here?" she asked.

I didn't know what to say.

"Arnold!" she called. "Alton and Toni are here!"

"Hi, Deborah," Toni said, then hugged her. "When did you get here?"

The best defense is a good offense.

A moment later we found ourselves surrounded by Lucy, Arnold, and Lucy's husband, Carl. There were hugs and handshakes all around.

"Are you two playing bridge?" asked Arnold.

"Of course they're playing," said Lucy. "What else would they be doing here?"

"Trapp had already paid for the airfare and hotel," I said, "so why not?"

"Fantastic!" Arnold exclaimed. "How's it going?"

Toni proceeded to tell everyone about the side game. ". . . If I'd had the queen of clubs, or if Alton had had the king of spades . . ."

They all remembered the hand. They had played in the two-session pairs game, which had used the same hand records we had.

"They bid six spades on that crap?" asked Deborah.

"You were fixed," said Arnold.

"Tell me about it," griped Toni.

"It's a tough tournament," said Carl. "Even in the side games, you're likely to face some world-class competition."

"So what event are you playing in tonight?" asked Deborah.

There was no use in lying, since they were likely to see us in the room. "Right here," I said. "National Pairs Championship."

"I'm impressed," said Arnold. "But that's the way to do it. No point playing in the novice game. The best way to learn is to play against the best."

"You're not in the top hundred, are you?" asked Deborah, who had seen me looking at the chart.

"Yeah, right," I said. "No, we're just playing for the experience."

"So are we all, I'm afraid," said Carl.

I was glad to hear that Lucy and Arnold had had a 46 percent in the afternoon, which was a percentage point better than their spouses had done. Don't get me wrong; it wasn't that I wanted them to do badly. I just didn't want them looking for their names in the top hundred.

They didn't even ask what our score was, presumably because they didn't want to embarrass us.

"No one's out of it yet," said Arnold.

"The main thing is to Q," said Carl.

I didn't know what that meant. We all wished each other good luck.

"Maybe we'll get to play against you tonight," Lucy said.

I'm sure she hoped she would.

Our table assignment for the evening session was H-10, North-South. I was glad that neither Lucy and Arnold nor Deborah and Carl appeared to be in our section.

The director reminded everyone to put away their cell phones. I was about to turn mine off, when I saw I had a new text message.

mom saw cliff @ pool

That was all. There was no further explanation or voice mail.

Leslie didn't own a cell phone. I decided she must have borrowed her friend Marissa's. Marissa's family had a membership in the country club. Leslie must have gone as Marissa's guest, and our mother had either driven her there or picked her up.

It probably took Leslie longer to type the @ symbol than it would have to type the word *at*, but that's the kind of thing she loves to do.

"You haven't talked to Cliff today, have you?" I asked Toni.

Toni's cheeks turned red. "Twice," she said. "Why?"

I was surprised, and also jealous. "When was the last time?" I asked.

"In my room after dinner."

"Did he say anything about my mother?"

"Your mother? No, we didn't, um, talk about your mother."

I turned off my phone.

68

Signals

I was glad to be sitting South. It meant I remained at the same table throughout the session, and so far, after the first three rounds, the reception had been very good. I was having no difficulty perceiving my uncle.

"What are your defensive signals, please?" asked the dignified woman in the East seat.

"Standard," I said, having memorized the answer to that question.

"Is your primary answer attitude or count?"

"Um . . ."

"Attitude," said Toni, "unless count is obviously more important."

"Of course," said the woman.

I should explain.

When you are on defense, if you are not trying to win the trick, then the card you play sends a signal to your partner. Just like in the bidding, you are not allowed to have any secret signals. The opponents can ask what signals you use.

I usually got by with saying "Standard."

It basically works like this. A high card encourages. A low card discourages. Let's say your partner leads the ♣3, and the ♣A is played from the dummy. Since you are unable to win the trick, you can signal your partner for later. If you held the ♣K62, you would play the ♣6, encouraging, telling your partner you had something good in clubs. If instead you held ♣862, you would play the ♣2, discouraging your partner from leading clubs again.

Those are called attitude signals because you are telling your partner your attitude toward clubs. But sometimes it's hard to tell. Is the six high or low? If you have ♣K32, the ♣3 is the highest card you can signal with. If you have ♣987, the ♣7 is a low card.

That's the problem I was having with Toni. I couldn't read her signals. I didn't know if she was encouraging me or discouraging me. And I'm not talking about bridge anymore.

"Seven of hearts," said Trapp.

I set the card on the table and tried to focus on the game. It was dangerous to let my mind drift.

I looked across the table at Toni. She was the picture of concentration.

Toni saw me looking at her. She smiled and winked.

"You shouldn't have done that," I told her after the opponents had left the table. If the opponents had seen her wink at me, they might have thought she was giving me some kind of secret signal.

"Done what?" she asked.

"Wink."

"Wink?"

"You winked at me."

"I did not!" she insisted. "Why would I wink at you?"

A new East-West pair sat down at our table, abruptly ending our discussion and saving me from further embarrassment.

I removed my cards from the South slot and sorted my hand.

"One heart," said Trapp.

I set the bid on the table.

She had winked. I could still see it in my mind: a slight upturn of the left corner of her mouth, then the quick but purposeful flick of her right eyelid.

Before I knew it, it was my turn to bid again. Trapp's voice was extremely fuzzy, no doubt because my mind was still thinking about the wink.

I looked at my cards, and at all the bids on the table. I bid two no-trump and hoped it was right.

Toni bid three no-trump and everyone passed.

I must have made the correct bid, because Trapp didn't call me a donkey. He was the declarer, and I forced myself to concentrate on his instructions.

Halfway through the hand, I realized I'd been wrong. Toni hadn't winked. There was no way she would have risked doing that in the middle of a bridge hand. She was also too shy.

The wink had come from Annabel.

69

Q

With two rounds to go, Annabel Finnick and Lester Trapp were first N-S in section H, with a 63 percent game. When the final results were posted they had dropped to 62 percent and second. They earned 1.68 platinum points.

There was also a capital Q next to their names. All around me, people were talking about whether or not they had Q'ed.

It took me a while, but I finally figured out that the Q meant we had qualified to play the next day.

I extricated myself from the crowd and looked for Toni. Instead, I saw Lucy and Arnold coming right toward me.

I hurried to meet them halfway. I didn't want them anywhere near our posted results.

"How'd you do?" I asked.

"We Q'ed!" said Lucy. "Fifty-eight percent."

I congratulated them. That more than made up for their 46 percent in the afternoon. "How about Deborah and Carl?"

From the way Arnold sadly shook his head, you would have thought they had died.

"How'd you and Toni do?" asked Lucy.

The question was obligatory. I knew she didn't think we had a snowball's chance in hell, but she had to pretend otherwise.

"We're still in it," I said, as if I didn't quite believe it myself.

You could tell Arnold and Lucy were experienced bridge players by the way they congratulated me without revealing any of their shock.

"Well, you had a great teacher," said Lucy; then, choking up, she added, "He would be very proud."

Arnold explained that for the next day there would be some carryover of that day's results, but only to a degree. It was like a car race in which after the race is half over, half the cars are eliminated. The remaining cars are kept in their same order, but they're bunched closer together, so even those at the back still have a chance.

"That's fair," said Arnold. "Some of the pairs may have gotten high scores today because they got to play against much weaker pairs. But tomorrow all of the weak pairs will have been eliminated, so it will be a much fairer test for the rest of us."

I appreciated the fact that he included Toni and me with the stronger pairs, even if he didn't believe it.

Lucy grabbed some hand records, and they invited me to join them for a drink in the bar and go over the hands. I reminded them I was only seventeen.

"Get a Coke, then," said Arnold.

"C'mon, it'll be fun to hear how you and Toni beat all the pros," said Lucy.

"I need to find Toni," I said.

I looked for her out in the hall, then over by the escalators, and finally at the bank of elevators. She wasn't there. I went back to the ballroom, then returned to the elevators and waited there for at least another ten minutes.

I felt like a fool. No doubt she was in her room, talking to Cliff.

He was her boyfriend, okay, I got that. Still, I was angry that she didn't stick around long enough to say good night before rushing off to call him. I took the elevator to the twenty-seventh floor.

There were no more messages on my cell phone, or on my room phone. That was good. At least my parents hadn't been trying to call me. Still, I would have liked to know more about what had happened between my mom and Cliff.

I didn't use the hotel pillow, just the pillowcase, which I stuffed with my dirty clothes. It was soft enough, but lumpy.

70

Canned Peas

Toni called after her morning swim, but I was already awake this time, having slept a good two and a half hours. My neck hurt worse than ever.

"Trapp and Annabel are in nineteenth!" she said, all excited.

I took a shower and tried letting the hot water pound on my neck, but the water pressure in the hotel was so weak I could just barely feel it. I was glad that Trapp and Annabel were up so high, but it was also worrisome. The higher they were on the list, the likelier other people would notice their names.

Toni and I met at the elevator and walked to the sandwich shop. She was energized after her swim, and talked excitedly about the upcoming two sessions, but I just grunted a few times. I was tired, my neck hurt, and I was still mad at her for rushing off the night before.

I remembered to check my cell phone when we got to the restaurant. There was a new text message.

"Yes?" said the girl by the cash register.

"Canned peas," I said aloud, still staring at my cell phone.

"What?"

"Granola and a lemon poppy-seed muffin," said Toni.

"The same," I muttered.

It was a good thing they didn't serve peas at that place, or I might have just ordered a bowlful.

At the table I told Toni about Leslie's latest text message and the one I'd gotten previously.

"So that's why you asked me if Cliff said anything about your mother," she said.

I nodded, or tried to. My neck hurt too much.

"He didn't tell me he saw her," she said. "I wonder what she means by a *password*?"

I didn't know. "The only passwords I ever use are on the Internet."

"His e-mail!" exclaimed Toni. "The hotel and airline reservations had been e-mailed to him. But why would we need his password? We had hard copies. Unless . . ." Her face lit up.

"What?" I asked.

"Unless *he didn't know* that Mrs. Mahoney had printed the e-mails!" she exclaimed triumphantly. "He thought you'd have to go online for them. And that's why he told you his password was *cannedpeas*!"

She banged her fist on the table, proud to have solved the *cannedpeas* question.

But that left another question: How did Leslie learn that

cannedpeas was Trapp's password? Only one answer came to mind, and I didn't like it.

"My parents know where I am," I said.

"What? How?"

"Mrs. Mahoney was the only person who knew Trapp's password," I said. "My mother must have spoken to her after running into Cliff at the pool. Mrs. Mahoney gave her the password so she could go online and check Trapp's old e-mail to find out where I was."

"You think they're coming here?" Toni asked.

I didn't know. It would explain why they hadn't tried to call me. They could be planning a sneak attack.

"Not again," Toni whispered fearfully.

"Again?" I asked.

"The last time they played," said Toni, "Annabel was dragged away."

"They won't come here," I said, sounding more certain than I felt. "They'd have to pay full fare for a last-minute plane ticket. No way they would do that."

We were walking back to the hotel when Toni suddenly asked, "Where'd you disappear to last night?"

I was shocked. "Where did *I* disappear to?"

"You were supposed to tell me the results, but I saw you talking to Lucy and Arnold. I didn't want to have to deal with them, so I went to check the results myself, and then when I got back, you were gone."

"I was looking for you," I said. "I figured you went up to your room."

"I wouldn't leave you like that!" Toni said, offended.

"Besides, I was hoping for some, you know, you-and-me time, without Trapp and Annabel."

"That would have been good," I agreed.

"Your neck's really bothering you, isn't it?"

"I'm okay," I said.

"Sit down on that bench," she said. "I'm really good at giving massages."

We had been walking beside a small city park, just a patch of grass, four trees, and a park bench. I sat on the bench and Toni came around behind me. She placed her hands on my shoulders and pressed my neck with her thumbs.

A lightning bolt of pain went screaming into the center of my brain.

"How's that feel?" she asked sweetly.

"Great," I said, fighting back tears.

71

Transportation

In the previous chapter, I mentioned that my parents wouldn't pay full fare for airline tickets. At least, I hoped not. When a bridge player talks about transportation, however, he's not talking about how he's getting to and from a bridge tournament. He's talking about getting from his hand to the dummy, or vice versa.

The declarer sometimes needs to be able to lead from the dummy, rather than from his hand. Expert declarers plan ahead in order to save *entries* to the dummy, so that they can win a trick in the right place at the right time. Similarly, expert defenders will do what they can to disrupt the declarer's transportation. It's often the game within the game.

Trapp was involved in such a contest. This was the situation with four cards left to play. The contract was three no-trump, and Trapp had taken six tricks. He needed three more.

Dummy (Toni/Annabel)
♡ QJ
◇ 93

West
♣ J962

East
♠ 7
♡ 9
◇ 65

Trapp (me)
♠ 94
♣ 103

If the lead could come from the dummy, it would be easy to take three tricks. The queen of hearts, the jack of hearts, and the nine of diamonds were all winners.

Unfortunately, he was stuck in his hand. The defenders had cut off his transportation.

I saw no way he could take three tricks. He could lead the ♠9. That would win, and it would get rid of East's ♠7. So then he could lead the ♠4 and that would also win. But after that, he'd have to lead a club, and no matter which club he led, West was sure to win the last two tricks.

The best he could do was settle for down one. That was what I thought.

"Four of spades," said Trapp.

Now, I didn't know exactly what cards were left in the East and West hands, but I was pretty certain that the ♠4 would lose. Even if I was wrong, why not play the nine first, just to be safe? For the first time ever, I wanted to ask, "Are you sure?"

Half expecting to be called a donkey again, I set the ♠4 on the table, and then, at his direction, discarded the ◇3 from dummy.

Sure enough, East won the trick with the ♠7. Now he was on-lead. He shook his head and said, "You got me!"

Whatever card he led would allow the dummy to win the last three tricks.

Trapp didn't have the transportation to get to the dummy by himself, so he purposely lost the trick in order to hitch a ride with a defender.

> Trapp purposely lost a trick he could have won, which allowed him to win the last three tricks.

"I never would have thought of that play," East said.

"Me neither," I agreed.

He looked at me oddly.

"I mean, I never would have thought of it until right then, when I did think of it."

Finnick and Trapp had a 61 percent game, and earned two platinum points. Lucy and Arnold met us afterward. They'd had a 57 percent game.

They knew they didn't stand much of a chance of winning the event, but even finishing in the top twenty could earn them 15 platinum points.

"What does the winner get?" I asked.

Lucy guessed it was around 125 platinum points.

Arnold asked how Toni and I had done.

"The best we could," I said, trying to sound like I was trying not to sound too dejected.

"That's a good attitude," said Arnold.

"What's wrong with your neck?" asked Lucy.

"He slept on it funny," said Toni, who then suddenly turned bright red and stammered, "That—that's what he told me. I wouldn't know!"

"Turn around," said Lucy. "I give great massages."

I'd heard that before.

Lucy placed her hands on me, and my relief was almost instantaneous. With each squeeze of her fingers I could feel the knot in my neck gently unravel.

"He doesn't like massages," said Toni. "He says it just makes it worse."

"Really?" asked Lucy.

That's what I had told her back at the park. I knew it had hurt her feelings, but I could only take so much pain. I wouldn't make a good spy. I'd crack after thirty seconds of torture.

I now had to weigh Toni's hurt feelings against the bliss of Lucy's massage.

"Yeah, you better stop," I said. "It only makes it worse."

My feeling of bliss abruptly ended.

Arnold invited us to join them for dinner. "Our treat," he said.

Toni and I glanced sideways at each other. It might be good to get a real meal for a change. I gave a half-nod.

"Okay," she agreed. "Thanks."

"Great," said Arnold. "Deborah heard about a sandwich shop not too far away that's supposed to have amazing food."

72

The Final Session

As we headed to the restaurant, I already regretted that we had agreed to go with them. Partly, I was afraid they might become suspicious if they started asking us questions about bridge hands. But even more than that, I realized that this was my and Toni's last night at the hotel. We'd be flying home the next morning. I would have liked some alone time with her.

Before entering the shop, I stepped away from the group and checked my cell phone. I had another text message from Leslie.

ur in BIG truble

Tell me something I don't know, I thought. I was getting annoyed with my sister's love for text messaging.

This time I tried calling the return number. Marissa answered. She said that Leslie had left a while ago, and asked if she could help me. For a second I considered that maybe

Marissa knew what was going on, but then decided I really didn't want Leslie's eleven-year-old friend involved in my problems.

Dinner was actually kind of fun. For one thing, Arnold had a strict rule: no bridge talk between sessions. He said it was important to give your mind a break.

I found out that Carl, Lucy's husband, was a retired judge. He had Toni and me laughing at all the stupid things that defendants, and *lawyers*, had done and said in his courtroom.

I held my head in such a way that I didn't look at Deborah. It had nothing to do with my stiff neck. It was just that every time I saw her, I couldn't help but imagine her coming out of that closet "in all my glory." Worse, even though the closet story had occurred when she was in her twenties, it was the present-day version of Deborah that I kept imagining.

When we returned to the playing area, Arnold checked the top hundred, starting at the bottom and working his way up. He and Lucy were sixty-ninth.

I started at the top and worked my way down. Finnick and Trapp were in ninth place. I wondered how big a game they would need to move to the head of the pack.

I noticed Lucy noticing me. "Syd Fox is in second place," I said, glad to be able to use him as my excuse. "Toni and I went to his lecture."

Our table assignment for the final session was A-5, East-West. I sat West. Arnold and Lucy were in our section, also sitting East-West, at A-12. At least we wouldn't have to play against them, but I knew they were sure to see the names of Annabel Finnick and Lester Trapp when the results were posted. I also noticed that Syd Fox was in our section, sitting North at table nine.

When the game got under way, I could actually feel a change in the level of intensity. Even Trapp's voice seemed to have an edge to it as he told me what cards to play. I doubted there would be any more winks from Annabel.

We played against Syd Fox in the fourth round.

"Hi," Toni brightly greeted him when we sat down. "We went to your lecture the other day."

"I hope it wasn't too boring," he said.

"No, it was great," she assured him. "Alton got his head chopped off three times."

"But on the fourth, I got to marry the princess," I said.

Syd Fox eyed Toni, then looked at me. "I think you came out ahead on the deal."

Toni blushed. "We're just bridge partners," she told him.

On our first board, Syd Fox was the declarer in four hearts, down one. One hundred for us. He didn't seem too concerned. In the post-mortem, he told his partner that it took good defense to set him, "but in this field, that should be the normal result."

On our second board, Annabel was the declarer in three no-trump, and made an overtrick for 630. When the hand was over, Syd Fox turned to Toni and said, "Next time, you should be the one giving me the lecture."

Three tables later we came across two other people I knew. (Who would have guessed I'd know so many bridge players?) They were the two women world champions that Trapp and Gloria had played against in the regional knockout. I guess I shouldn't have been surprised to see them here.

I didn't remember their names, but they remembered mine, and introduced themselves as Robin and Natalie. (In what other sport do you have the opportunity to play against the best players in the world? It would be like playing a round of golf and being joined by different people at each hole. "Hello, my name is Tiger, what's yours?") I introduced them to Toni. There was no point telling them she was Annabel Finnick, since they already knew I wasn't Lester Trapp.

"I noticed your uncle's name right up there among the leaders," said Robin, the younger of the two women. "Wouldn't it be wonderful if he won?"

"Yeah, it would," I agreed. Robin and Natalie must not have had a chance, or else she wouldn't have said that.

"I'm surprised we haven't seen him," said Natalie. "I guess he must have somebody else turning his cards for him."

"Yeah, a really cute guy," said Toni.

"Oh, really?" asked Robin. "And does he know you think he's so cute?"

"It's complicated," said Toni. "I've been going out with his best friend."

"A word of advice from someone who's been there," said Natalie. "You don't want to come between friends."

"Oh, I know," said Toni.

"Enough of this friendly chitchat," declared Robin as she removed her cards from the board. "Now it's war."

I didn't know what Toni was trying to do with those remarks, but it totally messed up my mind. I couldn't perceive anything from Trapp. Toni opened the bidding, 1◊. Robin passed, but all I could hear was "really cute guy" and "going out with his best friend."

I looked at my cards.

♠ J10
♡ K982
◊ 8643
♣ AJ7

I knew enough to set the 1♡ card on the table.

Natalie passed, Toni bid 1♠, Robin passed, and it was back to me.

Toni	Robin	Me	Natalie
1◊	Pass	1♡	Pass
1♠	Pass	?	

I had to choose between 1NT and 2◊. I think most experts would bid one no-trump, because of the scoring. You get more points in a no-trump contract than you do in a minor-suit contract. For example, you get 120 for making two no-trump, and you only get 110 for making three diamonds.

But I had something else to consider. I didn't know when my brain would settle down enough for me to hear from Trapp again. If I bid one no-trump, I'd be the declarer. In diamonds, Annabel would play the hand. I put my money on Annabel and pulled out the 2◊ card.

Everyone passed, and two diamonds was the final contract. As I tabled the dummy, I heard Trapp say, "Interesting bid."

At least he didn't call me a donkey. Of course I wouldn't have made that bid if I'd known I'd be hearing his voice so soon.

Either I made the right bid, or Annabel played it exceptionally well, or both, but she took ten tricks for a score of 130. In the post-mortem, Natalie and Robin agreed that the most I could have made in no-trump was 120. Those ten extra points would be the difference between an average score and perhaps a cold top.

I hoped that made up for the donkey hand.

73

The Final Table

Table four would be our final table. We had to stand aside and wait until the people there finished playing a hand from the previous round.

"Whatever happens," Toni whispered to me, "this has really been great."

I gave a half-nod in agreement, about as much as my neck would allow. "I hope Trapp and Annabel think so too," I said.

"Oh, they do," said Toni. "They've waited forty-five years for this!"

I smiled as I thought about Annabel, her wink, and the way she had purposely won a trick with the "beer card." Toni was right, I thought; Annabel was having the time of her life, although I guess that might not have been the most appropriate expression.

The people at table four were finished. They placed their cards in the slots on the board. The man sitting North recorded the score. The boards were passed to table three. The pair sitting East-West got up and moved to the next table and Toni and I took their place. A caddy collected the scores.

I removed my cards from the new board and looked at my hand. If it hadn't been for the jack of spades, I would have had a Yarborough. There was no other card higher than a nine. I had all four twos.

I remembered Trapp once telling Toni that these were the hands that separated the experts from the average players. I believe his exact words were *Even Alton can win a trick with an ace or a king.*

Okay, Trapp, I challenged him. *It's your turn. Let's see what you can do with this one!*

The guy on my right opened 1♣. I didn't hear anything from my uncle, but I had a pretty obvious pass, and set a green card on the table.

Our opponents had a very sophisticated bidding system. They made so many bids I actually ran out of pass cards. For my last two bids, I just pointed at one of the green cards already on the table.

I never heard from Trapp. Maybe he trusted my ability to pass.

They bid all the way up to six clubs, and I was on-lead. I waited, but still got nothing from Trapp, not even fuzzy mumbles. I chose one of my deuces.

The hand was over before it got started. After the third trick, the declarer laid his hand on the table for us to see and claimed the rest of the tricks. He took all thirteen, making his slam plus an overtrick.

North recorded the score of 1,390, but surprisingly, he wasn't happy about it. "Everyone else was probably in six no-trump," he muttered. "Or seven clubs."

"Only because she had the king of clubs," South griped. "If he'd had it, instead of her, six clubs would be the only makeable slam."

Their bidding system was so sophisticated, they knew that six clubs was cold even before I played my first card. Other pairs who weren't such expert bidders would not have known that, and probably would have tried six no-trump. That contract would have gone down if I'd held the king of clubs instead of Toni.

The pairs who had bid six no-trump got a score of 1,440. And those who had bid seven clubs scored 2,140.

In other words, we got a very good result even though we didn't take a single trick.

74

The Final Hand

Toni and I had played 103 hands, not counting the side game. These were my final thirteen cards:

♠ A108
♡ KQ2
♢ QJ10843
♣ 5

I've saved the hand records from the tournament, and have been using them to help me write an accurate account. But I didn't need to look at the hand records for this one. It's a hand I will never forget.

East was the designated dealer. Toni set the 1♣ card on the table. South passed, and it was up to me.

I had hoped that the reason I hadn't heard from Trapp on that last hand was because he knew it wouldn't make a difference, but I still wasn't getting anything from him.

I bid my longest suit, 1♢.

North passed.

Toni placed the 3♣ bid on the table.

She could have just bid two clubs, so Annabel's jump to three clubs showed extra strength. Since I had an opening hand too, we definitely belonged in game, and possibly slam.

South passed, and it was back to me.

I could use a little help here, I thought.

Maybe it had to do with the location of the table. Hell, for all I knew, it could have been the location of Jupiter, or the fact that the guy next to me was wearing a striped shirt, but for whatever reason, I was getting no help from my uncle.

I looked at my cards again, then at the bids on the table.

♠ A108
♡ KQ2
♢ QJ10843
♣ 5

Toni	South	Me	North
1♣	Pass	1♢	Pass
3♣	Pass	?	

I thought about bidding three diamonds, but I was afraid Annabel might pass, and we needed to bid game. I could try four diamonds, but that would take three no-trump out of the picture. But if I bid three no-trump, we wouldn't get to explore for slam. I considered just taking a shot at six no-trump.

I wondered what Lucy had bid when she had played the hand earlier. She was also sitting in the West seat. Earlier in the session she had held these very same cards.

I decided on the safest action, and set the 3NT bid on the table. I wouldn't want to be in slam without Trapp.

North passed and it was Toni's turn again. She sat there a long time without making a bid.

I wondered what Annabel was thinking about. I wondered if it would make a difference if she knew I was her partner.

Toni reached into her bidding box and pulled out a green card.

The final contract was three no-trump, and I would have to be the declarer. North led the six of spades and Toni tabled her cards.

Dummy
♠ 54
♡ A
♢ AK
♣ QJ1098732

Opening lead: ♠ 6

Me
♠ A108
♡ KQ2
♢ QJ10843
♣ 5

It looked easy. I could win one spade trick, three heart tricks, and six diamond tricks. That's ten tricks right there. And I might even get some club tricks.

"Thank you, partner," I said, then told Toni to play the four of spades.

The next person played the ♠Q, and I was just about to play my ace, when I suddenly realized it wasn't going to be as easy as I had first thought. I had a serious transportation problem.

My ace of spades was the only entry to my hand. All my other suits were blocked!

If I'd played the ace of spades immediately, I'd have won that trick. I could then have won the next three tricks in dummy, with its three red cards. But then I would have had no transportation to my hand to play the rest of my good hearts and diamonds. I'd have been forced to lead a black card from dummy. The defenders would have been able to take two club tricks and at least three spade tricks, setting the contract.

I stared at the cards in disbelief. I had all these high cards and no way to use them. Strange, but the dummy would have been a lot better if it had had the two of diamonds instead of the queen of clubs.

I have this rule. If you can see that plan A won't work, don't do it, even if you don't have a plan B.

I suppose experts always have a plan B, and even a plan C, but my rule had worked pretty well when I played in the side game.

Since I knew playing the ♠A wouldn't work, I ducked. I played the ♠8.

The opponents won the first trick. I could only let them win three more.

My other opponent was on-lead, and he set down the ♠K.

Again, playing the ♠A wouldn't work, so following Alton's rule, I ducked, playing the ♠10.

They'd won the first two tricks.

My best hope was that my opponent would now lead a red card. I suppose that was my plan B.

No luck. He led the ♠3.

This was what I had left.

Dummy
♠
♡ A
◇ AK
♣ QJ1098732

Lead: ♠ 3

Me
♠ A
♡ KQ2
◇ QJ10843
♣ 5

My ace of spades was my last spade, so I had to play it. The guy on my left played the ♠7, and I was just about to discard the ♣2 from dummy, when I suddenly spotted my plan C.

Since I had no transportation to get from the dummy to my hand, I just had to make sure that the dummy hand never won a trick. And that meant discarding the ace of hearts!

"Ace of hearts," I said.

A look of surprise came across Toni's face, but dummy has no choice in the matter. She discarded the ♡A.

I was on-lead. I led the ♡K, and once again had to discard something from dummy. "Ace of diamonds," I said, throwing away a second ace. Next I led the ♡Q and discarded the ◇K. I'd taken three tricks. I needed six more.

I started with six diamonds in my hand, and the dummy began with two, for a total of eight. That meant the opponents had five diamonds between them. If they split 3-2, I could run off six diamond tricks.

I led the ◇Q.

Both opponents played low diamonds. There were three diamonds still out.

I led the ◇J.

Again, both opponents followed suit.

My ◇10 took care of the last outstanding diamond. I ran the rest of my diamonds, for a total of nine tricks. The opponents took the last two.

> At first glance the hand seemed like it would be a snap. I had more than enough high cards. However, on second look, it seemed hopeless. Strangely, I didn't have enough low cards! I came up with a very unusual plan. Normally you only discard low cards. I discarded two aces and a king!

Maybe Trapp could have done better, but at least I made my contract.

"Let's go!" Toni said, jumping up from the table.

She was right. We needed to check the results and get out of there ahead of Lucy and Arnold.

When I stood up, I was finally able to hear Trapp's voice again.

He said just two words to me, but those two words caused me to stop and then grab hold of the top of the chair for support. I was still standing there when Toni returned three or four minutes later.

"Are you all right?" she asked. "You're trembling."

I didn't know it at the time, but those were the last two words my uncle would ever say to me.

He had said, "Nicely played."

75

Talk About Wow

"C'mon, we gotta go!" Toni said to me, grabbing my arm.

I heard Arnold's voice coming from where the results were posted. "If this is someone's idea of a joke . . . !"

We hurried across the room, then hid out in the middle of section H. Toni told me that with two rounds to go, Annabel and Trapp were leading with a 64 percent game.

That was just for their section, and Toni had only looked at the East-West scores. Sixty-four percent was good, really good, but we had no way of knowing if it was good enough.

"Our last round has to be good," she said optimistically. "First, they were in six clubs instead of six no-trump. And then on that second board, Trapp was amazing! I couldn't believe it when he told me to discard the ace of hearts! And then also the ace and king of diamonds! Talk about wow!"

I had no reason to tell her differently. Nothing she could say would top my uncle's last two words.

There were three printers on the directors' table, and they all began spewing out results. Caddies posted the printouts at various places around the room.

Section A was the first one posted, but Toni and I didn't dare go anywhere near it. It seemed to me that we should probably just leave and come back later after the room cleared, but we remained glued to our spot.

"May I have your attention, please?"

I could see the head director speaking into his microphone.

"The winners of the National Pairs Championship are . . . Annabel Finnick and Lester Trapp!"

Toni and I stared at each other. There were tears in her eyes, or maybe I only imagined them because I was looking at her through the blurriness of my own tears. The next thing I knew, her arms were around my neck, and I was holding her as tight as I could.

Since you've stuck with me this long, you know I don't do a lot of long descriptive paragraphs. I don't use many similes or metaphors. "A screaming lightning bolt of pain" is the only one that comes immediately to mind.

What happened next was that Toni and I kissed, and you're going to have to take me literally when I describe that kiss as cosmic. I didn't know where I was. I didn't even know who I was. I can't tell you how long the kiss lasted. Everything seemed to disappear, including time and space.

When I opened my eyes I looked at Toni looking at me.

"Talk about wow," she whispered.

"Was that you and me," I asked, "or Trapp and Annabel?"

"I think it was Trapp and Annabel," Toni said, then added, "but I liked it."

"Will Annabel Finnick and Lester Trapp please come forward?" the director called, for what was probably the third or fourth time.

I became aware that the pain in my neck was gone. It had melted away with the kiss.

"Annabel and Lester, please come up to the front to accept your trophy and to have your picture taken."

Toni and I held hands as we left the area. We walked quickly, but not too quickly, down the hall to the hotel lobby.

We didn't know who might come looking for us. Lucy and Arnold? My parents? A committee from the ACBL? The police? A crazed photographer?

We kissed again in the elevator. This time, it was just the two of us. Somewhere between the lobby and the twenty-seventh floor, Trapp and Annabel had left the building.

76

Philosophically Bent

Because I am now a member of the ACBL, I receive their monthly bridge magazine in the mail. In the October edition of *The Bridge Bulletin,* there was a very nice article written by Gloria about Lester Trapp, who during the last year of his life had played the game blind, "but could see the cards better than anyone in our club." The article mentioned that he had died on June 24. Elsewhere in the very same edition, Annabel Finnick and Lester Trapp were mentioned as the winners of the National Pairs Championship. It mentioned that Lester Trapp had reached the rank of Grand Life Master, but there was no accompanying article or photo. Still, you would have thought that some editor would have caught the fact that Lester Trapp had won the event *after* he had died.

We saw Lucy, Carl, Arnold, and Deborah the next morning at the sandwich shop. (Where else?) We told them the truth. They had already figured out that we had entered the tournament as Annabel Finnick and Lester Trapp. I called what we'd done "channeling," which seemed more credible than saying I heard my dead uncle speak to me.

They really had no choice but to believe us. It was either that, or they had to believe that two people who had been playing bridge for less than three months had outplayed all the best players in the world. The impossible is more believable than the highly improbable.

Consider the monkey and the typewriter. Imagine you walk into a room and actually see a monkey typing the Gettysburg Address, including all the punctuation and correct capitalization. Would you believe it was random luck, or would a different, totally impossible explanation be more acceptable to you?

Maybe that's what religion is all about. Is life just a highly improbable coincidence, or does an impossible explanation make more sense?

I've gotten way off track here. Like Trapp once said, I'm philosophically bent, and more so now than ever before.

Arnold, Deborah, Lucy, and Carl walked with us to wait for the shuttle bus. There were lots of hugs and a few tears when we left.

My parents grounded me for three months, but it only lasted about three weeks. They needed me to drive Leslie places, and then Leslie wanted to play at the bridge studio with me, and it would have been unfair to punish her for what I did. Pretty soon the whole grounding thing was pretty much forgotten.

The first time Leslie and I played at the bridge studio, we finished third and earned half a masterpoint. Leslie has gotten her school to start a bridge club, using a bridge teacher who's being paid by Trapp's school bridge fund. Only five kids showed up for the first meeting, but Leslie thinks they'll have at least seven next week. Counting the teacher, that's enough for two tables. The ACBL holds a youth national tournament every summer for people under eighteen, and Leslie hopes to put together a team.

I haven't heard from my favorite uncle since the nationals, but I think about him a lot. After Annabel's cruel death, his heart turned cold and hard, like a brick, but whatever kindness he did show was genuine. Just a simple "Nicely played" from Lester Trapp meant a lot more than a ton of praise coming from someone else. Each one of our conversations, whether about God or earwax, has a special place in my memory.

My dad still doesn't have a job. Our backyard is still a disaster area.

Cliff and I are still friends, but we don't spend much time together. It's awkward, because of Toni and me.

I cannot tell you the extent of my relationship with Toni. That is unauthorized information.

I'm working on my college applications, and I've gotten a job three days a week after school at a bookstore, the same bookstore where I dropped Toni off for her rendezvous with Cliff.

I've made a resolution that I will no longer let Cliff or anyone else manipulate me. Life will deal me many different hands, some good, some bad (maybe they've already been dealt), but from here on in, I'll be turning my own cards.

APPENDIX

Deciphering Bridge Gibberish
and Other Bridge Commentary
by Syd Fox

The kind of bridge you have read about is known as duplicate bridge, because in effect, the hands are duplicated. Everybody plays the same hands. This makes the luck of the cards much less of a factor.

The other type of bridge is known as rubber bridge or party bridge. It simply involves four people sitting around a table, shuffling and dealing after each hand. They talk and laugh and have a good time, and it's no big deal if somebody forgets the contract or whose turn it is to play a card.

Such perfectly normal social behavior drives duplicate players up the wall! We don't want to hear about Aunt Mabel's hip operation, or what somebody's precious child said to her second-grade teacher. To us, it's all about the cards.

Over the years I've played against people from all walks of life; young and old, rich and poor, Nobel Prize winners and construction workers, professional athletes and people who are physically disabled, famous actors and politicians. I've even sat at a table with two men who told me they had learned the game while in prison.

If you're interested in becoming a part of this amazing game, you can find out more at www.acbl.org. When you first get started, don't worry if you don't know a lot of complicated bidding systems or defensive signals. You will have plenty of other things to think about. Go ahead and make the logical bid or just the one that *feels right*. If an opponent asks what a bid means, or what kind of defensive signals you use, you can simply say, "We have no agreements." You and your partner are allowed to have no agreements. You're just not allowed to have any secret agreements.

As you become more experienced, however, you will find that these kinds of agreements are useful. Bridge is a partnership game, and the more you and your partner can cooperate, the more fun you will have and the better you will play.

I hope to meet you at the table someday.

A Note on the Scoring

Some eagle-eyed reader will no doubt notice that on page 178, Trapp's opponents scored 420 points for making a four-spade contract. Then, on page 193, Gloria also made four spades, but got 620 points. There are other apparent scoring discrepancies as well.

These are not errors. It has to do with something called *being vulnerable*.

Just as the board indicates who is the designated dealer for each hand, it also indicates which side is vulnerable. On board number one, nobody is vulnerable. On board two, North-South is vulnerable. On board three, East-West is vulnerable. On board four, both sides are vulnerable.

If you're vulnerable and go down in a contract, you lose 100 points per trick. If you are nonvulnerable, you only lose 50 per trick. You get a bonus of 500 points for bidding and making *game* when vulnerable, and only 300 when nonvulnerable. You also get bigger bonuses for slams when vulnerable.

Duplicate players will often take the vulnerability into consideration when deciding whether to bid or pass.

Running Commentary

Page 18:
There were two parts to a bridge hand, the bidding *and* the play. . . .

There's also a third part, the *post-mortem*. That's when you try to justify all the mistakes you just made, or better yet, blame them on your partner.

Page 21, the "Are you sure?" hand:

This was the spade situation described in Trapp's rant:

Dummy
♠KQ10

Gloria   Trapp

Declarer (you)
♠6532

Put yourself in the declarer's shoes. You lead the ♠2. Gloria plays a small spade. You play the ♠K from dummy, and Trapp plays the ♠4.

Now you return to your hand in another suit, and lead the ♠3. Again, Gloria plays a small spade. What card do you play from dummy?

Dummy
♠ Q10

Gloria   Trapp

Declarer
♠ 65

There's no easy answer. It all depends on the location of the ♠A and ♠J. If Gloria has the ♠A and Trapp has the ♠J, you should play dummy's queen. On the other hand (pun intended), if Gloria has the ♠J and Trapp has the ♠A, you should play dummy's ten.

How do you know? You don't.

Except earlier, when Trapp told Toni to play the ♠4, she asked, "Are you sure?"

Now you know Trapp has the ace, so you play dummy's ♠10.

This is what had Trapp so steamed. It was why he and Toni got into a fight, and why Alton became his new card-turner.

Page 26:
"I'm the only one to bid the grand, which would be cold if spades weren't five-one."

"Unless you can count thirteen tricks, don't bid a grand."

"I had thirteen tricks! Hell, I had fifteen tricks, as long as spades broke decently."

That last comment was a joke. You can never take more than thirteen tricks. Bidding a grand means bidding a grand slam. The speaker claimed he would have made it if the spades had been divided more evenly between his opponents.

If you are missing six cards in a suit, they will divide 5-1 or worse only about 16 percent of the time. So it does sound like bad luck, not bad bidding.

Page 26:
"Trapp!" she demanded. "One banana, pass, pass, two no-trump. Is that unusual?"

It sounded unusual to me.

"That's not how I play it," said my uncle.

You can't bid one banana. It isn't a suit. "One banana" simply means the bid of any suit except no-trump. One spade, one heart, one diamond, or one club—it doesn't matter.

"Is that unusual?" refers to a common bidding convention used by most duplicate bridge players, called the *unusual two no-trump* bid.

The *unusual two no-trump* bid is usually made directly after an opponent bids. Most commonly it shows the two lowest-ranked unbid suits.

So if an opponent opens the bidding with one heart and you bid two no-trump, you're telling your partner you have a hand with at least five clubs and at least five diamonds. If an opponent opens the bidding with one diamond, a bid of two no-trump would show five hearts and five clubs.

In the situation described here, the bid of two no-trump isn't made directly after the bid. There are two passes in between.

One banana—pass—pass—two no-trump.

Trapp indicated he would not take that as "unusual," and neither would I. In this instance, it would be the "usual" two no-trump bid, showing about twenty points including one or two high bananas.

Page 28:
She was nicely dressed, as were most of the women in the room. It was mostly the men who were slobs.

I have a theory about that. Bridge requires such a high degree of concentration, you want to be comfortable so as not to have to think about anything else. Women feel comfortable when they're confident about the way they look. Men feel comfortable when they're . . . well, when we're comfortable.

Not every man, and not every woman, of course, but it occurs often enough for Alton to have noticed.

Page 32, the skip:
It was like some sort of odd dance, with the people moving in one direction and the boards moving in the other. After the seventh round, every East-West pair skipped a table to avoid playing boards they had already played.

When there is an even number of tables (fourteen, in this case), a skip is needed to avoid playing the same boards twice. If there is an odd number of tables, no skip is necessary.

Pages 40–41:
One time it lurched a bit, and almost died, but I doubted Trapp noticed. We were driving back to his house after the Wednesday game, so his mind was on some bridge hand.
He would think not only about what he should have done differently, but also about what the opponents should have done, and what he would have done if they had done that. I could have driven into a ditch and he wouldn't have noticed.

Bridge players are famous for getting lost in their thoughts, especially when driving. Once after a tournament I drove forty-five miles past my exit before I finally looked around and thought, "Where am I?"

Page 69:
"Aces and spaces . . ."
"I had nine points, but it was all quacks. . . ."
"Odd-even discards?"

You often hear bridge players complain about *aces and spaces.* An example would be a hand like this:

♠ A43
♡ A65
◇ A432
♣ A42

323

Notice all the space between the ace and the next-highest card in that suit. True, a ten or a nine would be nice, but I like aces too much to ever complain about the spaces.

A *quack* is a queen or a jack. Nine points refers to the hand evaluation system that Toni taught to Alton. Charles Goren developed this system over fifty years ago, and while it's still used today, most experts agree it is not entirely accurate. Aces and kings are slightly undervalued, and queens and jacks, or quacks, are slightly overvalued.

Odd-even discards refers to a type of defensive signal. If a defender discards an odd card (3, 5, 7, or 9), it means she wants her partner to lead that suit. For example, if she discards the ◇5, she's asking her partner to lead a diamond the next time he gets a chance. If she discards an even card, the ◇4 for example, she's telling her partner she doesn't like diamonds.

The problem with this system is that sometimes you only have even cards in suits you like and odd cards in suits you don't like.

Page 81:
If you double, you're saying you think your opponents bid too high. If they make their contract, they'll get double the points, but if you set them, then you'll get double the points.

It's more complicated than that, but the general idea is correct.

The chart below shows how many points you get for setting a contract doubled or undoubled. The vulnerability applies to the side that bid the contract, not the side that doubled it.

	Nonvul	X	Vul	X
Down 1	50	100	100	200
Down 2	100	300	200	500
Down 3	150	500	300	800
Down 4	200	800	400	1,100
Down 5	250	1,100	500	1,400
Down 6	300	1,400	600	1,700
Down 7	350	1,700	700	2,000

I stopped the chart after down-seven, but you can actually go down as many as thirteen tricks on a hand (if you bid a grand and don't take any tricks). If you're wondering if any idiot actually has gone down as many seven tricks on one hand, yes, I have.

Page 90, Yarborough:
The odds of being dealt a Yarborough (no card higher than a nine) are 1,827 to one.

Page 97:
"Bidding's not that hard, once you learn the basics. Trapp and Gloria use a complicated system, but you don't have to do all that. You just have to know which bids are game-forcing, *which ones are* invitational, *and which ones are just* cooperative.*"*

Using the Goren point-count system, you should bid *game* if you and your partner have a total of 26 points. So if your partner opens the bidding (promising at least 13 points), and you have 13 points in your hand, you know you belong *in game*. Your partner, however, doesn't know this, and it's your job to let him in on the secret.

A *game-forcing* bid is one that tells your partner, "I want to bid *game* on this hand, so you must not pass until we have done so."

An *invitational* bid is one that invites game. Again, your partner made an opening bid, but this time you have about 10 to 12 points. You'll make a bid that invites your partner to bid game if she has a little extra.

A *cooperative* bid shows about 6 to 9 points. Your partner opened the bidding, and you have too many points to pass, but you're not interested in bidding game unless she has a lot extra.

There are many different bidding situations, but the key to good bidding is understanding whether a bid that you or your partner makes is game-forcing, invitational, or cooperative.

Page 125:
"After going into the tank for ten minutes, he leads a club, giving the declarer a sluff and a ruff! Then, in the postmortem, he asks me if there was something he could have done differently. 'Yes,' I tell him. 'Play any other card.'"

To *go into the tank* means to think for a long time before playing a card or making a bid. To *ruff* means to win a trick by playing a trump. To *sluff* means to discard. A *sluff and a ruff* occurs when a defender leads a suit in which both declarer and dummy are void, and where both hands have trump cards. It allows a declarer to ruff in one hand and to discard in the other, often giving her an extra trick. For example:

Dummy
♠ 8
♡
◇ A
♣ 3

Declarer (you)
♠ J
♡
◇ 5
♣ 4

Spades are trump. It looks like you have to lose a club trick, but if an opponent leads a heart, you will get a sluff and a ruff. You can discard a club from one hand and trump it in the other. This will allow you to win all the rest of the tricks. (Try it!)

Page 137:
The directors had a very specific rule for each situation. So not only were these mistakes really dumb, I realized, but they all had happened many times before.

And I've made every single one of them.

Page 159, the two idiots at table seven:
It was around this point that I noticed the blond guy squirming in his chair. When Toni won the next trick, the bushy-haired guy started squirming too.

If you see an opponent squirm, that's always a tip-off that he's being squeezed. If you're ever in such a situation, try not to squirm. Try to decide on your discards before it's your turn to play, and then calmly play as if you don't have any problem. Often a declarer won't realize you're being squeezed unless your body language tells him.

"First she squeezed me out of my exit cards . . . and then she endplayed me."

An *endplay* is when a defender is put in a position of having to lead a card, but whatever card he leads will give the declarer a trick.

There are many different kinds of endplays. Here's one example. These are everybody's last two cards.

Dummy
♣ Q4

West   East
(doesn't matter)   ♣ KJ

Declarer
♣ A5

If anyone else leads a club, East will be able to win a club trick (try it). But if East is on-lead, he is endplayed. If he leads the ♣J, dummy's ♣Q will win the trick, and then the declarer will win the last trick with the ♣A. If instead East leads the ♣K, it will lose to the ♣A, and then the ♣Q will win the final trick.

So Toni (or Annabel) first squeezed him out of his *exit*

cards, meaning he had to discard all the cards he could have led safely, and then she allowed him to win a trick, endplaying him in some manner.

Pages 177–78, the IMP chart:
Did you notice that as you win by larger and larger amounts, you get fewer and fewer additional IMPs? The chart is designed this way so that one peculiar hand won't decide an entire match. Rather, the winner is the team that consistently does better.

Page 204:
I knew what it meant to . . . pull trump.

To *pull trump* means to lead the trump suit and keep leading it until the opponents don't have any trump cards left.

Pages 218–19, Deborah in the closet:
We bridge players are unusual, to say the least. When the average male reads Deborah's story, he no doubt wishes he could have been there when she stepped out of the closet. When I read it, I wished I could have been there too, but I wanted to see that bridge diagram! If it had Trapp stumped, it must have been a very interesting hand.

Page 229, the post-mortem hand:

♠ Q109765432
♡
◇ 432
♣ 8

How did Trapp know he could make four spades on this hand?

He didn't. He was dealt nine spades. Do you know what bridge players call a nine-card suit?

Trump!

Page 231:
I won't go through the rest of the hand. Maybe you can figure out how to take ten tricks. I did, apparently.

I've made an approximate reconstruction of the hand based on what West said afterward. Look at West's hand. It's no wonder he doubled.

Dummy
♠
♡ J97643
♢ K87
♣ AQ62

West
♠ AK8
♡ AK5
♢ AQ96
♣ K94

East
♠ J
♡ Q1082
♢ J105
♣ J10753

Alton (Trapp)
♠ Q109765432
♡
♢ 432
♣ 8

Alton could only let the opponents win three tricks. When analyzing a hand, it helps to look at each suit separately.

By leading the ♠Q, Alton was able to lose only two spade tricks. He could afford just one other loser.

Since he had no hearts, he had no heart losers. He could play a trump any time an opponent led a heart.

Even though he only had one club, he should have taken the club finesse. When it worked, he could then have discarded a diamond on the second club winner.

That would have left this diamond situation:

Dummy
◇ K87

West
◇ AQ96

East
◇ J105

Alton (Trapp)
◇ 43 (he discarded the ◇ 2)

Alton now would have led the ◇3. West could have played his ace and won the trick, but that would have been Alton's last diamond loser.

In the end, he lost two spades and one diamond. Or, counting winners instead of losers, he won seven spade tricks, two club tricks, and one diamond trick.

Page 251:
"... *MUD from three small.*"
  "... *upside-down count and attitude.*"
  "*She was squeezed in the black suits.*"

MUD refers to a defender's choice of opening leads. There are *standard* opening leads from certain card-holdings. For example, if you have three cards in a suit, headed by an honor card, you would normally lead your lowest card. So from ♣K72, it is normal to lead the ♣2. If you have two small cards in a suit, you would lead the higher. So from ♣85, you would lead the ♣8. Where people tend to disagree is on what to lead from three small cards, say ♣852. *MUD* is one possibility. It's an acronym for Middle-Up-Down. If you agree to lead MUD, you would lead the middle card, the ♣5. Then the next time the suit was played you'd play "up," with the ♣8, and the third time "down," with the ♣2.

Personally, I don't like MUD, since the suit has to be played three times before I can figure out what's going on, which makes my partner's opening lead about as clear to me as the name implies.

Upside-down count and attitude is the reverse of *standard* signals.

In standard signals, a high card encourages and a low card discourages. If you play "upside down," then a low card encourages. That refers to attitude.

Count signals tell your partner how many cards you have in a suit. Playing standard signals, a low card says you have an odd number of cards. A high card shows an even number of cards. Your partner is expected to count the number of cards he has in that suit, and the number of cards the dummy has in that suit, and then figure out how many cards the declarer has in the suit.

If you play "upside down," then a low card shows an even number, and a high card shows odd.

Believe it or not, there are theoretical reasons why you would want to do this, and people have written entire books discussing the merits of different signaling methods.

"She was squeezed in the black suits" does not refer to a woman trying to fit into a bikini that's too small for her. A squeeze occurs when a defender has to make a discard, but whatever card she chooses will give the declarer a trick. When you're in such a situation, having to make discard after discard, it feels like you're in an ever-tightening vise.

You can never be squeezed in just one suit. For a squeeze to work, one defender has to be put in the position of trying to protect two suits. The black suits are spades and clubs, of course.

Page 261, 25 percent slam:
Taking a finesse is like flipping a coin. It will work 50 percent of the time. The odds of a coin flip coming up heads are 50 percent. The odds of flipping a coin twice and getting heads both times are 25 percent.

Toni was right to feel fixed. The odds of two finesses succeeding are 25 percent.

Before you feel too bad for them, however, Toni and Alton were most likely lucky on other hands. In every session of bridge, you will get some lucky boards and some unlucky ones. Bridge players tend to dwell on their unfortunate results, especially when they occurred during the final round, after all the other results were already water under the bridge (pun intended).

Pages 267–268, computer hands:
The boards had been predealt. There were tiny bar codes

on each card. A special card-dealing machine had dealt according to specific hand records.

You often hear bridge players complain about "computer hands," as if a computer designed them to be especially diabolical. That is a myth. Computer hands are just as random as human-dealt hands. The reason they are used is simply to make sure that the same hands are played in every section; and there's the added benefit of the players getting to see the hand records after the session is over.

Page 272, the donkey hand:
I told her about the donkey hand. She didn't think it was my fault. She said there were lots of times when it's right to overtake your partner's king with your ace. "You might need to unblock. . . ."

The diagram on the opposite page gives an example of when it would be right to overtake your partner's king with your ace in order to *unblock* the suit.

The contract is 3NT, and West makes the normal opening lead of the ♠K. If you look at the other suits, you will see that the declarer can take plenty of tricks: three heart tricks, five diamond tricks, and three club tricks. So it is imperative that East-West take five spade tricks before the declarer wins a trick.

If East plays the ♠4, the suit will be blocked. East will win the second spade trick with the ace, but will have no more spades left and will have to lead another suit, allowing the declarer to make the contract. So the correct play is for East to overtake his partner's ♠K with the ♠A

and then lead the ♠4. This will unblock the suit and allow
East-West to take five tricks and set the contract.

Dummy
♠ 973
♡ AKQ
◇ K8764
♣ 92

West
♠ KQJ52
♡ J65
◇ 95
♣ J104

East
♠ A4
♡ 10987
◇ J10
♣ 87653

Declarer
♠ 1086
♡ 432
◇ AQ32
♣ AKQ

Opening lead: ♠K

Page 305, Alton's Rule:
*If you can see that plan A won't work, don't do it, even if
you don't have a plan B.*

Alton's rule is a good one. If you're stuck, it often helps
to let the opponents win a trick. Remember, they don't
know what your problem is. They can't see your hand.
Quite often, they'll lead a card that helps you out.

Page 307:
I started with six diamonds in my hand, and the dummy began with two, for a total of eight. That meant the opponents had five diamonds between them. If they split 3-2, I could run off six diamond tricks.

If you are missing five cards in a suit, the odds of them splitting 3-2 are 68 percent. So really, it would have been unlucky if the diamonds *hadn't* split 3-2. Even if that had happened, however, I still think Alton would have gotten a "nicely played" from Trapp. An unlucky lie of the cards wouldn't change the fact that his line of play was both accurate and elegant.

About the Author

LOUIS SACHAR is the author of the award-winning *Small Steps* and the number one *New York Times* bestseller *Holes*, as well as *Stanley Yelnats' Survival Guide to Camp Green Lake*. His books for younger readers include *There's a Boy in the Girls' Bathroom, The Boy Who Lost His Face, Dogs Don't Tell Jokes,* and the Marvin Redpost series, among many other books. He is an avid bridge player.